TERMINAL IMPASSE

Books by Sara Driscoll

NYPD Negotiators

Exit Strategy
Shot Caller
Lockdown
Terminal Impasse

FBI K-9s

Lone Wolf
Before It's Too Late
Storm Rising
No Man's Land
Leave No Trace
Under Pressure
Still Waters
That Others May Live
Summit's Edge

Standalones

Echoes of Memory
Shadow Play

TERMINAL IMPASSE

By Sara Driscoll

KENSINGTON
PUBLISHING CORP.
www.kensingtonbooks.com

KENSINGTON BOOKS are published by

Kensington Publishing Corp.
900 3rd Avenue, 26th Floor
New York, NY 10022

All Kensington titles, imprints, and distributed lines are available at special quantity discounts for bulk purchases for sales promotion, premiums, fund-raising, educational, or institutional use.

Special book excerpts or customized printings can also be created to fit specific needs. For details, write or phone the office of the Kensington Sales Manager: Kensington Publishing Corp., 119 West 40th Street, New York, NY 10018. Attn. Sales Department. Phone: 1-800-221-2647.

The K with book logo Reg US Pat. & TM Off.

First Electronic Edition: June 2025
ISBN: 978-1-4967-5189-8 (ebook)

First Print Edition: June 2025
ISBN: 978-1-4967-5190-4

Printed in the United States of America

The authorized representative in the EU for product safety and compliance
Is eucomply OU, Parnu mnt 139b-14, Apt 123
Tallinn, Berlin 11317, hello@eucompliancepartner.com

For Shane.
Long before it became official, you were a part of this family. Many thanks for all your wholehearted enthusiasm for my writing over so many years and so many books. Thank you for all those trips to the gun range, opening me to the world Meg, Gemma, and Logan inhabit. Most importantly, thank you for always catching my mistakes and keeping my characters looking like the consummate professionals they are!

Chapter 1

"You're sure you want to do this?" NYPD Detective Sean Logan asked.

Standing at the open gate, Detective Gemma Capello looked past the low, wrought iron fence into St. Patrick's Old Cathedral's cemetery. Inside, a scattering of trees spread their bare branches over patchy grass, scattered headstones, and raised tombs that filled the space enclosed by a weathered two-hundred-year-old, eight-foot-tall brick wall.

Gemma's own words from more than a month before echoed in her head. *"Let's agree to do our best to close the book on it, but admit that parts of it will haunt us for a while."*

"I know we've talked this through to clear the air, but I'm not sure it's really put to bed. We're here, so I'd like to do that once and for all." Gemma met Logan's steady blue gaze. "You in?"

"I'm in." He extended one hand into the cemetery. "Lead the way."

Gemma stepped into the grass and Logan followed, closing the gate behind them with a squeak of rarely oiled hinges. She paused for a moment, taking in the quiet, centuries-old graveyard, so different from the last time she'd seen it this past summer, now with denuded trees and faded fall grass, and without the church's summer landscaping crew of a trio of sheep, back at their farm in upstate New York for the winter.

A cool breeze slithered down the back of Gemma's neck. She pulled the collar of her jacket higher to fend off the early December chill. "It's so...quiet."

"Compared to last time, you mean?"

"*Ferragosto* is always such a party." Simply saying the name brought back waves of emotion—hope, determination, fear, rage. "Little Italy was jumping that night, brilliantly lit, people everywhere. Everyone out celebrating." She had a vision of tables loaded with food, surrounded by her family. Love, support, unity—that was the Capellos. In the end, the strength of her connection with her youngest brother, Alex, had brought her through that nightmare of a day.

"That's what was going on?" Logan turned to look back out at Mott Street on the far side of the main gate. The windows of boutique shops and restaurants glowed bright in the evening gloom, and steady foot traffic marked New Yorkers on their way home from work, to dinner, or to do a last bit of holiday shopping before the stores closed at 7:00 PM. "I knew it was some kind of celebration, but wasn't sure what. The streets were packed. We had to force our way into the area."

"It was August fifteenth, the Sicilian Feast of the Assumption. A perfect summer evening and the streets were humming with people and music." Her gaze wandered back to the street, a shiver running down her spine as she saw it as it had been that night, bustling with foot traffic. "I spent the whole time terrified Boyle would kill someone at any moment, and I'd be powerless to stop him."

"We've talked about the end of that night, but never about what led up to it. I mean, I read your report—"

"You did?"

"Yeah."

To Gemma's surprise, Logan didn't meet her eyes, but instead focused on a nearby charcoal marble headstone topped with a cross. "Do you normally read case files afterward?" she asked.

"No. This one was special." He turned to meet her gaze. "I knew you hated me that night for what I'd done. Even before I read it, I knew that. I could tell you tried to keep it out of your report, but anyone who knew you well could hear it. I could."

"Sean." Gemma closed her hand around Logan's wrist, his skin warm under her cold fingers. "I don't hate you."

"Not now. But that night..."

Together they turned to stare down the length of the cemetery. To where it had all ended.

The night when Gemma and Alex were in pursuit of retired NYPD Sergeant John Boyle after he took hostages in New York City Hall and then murdered First Deputy Mayor Charles Willan in cold blood in retribution for the loss of his son, a fellow NYPD officer. Gemma and Alex had cornered Boyle in this cemetery, while Logan, deployed as part of the NYPD Apprehension Tactical Team—the A-Team—was stationed across the street, six stories up in a sniper's nest, positioned on the roof with his M4 Commando rifle, ready to save the lives of the officers below and stop a killer if needed. His lieutenant had already given him the green light to take the shot, but the final decision had rested in Logan's hands.

Gemma had spent hours with Boyle by that time and thought she could anticipate his next moves. He'd lost his son in a line-of-duty death, had exacted his vengeance on the men he felt were responsible—one dead, the other to live with that tragedy for the rest of his life—and had nothing left to live for. He also knew the justice system and a long jail sentence lay before him. Gemma had known in her gut he'd try to end his own life that night.

Gemma had tried to lean on her long-ago shared history with Logan—six intense months together at the academy culminating in a single, unforgettable night in his bed before they went their separate professional ways—for him to trust her judgment with Boyle. To refrain from taking Boyle's life because he wasn't truly a threat to her or Alex.

"Sean, don't do this. He's going for suicide by—"

Her frantic plea to stay his hand had been interrupted by the shot that killed Boyle.

It had taken months for Gemma to talk to Logan. In the end, he'd forced her hand in a dim room on Rikers Island in the middle of a hostage incident when their inability to work the situation together had called for a come-to-Jesus moment between them.

They'd rebuilt their friendship from there, but the attraction between them never wavered. So much so, following the South Greenfield shooting only three weeks before, they'd agreed to meet for dinner and an evening out. It had taken some time around the Thanksgiving holiday to find a date when both were off duty for an evening as well as the next day so they could enjoy a late night, but it had finally come together.

They'd begun an hour before with coffee at La Cassatella, the café and bakery run by Gemma's best friend, Francesca Russo—affectionately

known to the family as Frankie—before walking through Little Italy while
Gemma showed him the sights of her childhood. Until they had ended up
at St. Patrick's Old Cathedral.

Now they stood on the cusp of starting something as mature adults,
instead of competitive young police cadets constantly trying to outdo
each other to make their own professional mark. For Gemma, whose
partners from the past had somehow never measured up to some impossible
standard she hadn't realized had been set, it held the potential of coming
full circle to what could have been if she hadn't been so focused on only
one facet of her life at the time. She wasn't entirely sure where it stood for
Logan, except he'd been the one to ask her out to dinner, so she suspected
something was pulling him as well.

Yet one moment from this very cemetery still stood between them.

"I'm glad we're here," she said. "Let's do this so we never
need to look back."

Gemma released him and crossed the cemetery, through a grouping
of tombs and headstones so old and weathered, the identity of those buried
below was wiped clean except in church records. Past a steel-and-wood
bench under the bare, spreading branches of several towering trees, with
the crunch of the last of the season's leaves underfoot as Logan followed.
Around the obelisk where Alex had taken shelter before moving into his final
position, where he'd hoped to be able to disable Boyle rather than kill him.

She stopped beside the raised granite tomb standing about twenty-five
feet inside the brick wall. Boyle had sheltered on the far side of the tomb,
in full view of Logan across the street, even as he'd leaped onto the pitched
stone roof and aimed his handgun at her brother.

Gemma looked up the long line of the six-story redbrick building
rising above the weathered brick wall and over the street. "You had a good
view from up there."

"With the night-vision scope? I could see every detail from only a
hundred feet away." He paused for a moment as if weighing his words. "I
could see what he'd done to you." His tone was ice cold.

Gemma's gaze shot to Logan, taking in his flat stare. "To me?"

"He'd battered you. The trails of blood on your face were crystal clear
through the scope."

"To be fair, we'd battered each other. But yes, while we were fighting
in the crypt, he hammered my nose with his elbow. I knew it was bleeding

but didn't know how badly. Got cleaned up by a paramedic, so I never saw it myself."

"You bled quite a bit."

"Good scope."

"Great scope. If I could read lips, I'd have known what you were saying." He gave her a sidelong glance. "I could see you were talking to him off comms so Sanders couldn't hear you trying to talk him down. So I couldn't hear."

"Goddamn Sanders." She held up a hand to forestall whatever defense he might give of his commanding officer, knowing they were never going to agree there. "I had one shot at it and I didn't need anyone in my ear telling me what they wanted me to do." Her gaze dropped to the tomb. "And then Boyle burst from his hiding place, jumped on the roof of the tomb, and pointed his gun at Alex. And it was game over."

"He knew what he was doing. Even before you came over comms telling me he was going for suicide by cop, I knew there was a chance that was his goal. He was a good cop. He knew his life in prison would be hell because he'd jailed people himself. Are you finished being mad that I didn't listen to you?"

His rapid left turn didn't throw Gemma; Logan had a habit of shooting straight from the hip as his preferred method of dealing with people. Also, it was the real reason they stood in a cemetery in the gloom of a chilly December evening—her fury with him over Boyle. "Once you explained you did it for me, to save Alex's life, but really to save me his loss...all the rage I'd held and stoked for you died away. You burned out months of fury in seconds. That was my fault for not seeing the situation from your side."

"You were too invested."

"That was definitely part of it. You and I come from radically different sides of law enforcement. A-Team members are told time and again, if push comes to shove, taking a life is an acceptable consequence to save someone else. Whereas hostage negotiation training stresses taking as much time as needed to save every life in play, if you can." She blew out a long breath. "We were never going to meet in the middle."

"There was no middle ground."

"You may be right. I remember looking up at you that night as I sat on the grass beside Boyle's body. All I could see was your silhouette as you stood on the roof. I knew you were looking down at me. I was so angry

you'd shot him. Alex was just as angry; he had to walk it off before he did
something stupid like punch a headstone."

Logan stepped a few feet away, his head tilted back as he gazed up at
the roof of the building, at where he'd perched in the darkness. "I watched
you afterward, sitting down here beside the man you'd tried so hard to
save." His gaze slid down to the ground under his boots as if he could still
see the blood that had drenched the grass four months before. "Standing
there, I wasn't using the rifle scope anymore, so I couldn't see details, but
six stories up, I could feel your fury. I think you really hated me in that
moment. Even knowing that, I didn't regret it. I'd rather have had your
rage than your grief. Not after you'd watched your mother's murder at ten.
I had your anger; you had Alex. I considered it an even trade."

Gemma couldn't mistake Logan's sincerity—it was clear in both tone
and demeanor. Dimly illuminated by the single light high on the church,
scattered through the overhead branches, he stood stiff, his hands jammed
in his pockets, his tight shoulders riding high, with his jaw set and mouth
tight, his blond head bent. She realized she so rarely saw him out of his
all-black Emergency Services uniform; to see him in color—brown leather
lace-up boots, tan cargo pants, navy collared shirt with the top two buttons
open, and hunter-green ski jacket—was as jarring as his naked honesty.
But this was exactly what they needed, to be out of uniform and to explore
the depths of the other's nonprofessional side. It's what they hadn't done
fifteen years ago; much, if not all, of which was her fault. She'd left the
academy with her sights set on living up to the Capello name inside the
NYPD and hadn't wanted any distractions to stand between her and her
potential success. She'd walked away from him then; she wouldn't make
that mistake again now.

She slid her arm through his, closing her fingers around his forearm,
to stand *with* him rather than simply beside him. "I'm not sure 'grief'
would have covered it, had Alex died that night after answering my call
for help. I'm not sure 'devastation' would cover it either, but it would
come closer. Thank you for saving me that experience. Thank you for
transferring that load from me to you, because I know you bear it still.
It's one reason you're here."

"The goal is never to take a life, but sometimes you have no choice.
You carry a piece of every life you take with you. Even when it wasn't
your choice and your hand was forced." His voice was quiet, and his eyes

stayed fixed on the ground where Boyle had fallen, already dead from Logan's precisely placed shot.

"I'm sorry for that. For Boyle and for the others." She gripped a little tighter. "But no more blame from me about Boyle. We both did the best we could that night under an incredible amount of pressure. It's now put to rest for good."

He pulled his hand from his pocket, dislodging her arm where it wove through his, but caught her hand before it could drop away, intertwining their fingers and holding tight. "We're done here?"

She met his gaze, saw her own hope for a fresh beginning mirrored. The years and their careers had instilled too much distance; they'd waited long enough to see if there was really something there between them. "We're done. It's behind us. This is a new beginning."

"I like the sound of that. How does dinner sound?"

Gemma laughed, feeling so much lighter than when they'd set foot inside the cemetery. "As Alex would say, I could eat."

"Then you'll love O'Callaghan's. Seriously good food, great crowd. Nice selection of cocktails and beers."

"I've been looking forward to this place since you sold me on it last week. It sounds just right."

Hand in hand, they left the cemetery, putting St. Patrick's and all its bad memories behind them.

Chapter 2

"I meant to ask you—how did the interview with Coulter go?" Logan asked as they stepped off the escalator rising from the depths of the subway and into the bright length of Grand Central Terminal's Lexington Passage. "I assume it's done?"

Gemma groaned, remembering the media interview her superior officer had arranged for her in exchange for critical information ABC7's Greg Coulter could provide about the hostage takers during the South Greenfield shooting a few weeks earlier. "Don't remind me. What a disaster."

Logan's gaze went sharp. "It didn't go well?"

She had to refrain from rolling her eyes and instead fixed her gaze on the brilliantly illuminated boutique shops they passed by, their floor-to-ceiling windows filled with expensive jewelry, designer luggage, and unique perfumes. "Coulter rubs me the wrong way, so I instantly go on the defensive whenever I'm near him. He doesn't even have to open his mouth; just the sight of him puts my back up. He wants every story to be bigger than the last and lives for spectacle. I don't do spectacle, especially not at the expense of grieving families. Those who lost their children to death. Or prison."

"You mean Russ Shea's parents."

"Yes. I met them, you know. They made a request of the NYPD to meet the negotiator who saved their son's life."

"Garcia approved it?"

Gemma sidestepped a man power walking through the passage, pulling a rolling carry-on behind him, bumping shoulders with Logan. "Sorry."

"No worries. It's rush hour. It's impossible to get through the Terminal without potentially running into someone. They say seven hundred fifty thousand people pass through here every day."

"Feels like most of them are here right now."

"I'd have suggested heading out to the sidewalk to circle around to Madison, but it'll be just as crazy out there as in here. And colder. Anyway, the Sheas?"

"Garcia green-lit the request, so I met with them and tried to give them insight into the son they raised but couldn't recognize from his actions that day. They had no idea he was in such a bad place. He never let it show with them. If Hank hadn't gotten his claws into him..."

"Those seventeen dead kids and teachers would be getting ready to celebrate Christmas with their families."

"Exactly. Of course, Coulter wanted to get into what made Russ tick, which I wouldn't even attempt to theorize. It will take top psychiatric minds time to talk to him and review his writings to get a clear picture of his motives that day. My job is to connect with the hostage taker enough to save lives—which, thanks in large part to you, we succeeded in doing—not to psychoanalyze. But the more drama the better, as far as Coulter's concerned. I know I wasn't happy with the interview. I'm pretty sure he wasn't either. Neither of us got what we wanted."

"You wanted to not be there in the first place."

"Exactly. I was unhappy before the cameras even started to roll. He became unhappy when I wasn't the open book he expected. But enough about Coulter. I want to enjoy my evening and he makes me want to hit something."

"I have a speed bag at home that could help."

"I'm thinking a glass of Harp could also do the job."

Logan hummed his approval in the back of his throat. "Nice choice, though I'm more of a Guinness Extra Stout man myself."

"Why does it not surprise me a heavy hitter like that would be your choice? You really haven't changed much in all these years."

"Not where it counts. I could say the same for you."

They crossed under a draped garland of dark evergreen, shot through with tiny white lights and accented with large, gold-trimmed red bows at each attachment point on the pale marble archway, and stepped into the Main Concourse between the long row of ticket counters and the double marble staircase leading to the East Balcony.

Gemma had lived in New York City her entire life, but Grand Central Terminal's Main Concourse never failed to catch her breath. She supposed if she traveled through it daily on her commute to work, she might take its glorious barrel-vaulted ceiling and miles of lustrous marble for granted, as did many of the hundreds rushing through, heads down, all with somewhere to go as quickly as possible, oblivious to the beauty overhead. But much of her life was contained in Lower Manhattan with the family homestead in Brooklyn, so she always enjoyed the beauty of the concourse on her occasional visits.

The same hazelnut-veined pearl marble lining Lexington Passage rose 120 feet overhead in massive columns and twice as long across the concourse to the far side. Overhead, the turquoise ceiling was gilded with a soaring mural depicting a line of heavenly zodiac constellations, lit with embedded lights to draw the eye. Five arched lunette windows lined the north and south edges of the ceiling, each embossed with plaster reliefs depicting transportation—a ship's helm, wings, locomotive wheels and tracks—spotlit in alternating green and red for the holiday season. Beneath their boots stretched alternating lines of large oblong tiles of gleaming black-veined Tennessee pink marble. Huge evergreen wreaths, twinkling with white lights, each cradling a gilt-edged red velvet bow, hung stories high on each side of the concourse on the outer two massive columns, the columns between draped with banners proclaiming the holiday fair taking place in Vanderbilt Hall until Christmas Eve. Each passage entrance into the concourse was topped with a garland identical to the one they'd just passed under, as was the archway over the four escalators connecting the Terminal to the adjacent MetLife Building. Jazzy Christmas music filtered through from the wine bar on the far side of the ticket booths.

Gemma's eye naturally found the iconic four-face opal clock over the circular information booth in the center of the concourse, so often considered a primary symbol of the Terminal since its opening in 1913. Over a century in use and the Terminal had changed very little through the years—renovations had cleaned and brightened the space, and the East Balcony had been added, but so much of the building was true to its original roots. She found it comforting—in a city that too often discarded its historic architectural gems over the years, Grand Central Terminal remained a mainstay.

"It's crazier than usual tonight," Logan said. "I'm here every couple of weeks to go to O'Callaghan's and it's not usually this packed. Careful there." A shouting, laughing gaggle of teenage boys darted past and Logan slipped an arm around Gemma's waist, tugging her against his side and out of the danger zones of flying hands and elbows.

She looked up to find him grinning down at her. "Thanks."

"No problem." But he left his arm curved around her.

They crossed the concourse as quickly as they could around tourists and commuters. It felt like all of Manhattan was here tonight and Gemma's gaze fell across the churning crowd: an older pair, clinging to each other so neither would be knocked down by the throng as they passed under the giant American flag hanging over the entrance to Vanderbilt Hall; a young couple, the mother pushing a stroller while the father dragged a full-size suitcase behind him; three army officers in camo fatigues, each shouldering a stuffed duffel bag; scores of commuters in both business and casual wear, carrying briefcases, backpacks, laptop bags, purses, or gym bags.

Every gender, race, age, status...all part of New York City's melting pot.

Twenty feet ahead, people gathered around the circular information booth to check the timetables or to talk to those within about train schedules. On the arrivals screen, the horizontal bars detailing incoming trains shifted as a new train pulled in.

"You said this place was on Madison?" Gemma asked.

"On 47th, just off Madison. You're going to love it. Not a huge menu, but everything they do is stellar."

"What do you recommend?"

"You used to be able to nearly eat me under the table. You haven't gone vegan on me, have you?"

Gemma laughed. "Definitely not. There would be a lot of angst from my brothers if I stopped making *spiedini* or *involtini di manzo*. Speaking of...you should come for dinner some night. I promise you won't regret it."

"I remember you making desserts to die for back in the academy days."

If you're seriously going for this, you might as well go all in. "I'm so much better now than I was then." She threw him a look under lowered lids to make her double entendre clear.

Logan's arched eyebrow paired with an expression of pure intrigue told Gemma his mind went exactly where she intended—back to that night fifteen years before when they'd practically scorched his sheets. She'd never been able to shake it; the look in his eyes said he hadn't either.

"I'll file that away for later." Logan cleared his throat, as if forcing himself back to a topic suitable for a public place and packed crowd. "As I said, you'll like O'Callaghan's. It's carnivore heaven there. Burgers, chicken, excellent fish-and-chips. An outstanding New York strip, which is where I'll probably land. This is my treat, so get whatever you want. If you want something done special, I can get—"

The earsplitting staccato crack of machine-gun fire boomed, stunningly loud in the open space, followed by a brutal echo off marble walls and columns. Terrified screams added to the din as everyone exploded into motion.

Gemma and Logan automatically sprang apart to protect those around them, rather than take cover themselves.

Gemma had a brief glimpse of a figure, all in black, wearing a black balaclava, bursting from the entrance to track 24, to the right of the escalators traveling up to the MetLife Building. The figure turned toward the compact wooden MTA NYPD desk tucked against the wall, just to his left, and loosed a stream of bullets directly into the two officers standing behind it. Blood and brains splattered against the marble behind them as they fell from view.

Cops would be the first to die.

She couldn't dwell on that; there were lives to save.

Gemma caught two teenage girls by their arms where they stood, frozen like deer in headlights, and threw them behind the bulk of the information booth. "Get down!" She turned as more shots rang out and the older gentleman beside her took a round in the throat. Blood spurted, a warm spray against her left cheek. Her body jerked in horror; then she pushed her reaction down and dove for the screaming woman beside him, pulling her to the floor, then dragging her past the man's corpse toward shelter, the marble floor slick with blood spray, making her job gruesomely easier.

"Leave your bags! Take cover!" Gemma waved in several shell-shocked tourists talking in short snatches of what she thought was German. "Stay out of the line of sight!"

A middle-aged woman with a teenage boy—mother and son?—their arms loaded with shopping bags, tried to bolt for the entrance to Vanderbilt Hall, but a second round of gunfire, this time coming from the west side of the information booth, had them falling to the floor and cowering.

Sitting ducks. At least if they were moving, they'd be harder to hit.

Gemma waited for a few seconds' break between bursts of gunfire, and ran toward them. "You can't stay here. You need to move." She eyed the distance to the walkway to Vanderbilt Hall, knew their chances of making it were slim. She grabbed the mother's arm, pulled her to her feet, leaving the bags behind, and moved her toward the shelter of the information booth, her son scrambling after. More gunfire sounded and they dove for cover below the chest-high marble base, below blood-splattered windows.

From the amount of spatter, at least one person had likely died inside.

Another rapid-fire stream of bullets sounded as Logan slid in behind the information booth on his knees like a rock star finishing a guitar solo. It would have been a painful dive on an unforgiving surface, but it kept him upright enough that the head of the woman draped over his shoulder stayed clear of the marble floor. Gemma pushed past several terrified people huddling together to reach for the elderly woman, helping Logan lower her to the ground as gently as possible, positioning her with her back against the marble base.

It was only about fifteen seconds, though the attack had felt like they'd been moving in slow motion. People were still rushing to the outer exits, and footsteps pounded through the back corridors and up the last of the stairs and out onto Vanderbilt Avenue or through the emergency exits.

Then the gunfire fell silent, and Gemma could only hear her pounding heart in her ears, and the rasp of her labored breaths, matched by Logan's.

How many gunmen were there? Was that one figure the only shooter?

Gemma's gaze frantically scanned the now open space, the scattering of bodies across the marble floor.

There was no denying she, Logan, and the people huddling beside them had been in the wrong place at the wrong time.

But now the bigger question was—why had this happened and what would it take to come out of it alive?

Chapter 3

The shots came out of nowhere.

One moment Logan was strolling across the concourse with Gemma, looking forward to a good meal—and who knew what might follow after Gemma's reference to their one night together—and the next, the swift tattoo of gunfire blasted through the air. Not a handgun—that was immediately obvious from the rapid-fire cadence of the shots—but small-arms fire, a machine or submachine gun.

A deadly high-capacity weapon that could mow down a crowd in seconds.

He jerked away from Gemma at the same moment she stepped clear of him—after nearly a decade and a half on the force, their training was ingrained down to the bone. "To Protect and Serve" might be the official motto of the LAPD, but it was the heart of every police department in the country.

The NYPD motto was *Fidelis Ad Mortem*. Faithful Unto Death. In this situation, they both might be, with death standing so near.

Logan's hand automatically fell to his upper thigh where his Glock 19 was normally strapped when he was geared up for A-Team duties. But his hand met only with the top flap of the pocket on his cargo pants. *Unarmed.* He sprang forward, tackling a woman with a backpack young enough to be a university student, sliding with her along the slick floor, until they struck the information booth. "Stay here!" He rolled to his knees under the cover of the marble base of the booth. A middle-aged man clutching a DSLR camera dove behind the bulk of the information booth, slamming into Logan's right side, nearly sending him sprawling. He caught his balance and staggered to his feet, maintaining a crouched posture, keeping his body below the glass.

All around, people were sprinting for the nearest exit. A man in a trench coat pelted for the Lexington Passage, his briefcase nearly taking out an older woman with a large purse on her shoulder, leaning on a cane, caught in the middle of the floor.

Shit.

She was never going to make it on her own and, as people scattered, was a wide-open target. He had two options—watch her die or get her out of there.

Logan didn't know how many gunmen there were or if it was a solo shooter, but whatever weapon they were shooting, they were going to have to reload at some point. That would be his chance.

More gunfire exploded from the western side of the Terminal—two shooters, or had the shooter moved?—and then there was a heartbeat of silence. Two.

Move.

Logan burst from behind the information booth, his attention focused on the terrified woman. He covered the twenty-five feet between them and didn't waste words, but simply bent, threw her over one shoulder—her cane clattering to the floor—spun, and sprinted back to the information booth. It wasn't gentle handling, but injured was better than dead, and there was no time to set up a secure fireman's carry over both shoulders.

He had a brief glimpse of two figures in black, both with dark weapons and standing just outside the entrance doors to the lower train shed, before they opened fire in different directions. He swore he could feel the bullets fly past his head as he crashed to his knees, sliding the last three feet to shelter.

Then Gemma was in front of him, reaching for the load he carried. Together they got the older woman onto the ground, her back against the base of the information booth. She'd be sheltered from any approaching gunmen until they came around the circular structure, after which nowhere in the open concourse was safe.

Logan rolled to the balls of his feet, ready to spring, to act, to retrieve the next victim. But a rapid scan of the concourse floor told him it would be futile—no one on the open floor was moving, and with no one else in the area, any mission to go after anyone now the chaos had cleared would be a deadly trap.

His gaze roamed across the floor, at dark puddles and smears of blood leading toward the exits. Others had been hit but had gotten themselves clear or had been helped. Those who were left were beyond help, either from instantaneous death or from oncoming death because he was helpless to save them without it being a suicide mission. A glance at the dead man sprawled closest on the floor—bloody arcs splashed across the tiles telling the tale of arterial spray, his pale blue eyes sightlessly staring into forever—only reinforced what he already knew in his gut.

Stand down. He turned back to those gathered around him. *Save the ones you can.*

He sat down heavily, sliding to sit beside Gemma, their shoulders touching and his back to cold marble.

It became very quiet, with only the sound of shouts and pounding feet echoing from the farthest reaches of the Terminal.

The gunmen were silent, except for the sound of something solid hitting the floor, followed by a metallic snap.

Logan met Gemma's gaze and mouthed, "Reloading."

Then he really looked at her. Her brown eyes scanned the space, sharply assessing their situation, and her curly, shoulder-length brown hair was tousled, but it was the splatter of blood over her paler-than-usual olive complexion that focused his attention.

Her gaze came to rest on his face, seeing where his attention was centered. She pulled the sleeve of her sweater over her hand and wiped at her cheek a few times. "Not mine," she whispered.

Relief surged. If they were going to get out of this, they both needed to be at one hundred percent.

In the distance, a door slammed, likely one of the emergency exits from the balcony level as one of the last commuters escaped the carnage below.

Logan only had seconds to take in the small group of people who had taken cover behind the information booth, the only protection in the middle of the wide-open space of the concourse. He scanned the group, each of them sitting with their backs to the marble, their legs pulled in or up, being as small a target as possible if the gunmen circled around to them.

Logan knew they would. The only question was whether they'd die then and there or be used as hostages. It had truly been a catch-22 scenario.

Multiple gunmen with high-capacity submachine guns and the closest exit had been a full fifty feet away.

The bodies on the floor showed how futile that escape attempt might have been. Though in taking cover, they'd exchanged one risk for another.

Gemma hissed his name as she rummaged through the cross-body bag she still wore. Then she pulled out her flip case—the small black leather folding case holding her NYPD identification on one side and her detective's badge on the other. "They killed two MTA officers. They can't know who we are or we're dead," she whispered. She jammed her flip case down one of the tall riding boots she'd paired with blue jeans and a deep burgundy sweater for their dinner, pushing it all the way down so it slid behind decorative strapping and a large gold buckle at her ankle to help camouflage the bulk.

Logan wore shorter boots, but he'd make it work—it would be the last place they'd look if they went to the extent of patting each of them down. He pulled his flip case out of his back pocket and quickly unlaced his left boot, pushing it down to the sole. Next came the folding tactical blade he carried in his right cargo pocket, the only weapon available and one that might be crucial to their survival of the next few minutes or hours. It wouldn't stand against the firepower they currently faced, but it wasn't only a close-quarters weapon but a tool, and, at this point, they needed every advantage they could scrounge. He relaced his boot. Not comfortable, but he wasn't about to be running a marathon like this.

In fact, any movement would likely get him killed. After what these attackers had done, they wouldn't hesitate to take out anyone they identified as a threat.

The continued silence grated on him. *Come on...show yourselves. Let's find out what we're up against.*

As if he'd spoken the thought out loud, a shooter stepped into view to Logan's left.

Wide build, muscular, 220 pounds, likely male from size and stature. Face is masked. Wearing a Kevlar vest under the jacket.

He focused in on the real issue at hand—weaponry. He instantly recognized the short, squat design of the compact assault weapon in the man's hands—a P90 submachine gun. Not the longer-barreled PS90 authorized for personal use, but the military model from its short barrel. It would be an easier weapon to smuggle into a public place, especially if, as it appeared, they'd come in via train into the upper train shed, only revealing their weapons as they entered the concourse.

The P90 was a formidable weapon, with a fifty-round magazine snapped flush into the top of the frame; changing the magazine would only take seconds in experienced hands. It would contain high-velocity 5.7x28mm cartridges, a hollow-point model that would expand into razor-sharp spinning petals of death as soon as it entered a victim, shredding any tissue and blood vessels in its way as it ricocheted around the body. A smaller round with not as much stopping power as a 9mm, but still incredibly deadly in its own right.

Those who'd died under a barrage of bullets never had a chance.

As for himself, not having his Emergency Services Unit—ESU— level IIIA Kevlar vest wouldn't be an issue, as those rounds could pierce it at this range and he'd be equally dead with or without it. The P90 was a weapon meant to kill indiscriminately, as the bodies strewn across the floor demonstrated.

He became aware of Gemma's stiffness beside him as the impact of the situation for her clarified with a snap. *Not again.* She'd lost even more color and couldn't take her eyes off both man and submachine gun.

On Gemma's far side, a second figure—another man, Logan estimated— stepped into view from the west side of the concourse, similarly carrying a P90, sweeping the barrel back and forth over the group of men and women who had taken cover behind the only protection in the entire concourse. He was clearly weighing opening fire again.

They were in serious trouble.

Chapter 4

Gemma relaxed fractionally when Logan got his boot relaced before being seen. Now they both only overtly carried standard identification, and unless one of the shooters actually recognized one of them as NYPD, or they did something that specifically identified them as law enforcement, they were as safe as any of the group.

Which wasn't safe at all.

A figure, all in black and with his face covered, stepped into view from the west side of the concourse carrying an assault weapon, and, unbidden, memory flooded back.

Sitting on cold marble under a soaring rotunda, her face pressed against her mother's shoulder, her hand held in her mother's firm grip, surrounded by terrified adults. Two gunmen, one watching the hostages, one at the teller, demanding cash. Tautly balanced order and calm until the NYPD arrived, then it was all shouting between the hostage takers and terrifyingly loud gunshots into the ceiling. Wanting to crawl inside her mother's coat for protection, covering her ears with both hands to blot out the sounds of fury and violence. Her mother's quiet murmurs as she prayed to St. Jude, the patron saint of hope and impossible cases, and then the familiar words of the Hail Mary.

Hail Mary, full of grace...pray for us sinners, now and at the hour of our death.

The terror of watching her mother bravely rise from the floor to try to reason with the gunmen. Her words of logic and of patience, the words of a cop's wife, one who likely thought she had knowledge other hostages didn't and could end this situation peacefully. All snuffed out, along with her life, when the gunman silenced her forever with a single shot to the head.

The reverberating boom of the gunshot; the splatter of blood; her mother's boneless fall; the cooling of her mother's skin as Gemma sat holding her limp hand for hours, surrounded by people, but so very alone.

The warmth of her father's arms, the security in his words as he carried her away from her mother forever and back into the waiting arms of her family. A family that would never be the same.

She gave herself a mental shake. *Stop that. You're not a defenseless ten-year-old anymore. And you're not alone.*

As if Logan heard her thoughts, his hand dropped over hers where it pressed flat against the marble floor, fingers splayed with stress, his fingers slipping under hers to gather and grip tight. "This won't be the same." His barely there whisper only carried as far as her ears, his head bent so the man with the gun couldn't see his lips moving. "We can do this."

She blew out a breath through pursed lips and returned the pressure of his grip. Logan knew about what had happened to her as a child—not every last detail, but enough to foresee where her brain would go at that moment. *This family is cursed when it comes to these kinds of situations. Logan's going to be sorry he stepped out in public with you.*

As if Logan could hear her thoughts, he gave her hand one more squeeze, then let go, purposely setting his hands on his drawn-up knees.

Logan clearly didn't want to mark them as a couple. Giving the gunmen that information could lead them to use one of them as leverage against the other. Better to look like strangers sitting side by side.

A second figure stepped into her field of view from the west side of the open space and Gemma pushed through the shock to study his weapon. She didn't know firearms to the detail Logan did—it was an integral part of his job, where dealing with individuals took that role for her. Still, she recognized the compact form with the rounded edges. *P90.*

It gave her the kick she needed. *Stay in the game. Think like a cop. You're not a victim; don't be one.*

A quick glance in the opposite direction confirmed both figures carried the same weapon. Double the same firepower, the kind that could kill each of them with a fraction of each magazine load, in a fraction of a second.

Who are they?

She bent her head, letting her hair fall forward to shield her face as she looked at the closer of the two men. As a hostage negotiator, she needed every minute detail about the hostage taker to strengthen her position with them. Often, she was on the phone with them, and while she might like visuals, she didn't have them. In the South Greenfield shooting, the NYPD had managed to get visuals of the classroom, and being able to see Russ Shea's physical reactions to her or the students around him had given her a significant advantage. She had a similar advantage here.

The shooter was tall, over six feet of bulky muscle, and handled the P90 like someone used to dealing expertly with weapons. The build said male to her, as did the slightly outward angled stride. He was all in black—heavy military-style boots; cargo pants, the pockets of which bulged with unknown supplies; and a crew-neck shirt under both a Kevlar vest and an unzipped bomber jacket. A balaclava covered his face, hiding his features as well as his age, but holes around his eyes and mouth showed pale skin. His eyes were light, the color ambiguous from this distance but either blue or green, and his lips were thin. The tight, smooth fit of the mask made her think he was clean-shaven.

She surreptitiously appraised the other shooter, finding his traits similar to his teammate's, though his eyes were dark.

White men, likely in their twenties or thirties from the way they move. Fit. Strong.

She had no illusions about the situation. Their choice had been to flee with a good chance of death due to their open position when the shooting started, or to take shelter from the bullets. Perhaps if it had been just her and Logan in the concourse with the shooters, they might have chosen differently, but when they'd pulled away from each other, both had the same purpose—to save those around them, rather than just themselves. That had meant cover behind the information booth.

The end result: they were now hostages along with the others.

She knew what this would do to her family. More so, what it would do to her father. She might not have done it purposely—as opposed to last August when she'd traded herself for the hostages when Boyle had holed up in city hall—but here she was once again in a situation out of her control, where she was being held at the whim of someone with an agenda. Unlike her helplessness at ten, and even in August, when she was essentially on her own until she managed to get a message through Frankie to her brother

Alex to come to St. Patrick's Old Cathedral, she knew help was coming. She could only imagine the messages flooding into 911. Help was most assuredly on the way.

More specifically, her team was on the way. As was Logan's. Little did they know the teams each had one of their own within the pool of hostages. There had to be some advantage there. She and Logan needed to figure out how best to work the scenario from the inside.

But her father and her three NYPD brothers... Part of the job of the hostage negotiation team—the HNT—was to identify both the hostages and the hostage takers. While her identity was unknown, her family would go about their duties. Her father, Chief of Special Operations Tony Capello, would run the operation to manage the unfolding crisis. Her older brothers, Joe, the oldest, a lieutenant in the Gang Squad, and Mark, a patrol sergeant in the 5th Precinct, would have no place in this operation. Her remaining older brother, Teo, who had broken with family tradition and had instead joined the FDNY, wouldn't have any immediate reason for personal concern.

The exception was Alex, her sole younger brother, an officer in the NYPD Internal Affairs Bureau. Not because of his professional position but because of his familial one. No one in the family but Alex knew she and Logan were out for dinner tonight. They lived in the same Alphabet City building; even as adults they were extremely attached, so it was his habit to hang out at her more spacious apartment. As a result, he knew of her plans in detail for the evening. Alex would hear of the shooting, would call, and when he didn't get an answer, would start to worry. At first, he'd assuage himself that his sister was busy—being social, having dinner—but that would only last so long; then he'd raise the alarm. The Capellos were a tightly bound family. If there was any concern for one, everyone came together, as they had when Joe's oldest son, Sam, had disappeared during the school shooting three weeks before. Everyone had sat vigil while Gemma had negotiated with the shooter, using Logan as a go-between.

Her father would be concerned when Alex raised the alarm. And really, who could blame him? Widowed with five children ages fourteen, thirteen, eleven, ten, and nine, he'd been not only devastated by the loss of his beloved wife twenty-five years before but by how he lost her. Additionally stressful was the psychological damage done to his only daughter, who had been so affected by the trauma, she hadn't spoken for a full twenty-four hours afterward. This current situation would gut her father once he realized she was one of the hostages.

She needed to calm her mind and think this through. She and Logan had proven in the past they could be an unbeatable team with complementing skills. More than that, essentially being undercover cops gave them a huge advantage. Unlike twenty-five years ago, she had the skills and the ability to deal with this situation. Furthermore, she had a partner to do it with.

The only question was how to do it without giving away their roles as NYPD officers.

Chapter 5

"No one move."

The gunman on Logan's left rumbled out the order, though it was unneeded, as most of the hostages were too terrified to even twitch. Logan tried to blend in, to look slighter and less threatening, slouching down, hunching his shoulders, bowing his head, even while peering sideways at the shooter as he pushed away the corpse of the older man with his boot. A moan came from his left, past Gemma, where an older woman sat with her hands pressed to her mouth as tears flowed.

The man's wife?

An almost silent squeak of rubber on tile had Logan's attention snapping back to the gunman just as a third man stepped from behind the information booth carrying a duffel bag in one hand. He set it on the ground about twenty feet from the hostages and turned to the group.

Logan's heart kicked into overdrive as the soft catch of Gemma's breath whispered beside him.

Holy shit.

And he'd thought they were in trouble before.

The man was dressed similarly to the two gunmen—black boots and cargoes, balaclava, and bomber jacket. But his open jacket revealed the horror beneath. A suicide-bomb vest was strapped around his torso with two rows of pale bricks running across the front of the vest, a connecting wire running from one to the next.

A-Team detectives knew where their strengths were and were not—if explosives were ever found on an op, the A-Team would pull back and wait for backup from the Bomb Squad to arrive to safely disarm the bomb without killing the officers involved. Logan knew a lot about explosives but wasn't trained as a bomb technician to the detail required to dismantle a bomb. He could do it with instruction, but not on-the-fly solo.

However, he knew enough to piece together what he was looking at—blocks and blocks of plastic explosives, likely C-4, each wired with a detonator that led back to a control box. If the explosives circled the vest, from the number he could see from this angle, there were likely at least twenty half-length blocks of C-4. He did a rapid calculation—that would be over twelve pounds of C-4, not enough to bring down the building, but enough to kill everyone within range. And that kind of explosive meant—

His gaze shot to the hand the man kept hidden in the pocket of his jacket, but at that moment he pulled it out to reveal a closed fist clutching a cylinder connected by a wire back to the vest.

Despite wearing a well-insulated ski jacket indoors, a chill coursed through him.

A dead man's switch. They'd stay alive as long as the circuit inside that bar switch stayed in its current open position. The moment the switch was released and the circuit was closed, it would detonate the bomb.

They'd all die.

This team of suspects had the attack completely planned out, and apparently taking hostages was their primary goal. They'd also concocted a perfect use for the space in the Terminal. To use this location for hostages held at gunpoint was insanity; it was simply too exposed. There was no space in or around the concourse where the suspects could shelter from the incoming onslaught of A-Team snipers and officers.

The biggest risk was the huge trio of windows at both the east and west sides of the concourse. Each window was about sixty feet high but was actually two windows with a glass walkway between, allowing workers in the offices in the four corners of the building to travel between sides while avoiding the chaos of the concourse floor. From an A-Team perspective, those walkways would make perfect line-of-sight sniper nests. Moreover, in certain spots, the glass was actually an inset window that could be opened for an unobstructed view of the concourse below. Not that any sniper would use those exposed locations, as that would put them easily in range of the P90s below, but it was an option if needed. More than likely, the A-Team officers would use the massive supporting columns as cover and would shoot straight through the glass to make the shot. Or, because of the potential of a one-to-five-degree deflection of the bullet as it passed through the glass, they might consider the first shot simply a proof-of-concept targeting, rapidly followed by a second, deadly-accurate shot through the unobstructed hole in the glass. They might get lucky on the first shot; they'd be precisely on target with the second.

From a tactical standpoint, it was a difficult building to lock down: Multiple public entrances and exits—from street level to the sunken concourse level to the stairwells in every corner. Access to the lower level and the Dining Concourse, as well as the entrance to Grand Central Madison, the commuter rail terminal of the Long Island Rail Road, the newest addition to the complex just north of Grand Central Terminal. The upper and lower train sheds, with their tracks buried deep under Park Avenue, yet accessible via necessary pedestrian and emergency exits, including the Park Avenue East and West Walk staircases, and the 45th and 47th Street Cross-Passages. Then there were the surrounding balconies, each of which could be a sniper nest location following a short commando crawl, from which any of the A-Team could take out the suspects, saving every hostage. It was an easy, though bloody, solution.

Unless there was a bomber with a dead man's switch in his hand. One hardwired into the explosives so there would be no way to jam an over-air signal.

Clearly, the bomb was the linchpin of the plan. There could be dozens of A-Team snipers arriving to surround them and not one of them would take a shot knowing the first bullet would mean the death of every hostage in the room. They wouldn't even need to shoot the bomber if the three men had a one-for-all kind of pact. One goes down, they all go down, taking every hostage and possibly every A-Team officer with them.

Ingenious. Cold and devilishly evil, but ingenious.

Brute force wasn't going to get them out of this situation. Guile might, however. And where he might be a better strategist than Gemma, she had him cold with her ability to talk to people, to convince them not to jump off a bridge, or to release a hostage in exchange for something they wanted or needed. If guile could win the day, Gemma would be the one to make it happen.

He looked sideways at her, found her eyes fixed on the bomb vest.

"C-4." Logan managed the whisper without moving his lips, knew she'd heard from the tiny tip of her head. But there was no surprise in her eyes, and Logan knew she'd already made the same leap.

Bomb-vest guy leaned in and said something to his comrade, who then disappeared behind the information booth while the remaining gunman held his weapon locked on the hostages. Logan closed his eyes, concentrating on his soft footfalls, the odd scuff along the floor, and then back around on the other side of the information booth, the tracking made easier by the terrified silence of the hostages. Then he reappeared on the west side, circling the other gunman, and dropped a second duffel bag on the floor just past him.

The bag nearly tipped as he dropped it, and the gunman had to bend to right it, but in that instant, the unzipped top of the bag revealed more horrors.

Logan hadn't meant to react—he didn't want the suspects to know they had someone in their midst with knowledge of weapons and explosives or he and Gemma would lose their most important advantage—but he couldn't help a slight jerk of shock. Gemma's gaze shot to him even as he quickly got himself under control. The question shone in her eyes—*What do you know that I don't?*—but he couldn't respond, not while he was calculating the impact. The damage. The catastrophic loss of life.

The bags must have been used to hide the two P90s—each only twenty inches in length—when they got on the train that carried them toward Grand Central Terminal. To any passerby, they'd have looked like three guys wearing winter coats on a chilly December evening, one who could stand to lose some weight from his portliness, the other two carrying duffel bags loaded with gym or travel clothes. The bags had some heft, but these were big, muscular guys, and they could have easily managed the weight without strain.

Because inside the bag, under a few stacked P90 magazines, were more blocks of C-4. Many more. And though he hadn't seen into it, the second bag likely held the same.

The intent wasn't just to take out the hostages if snipers took them out. The intent was to take out Grand Central Terminal, and possibly a number of the surrounding skyscrapers.

C-4 on its own was actually a stable material. As a plastic explosive, you could mold it into any shape needed for the job, and it would remain inert until detonated with a high-speed shock. However, the shock wave resulting from the detonation of C-4 would be sufficient to detonate any nearby C-4. The suspects didn't need the duffel bags of C-4 to be wired to blow; simply blowing the vest would detonate every block of C-4 in the room, creating an exponentially catastrophic explosion.

On the bright side, they'd all be dead in milliseconds, so they wouldn't have to worry about the fallout. The city, however, would never be the same after such an act. If the blast happened before the NYPD could evacuate the area, the death toll could approach that of 9/11.

It wouldn't just be the loss of a structure on the National Register of Historic Buildings, but the crippling of one of the city's main transportation hubs with the destruction of Grand Central Terminal, Grand Central Madison, much of the underground track system, and possibly the buildings perched above it on Park Avenue. It would cause chaos within the city and the surrounding region for years at a minimum.

"NYPD!"

Logan's head shot up at the sound of the bomber's voice. The man was standing about twenty-five feet away, about fifteen feet from the gunmen on either side of him, his arms thrown wide, pulling his coat open farther as he spun in a slow circle.

"NYPD! Do not shoot! I'm wearing a suicide vest with a dead man's switch. If you shoot me or either of my two friends, I'll release the switch and the vest will explode."

One of the women in the group shrieked; then the sound was muffled like someone had covered her mouth in fear of retribution. But Logan didn't see; he wouldn't take his eyes off the man who held all their lives in his hand.

"I also have two bags of additional C-4," the bomber continued at a bellow. "They'll also blow and it could take out this whole city block. Do not enter the concourse. Do not engage your snipers. Or we *all* die." His emphasis on "all" was unmistakable. He didn't just mean his group and the hostages.

Logan hadn't seen a single NYPD officer of any variety but knew by this time there had to be a mass gathering outside the building with the first officers preparing to enter. Because the shooting had stopped, they'd be weighing active versus passive shooter protocols. But it was so much more than that now. The suspects had arranged a scenario where they could stand in view of every sniper the department had at their disposal and no one would touch them.

He knew one of his commanding lieutenants, Sanders, who had a tendency to lean on force more than some in the department would like—Gemma among them—would want to get men into position immediately with the intention of multiple, simultaneous shots to take out all three quickly. There were more than enough men and available positions to make it work. But now that option was entirely off the table.

Only minutes into this scenario and they were already at a stalemate.

Chapter 6

Gemma had shared Logan's jolt at the sight of the suicide vest, but his clear alarm—at least to her—at the duffel bag made her own concern soar. Logan was known for his cool head in a crisis; if he was worried, they had a real problem. Now, with the announcement of the blast power of the total amount of C-4, she understood his reaction.

"Do you hear me, NYPD?" As if satisfied, the bomber stopped his slow spin, making sure whoever might have eyes on the situation—and there were so many directions from which to do that—could see what they were up against.

But silence was his only answer.

For the first time, the bomber turned to look at the group of people huddled against the information booth. His gaze tracked briefly to the blood-spattered glass over their heads, and then down again. Most of his face was covered, making it hard for Gemma to guess at his expression, but the tiny tilt to one corner of his lips conveyed his satisfaction.

The attack must have gone according to plan. The three of them were still alive—killing the MTA cops in the opening seconds had tilted chances of survival in their favor—and they had a group of hostages to use for leverage.

Gemma noticed the man's gaze never strayed toward any of the bodies strewn about the floor. She didn't want to take her eyes off him to count, but there had to be at least a half dozen visible, knowing she could only see just under half the space. But he remained focused on the living, those who had a purpose in his cause as far as he was concerned. Those who had already passed were not useful, and therefore beneath his concern.

"What do you want from us?"

Gemma's head whipped sideways at the sound of a man's voice coming from her right, on the other side of Logan. A business type sat tall, a blond man in a navy suit and tie under his unbuttoned trench coat, his eyes locked on the bomber. Unlike most of the other hostages, who cowered, this one seemed pissed his Friday night had been disrupted.

The bomber slowly turned to stare at him unblinkingly and then held the stare so long the businessman actually shrank back slightly. "Trust me. When I want something from you, you'll know."

Forceful, commanding tone. No hesitation. English is likely his first language. No strong accent from any of the five boroughs. Possibly not from around here.

"But now that you mention it, there are things I want. First off, I want everyone to toss their bags and coats on the floor out in front of them. Everything out of your pockets, most of all your cell phones. Then we're going to search you to make sure you did as directed." His eyes narrowed into a mean squint. "You won't like what happens if we find something."

Gemma knew it wouldn't matter if they found her badge in her bag or in a body search; she'd be dead either way, probably used as a demonstration to the NYPD of what they'd do if the department didn't do what they wanted. Logan wouldn't be far behind.

When most of the hostages stayed frozen, the bomber bellowed, *"Now!"*

The hostages flew into action. Gemma pulled off her cross-body bag—which contained her cell phone and personal identification—and tossed it onto the marble floor several feet in front of her boots.

A few feet away, a middle-aged man took off his coat, laid a DSLR camera in its folds and rolled it up inside to protect it, then pushed it away from him to slide across the floor. Farther to her right, two teenage girls were taking off their coats but seemed reluctant to part with their precious cell phones, and with them, their connection to the outside world, to help, to family. The dark-haired girl tucked her phone in her purse, then grabbed her friend's and added it before zipping the purse shut and sliding it away from her.

Beside Gemma, Logan tipped toward her as he jerked his arm as if he were getting tangled as he struggled to get free of his jacket. "Confirmed. C-4 in the bags," he murmured.

She continued removing her jacket, purposely leaning into him as she did so to facilitate conversation. "As much as he said?" The words were only a whisper of sound.

"Enough to blow the block when he blows the vest." He straightened, shrugging out of his jacket. He tucked his phone and wallet into one of the jacket pockets, zipped it shut, and then lobbed the jacket onto the floor next to her bag.

Gemma finished wriggling out of her winter jacket, balled it, and threw it on top of her bag.

A tap on her thigh pulled her attention back to Logan. He was looking down, and she followed his gaze toward the floor. He held out an index finger, then pointed with it at the bomber. Then he unfolded a second finger and pointed with both to the gunman on their left. Next, he pointed three fingers at the gunman on their right.

She understood his shorthand. To be able to come up with a plan, to be able to strategize how to get out of this crisis, they'd need to be able to discuss the hostage takers as individuals. Numbers would do nicely— Hostage Takers One, Two, and Three, it was.

"Stop sniveling and move!" Three turned his P90 on one of the two teenage girls a few hostages to Logan's right. The smaller of the two, a petite girl with a messy blond bun, dressed in pink low-cut sneakers, black skinny jeans, and a black-and-white long-sleeved T-shirt, cowered, curling into herself, a terrified squeak rasping from the back of her throat.

"She'll move faster if you take that gun off her." Gemma's voice rang out in the nearly silent echoing space.

Three immediately turned his P90 on Gemma, which had been her goal. The point of hostages was to use them as live leverage. A dead hostage was no good for them. But still, staring down the darkness of the barrel of a weapon of mass death left her chilled.

"This work better for you?" he asked.

"Gem..." Logan's murmur to her right warned her to watch herself, but she couldn't let a teenage girl cower under the barrel of a P90.

Been there, done that. No child should live through that.

"Not really." She kept her tone as nonconfrontational as possible. "But you're scaring her. She's a child. Let her do what she needs to do."

"Then why don't I do what *I* need to do." He looked at Two while One stood farther away, watching the greater concourse space. "Cover them. Anyone moves without our say-so, feel free to fire."

"Works for me."

No one had spoken for long, but Gemma had now heard all three hostage takers speak, and what she heard was typical for East Coast Americans without the obvious indicators for Boston or the Bronx. She wasn't sure, but there might be a little Philly in Suspect Two's vowels.

Three set down his P90 on top of the duffel bag—the warning not to touch it had essentially already been given—and strode toward Gemma. "Get up. We'll start with you."

Gemma rose to her feet but didn't move. She wasn't about to make this easy on him in any way but would follow his directions to the letter.

"Step out here." He stopped about fifteen feet from the hostages, well out of reach if any of them attempted to lunge at him.

Gemma stepped over her coat and bag and walked calmly to him. She was glad that while her sweater was snug over her torso, it was also high-necked; she was sure while she exuded calm, her carotid was likely visibly pulsing against the skin of her throat, based on the hammering of her heart.

She wasn't a terrified ten-year-old this time. She'd be damned if she would let him see her fear.

"Turn around."

Gemma wordlessly turned her back to the gunman, who proceeded to run his hands down her sides, over her hips, and down to her knees. She met Logan's gaze to find it laser-focused on her, holding hers as a strange man freely ran his hands over her body. Straightening, the man did an extra, noticeably slower pass over her torso. She winced as he gave her left breast a hard squeeze as he lingered there. Across from her, Logan's eyes flared wide with fury, but he held still, knowing better than to react.

Three's hands dropped away. "You're clear. Sit down." Three pointed a gloved finger at the man who sat beside Gemma's empty spot. "You."

A man in jeans and a sweatshirt rose and walked around his backpack and coat to change places with Gemma.

Gemma sank down cross-legged on the floor beside Logan and let a shaky breath slip free.

Logan dropped his head while giving her a hard sideways look. "You okay?"

"Yeah. Handsy bastard." She sat up straight and kept her eyes directly ahead, staring at Three, refusing to be cowed.

But they both recognized the most important aspect of what had just happened—Three had been so focused on the female form beneath her sweater, he'd missed the flip case hidden in her boot. Safe...for now.

Logan was next. His pat down was impersonal but thorough, though Three continued his blind spot with footwear, and the flip case and knife remained undetected.

Three moved swiftly through the rest of the crowd. Both Gemma and Logan kept their gazes locked on whoever was being searched, though Three's preferences quickly became evident. Men—quick and efficient searches. Older women—ditto. Younger women—slower, with liberties taken.

It gave Gemma a chance to see exactly who the hostages were and to get a final count.

There were fourteen of them in total, including herself and Logan. The two teenage girls, the older woman who'd lost her husband when he was shot in the throat, a young woman likely in her early twenties who had gritted her teeth through the obvious and degrading groping, the middle-aged woman and teenage boy, the man who owned the camera, the older woman Logan had carried to safety, two German tourists, who luckily seemed to understand enough English to follow the instructions, the mouthy businessman, and the man in the sweatshirt who sat beside her.

The hostages appeared to be physically unharmed with the exception of one of the German men, who clutched his left hand over his bloody right sleeve. While clearly hurt, the injury didn't appear life-threatening, so perhaps he was only winged by a bullet.

When the mother went to sit down again beside her son, she had a quiet conversation with one of the gunmen, who nodded his assent, and she snatched a bright blue scarf off the coat piled in front of where she sat. Gemma turned her attention away from them, but not before seeing the woman begin to wrap the injured man's arm.

When the two teenage girls were searched, Gemma tried to lock gazes with each of them in turn, trying to give comfort across the distance. The blond girl who'd been so upset before met her gaze and desperately held it, her face crumpling when Three was overly hands-on with her. The other girl, taller than her friend, with a spiky black pixie cut, dressed in ripped blue jeans, a blue V-neck sweater, and black leather ankle boots, stood stoic as she was searched, her face set in stone, her eyes locked on the clock over the information booth.

As the last of the hostages returned to sit down—the stone-faced woman who had lost her husband in the opening moments of the attack—One bellowed out his instructions to the NYPD again, no doubt wanting to ensure his message made it through to everyone from patrol cops to the chief of the department.

Gemma had no doubt the news had rocketed all the way to the brass by this point. She could only imagine the scrambling taking place at One Police Plaza and throughout the whole ESU.

One strode over to the piles of coats, bags, purses, and technology, staring down at it for a moment. "Move this so it's not in the way." He pointed at Two while Three stepped closer to the group, where he could cover the hostages. Could take them out in a single stream of bullets without needing to reload, if provoked.

Two made quick work of kicking the bags and coats toward the West Balcony and out of the way.

"Now, time to make sure you're not going anywhere," said One.

Two put his P90 down on the nearest duffel bag and shucked off his bomber jacket, revealing the Kevlar vest strapped over a long-sleeved black T-shirt, then rummaged through a side pocket of one of the bags and pulled out a handful of long zip ties, which he stuffed into the back pocket of his pants.

Beside her, Logan growled low in the back of his throat. She understood his frustration.

If they were each going to be tied hand and foot like slaughtered deer, getting free to deal with this situation just became much harder.

Chapter 7

As Three moved to stand near the middle of the group, where he could keep an eye on everyone, Two started at the west end of the hostages with the mother-and-teenage-son pairing. Two initially stepped toward the son, but the mother asked to be done first even though her son was on the end.

Keeping her head down so it looked like she was staring at the floor, Gemma kept her gaze sideways to watch the transaction, trying to get a feel for the personalities of the hostage takers. She had a good handle on Three already—confident, brash, willing to stomp on personal rights, more than happy to cop a feel of an unwilling woman. So far, her impression of One was he was in charge, the one who ensured control of the most sensitive part of the operation—the suicide vest. He was hands-off when it came to the hostages, but that likely was to ensure no one jostled the dead man's switch out of his hand, ending the crisis early with catastrophic results. Additionally, she got the feeling he held himself separate from his two teammates, always watching for compliance from them as well as from the NYPD.

This was *his* op.

Was that because he had the most to lose? Or was he simply a psychopath with no empathy for what he was putting the hostages and the city through? If so, his lack of remorse after the fact wouldn't be a factor if the vest detonated, as he'd be gone with the rest of them.

Two was proving to be a little harder to discern. Granted, with their faces being mostly covered, it made deciphering their emotions considerably harder, but Gemma was getting the impression that while he was going along with his partners, and while he'd certainly been responsible for some of the loss of life in the initial minutes of the attack, he was perhaps a little less likely to use force for no reason. He would be the participant most worth watching, and potentially might be a conduit of coercion of the greater group.

Two zip-tied the mother's hands first, then her feet. She looked up at him, and while Gemma was sure his two colleagues couldn't hear her words, thanked him for allowing her to go first. He froze for a fraction of a second before turning to her son.

Was he having second thoughts now the initial carnage was over? Was he a parent and recognized a connection between the mother and himself?

Gemma's experience of over fourteen years on the force, the last two being with the HNT, told her this was the most dangerous moment of the hostage standoff, barring the situation that got them there.

No hostage taker ever considered they could form a bond with their hostages, but familiarity over time eventually started to form the threads of one, even if unwittingly and unwillingly. As the hostage taker spent time with a hostage, as they came to know that person, a connection was formed. The stronger that inadvertent connection, the harder it would be to harm them. Even something as simple as a hostage's name could be enough to begin to turn the tide. Killing a stranger was one thing, killing someone you knew something about—their name, family status, or history—became so much harder, and that was a layer of protection for each hostage.

But in these crucial beginning moments, there was no connection to speak of, and anyone who acted out of turn, who resisted the will of the hostage taker, was at a much higher risk of injury or death at the hands of the hostage taker. Currently, everyone was as disposable as the two MTA cops lying dead behind their desk.

Those deaths and the deaths of the victims around them actually made for a much more perilous situation. In any hostage situation, all negotiators knew there was an invisible line to cross—the first hostage death. Taking hostages was one thing, but the punishment for taking a life was much higher. Once that invisible line was crossed, the risk of subsequent death went up dramatically—what's two life sentences when you already had one?

That line had been crossed in the opening seconds of the attack, which made the job of any negotiator that much harder. And, in this case, the line hadn't just been crossed; it had been annihilated with the killing of not one but two police officers.

There was nothing to hold these men back from killing again. Especially when they knew no tactical officer would hesitate to kill them after they'd murdered a brother in blue.

The suicide vest had been key to their plan. Anyone who researched Grand Central Terminal, anyone who came to scope out the facility as they surely had, would have known about the manned police desk opposite the information booth, a similar desk in the Dining Concourse below them, the golf-cart-size police vehicle parked just outside the Main Concourse, and the police station on the lower level, near the Dining Concourse. Lost in the crowd of travelers, who could have guessed their intent as they plotted and schemed? But to pull this off, they knew they'd have to not only kill any officers present in the opening seconds but find a way to protect themselves from any return fire once local officers and, more importantly, the A-Team arrived.

Now that they were here in this situation, what was the plan to open communications to the outside world? They'd made this stand; there had to be a reason for it. And whatever it was, she needed to find a way to insinuate herself into the negotiations to be able to feed information to her team. Maybe if she—

"Hold still!"

Two's snapped order brought Gemma back to the current scenario. Two had moved down the group, binding the wrists and ankles of the mother and son, the two male tourists, and the dark-haired teenager. But the blond teenager was starting to crack. She was shaking and kept jerking her hands away from Two while he tightened the zip ties.

As he tried again, and the girl pulled one hand from the loop, Two pulled away like he was going to backhand her, and she cowered in terror against the marble wall. Beside her, her friend was trying to calm her down, to no avail.

Gemma understood the terror. When she'd been trapped in Dime Savings Bank with her mother that fateful day, her reaction had been to become as small and quiet as possible, hoping the gunmen wouldn't notice her. The adults around her had reacted in various ways that morphed over time. Some were meek, and some looked like they were considering jumping one of the gunmen but held back because of the second shooter. Some had reacted more like this teenage girl, weeping and shaking, irritating the gunmen as their carefully crafted plan had gone to hell when a police car cruising by spotted the robbery and had ruined their getaway plan. One woman had become so strident, Gemma had feared for her life, but her extreme panic had been beyond her control.

Her mother had remained calm. Too calm. So calm and controlled, she thought she'd be able to talk the gunmen out of harming the hostages.

She'd been so very wrong. It had been a fatal mistake.

Gemma didn't want to step in again in the girl's defense but would if there was no other choice. She'd already called attention to herself, and if she was going to find a way to connect with these men so they'd allow her to speak for them, she had a very fine line to walk.

"For fuck's sake," the businessman beside Logan hissed. "You're going to get us all killed." He grabbed the girl's forearms, ignoring her shriek at his rough handling, and looked up at Two. "Do it."

It was quick work to bind her hands, then her feet, now that she was being held down. Gemma could feel Logan beside her, his body tense, fighting the need to give the guy sitting beside him a shot for his rough treatment of a frightened girl but knowing they had to lay low. Gemma was female and might be somewhat discounted in their eyes because of her gender—something she normally despised but was happy to work with right now—but Logan, tall and strong, with a commanding presence as a law enforcement officer, would be instantly considered a threat to be dealt with. He had to lay low, saving his offensive moves for a single, best-placed moment. Gemma knew what it cost him to do so.

"Here." Business Guy stuck out his balled hands, the insides of his wrists pushed together. "Just remember I helped when you needed it."

Oh, yeah, you're a real hero. Gemma struggled to keep her face in neutral lines and to not give away her disgust; she could tell by the way Logan's jaw went rock hard and his eyes flinty, he was thinking the same thing.

But the teenage blonde couldn't be calmed. Her friend's whispered pleas for her to calm down were getting louder as she continued to be ignored, the desperation in her tone cranking higher and higher. She sat with her bound hands curled under her chin, her knees drawn up, the zip ties noticeably digging into her ankles, rocking and sobbing, letting out a high keening wail.

This couldn't continue. Someone was going to lose it, and this child was going to be the next fatality.

Two cast a furious backward glance at the girl as he moved on to Logan. "Wrists," he ordered.

Logan held out both hands, about four inches apart, not making it easier on the man.

"Together," Two barked.

Gemma winced as the keening rose in pitch. She could swear her eardrums were vibrating at the frequency—

"*Shut up!*" Three swung the P90 to point the barrel at the girl's skull. The brunette teenager cried out and pulled back from her friend as the blonde suddenly stopped all sound as if her lungs had iced over.

Two froze in the act of slipping the loop of a zip tie around Logan's wrists, the white plastic band lying loose as Two looked back at the blonde.

Time to make the best kind of distraction Gemma knew how to make.

"This is getting us nowhere." Gemma didn't have to raise her voice much to be heard over the frozen silence of the hostages.

Three's P90 swung in her direction, but he had to step farther away from the hostages to get a line of sight on her around Two. "You think so?"

Gemma held still under the barrel of the P90. At least it was off the girl, which might give her a chance to calm down. In the meantime, she'd keep the attention on herself. And hope to God that attention had a better outcome than when her mother had attempted the same thing twenty-five years earlier. Gemma at least had the skills needed for this challenge, something her mother had lacked. "I know so. You want something or else you wouldn't have done this. But standing here yelling at the NYPD isn't going to get it. Haven't you seen *Dog Day Afternoon*? You need a conversation to get what you want, and not one where you're screaming your demands. You won't get your message through that way. Trust me, I know."

Logan's elbow dug into her side, a warning for her to back down, but she knew this was how it had to be. If she was going to insert herself into the negotiation, she had to convince these men they *needed* her.

Three drew in a breath as if to bellow a response, but a cooler voice cut him off.

"How exactly do you know?"

Gemma's gaze tracked toward One, who stood back about ten extra feet from Three, standing across from the middle of the group so he could constantly watch both his own men and the hostages. "Because I'm a professional negotiator." She sensed Logan's sudden stillness and wished she could reassure him, could tell him to trust her. *You didn't fully trust me in the cemetery with Boyle. Trust me now.* "A business negotiator. I've negotiated deals with top businesses nationwide, many against unions who had their own professional negotiators. I've been extremely successful." She sat a little straighter, held her chin higher, a picture of someone sure of herself and her skills. "I'm very expensive and in great demand."

"And why would I care about that?"

Out of the corner of her eye, Gemma noticed as Two had been distracted by the disruption of the teenager, Three's fury, and her conversation with One, Logan had subtly shifted how he was holding his wrists, no longer facing but side by side, his fists clenched, building in as much space for possible escape as he could before the ties were tightened. "Because I can help you."

One let out a bark of laughter. "And why would you do that?"

"Because currently you're the highest bidder for my services. And I negotiate for whoever is paying for those services." Her gaze slid to Three and she let her lip curl slightly. "I don't see you have anyone competent to fill that role so far. And it obviously shouldn't be you."

"Why is that?"

Gemma pointed at Two's balaclava where he bent over Logan, tightening the zip ties around his wrists. "Besides the fact you obviously don't want to be identified and you could give yourself away in direct conversation? Because when those directly involved take part in a negotiation, emotions become part of the strategy. Why do you think businesses and unions hire professional negotiators to get a deal made? Because they want someone who can come in and use cold logic and their knowledge of people and what makes them tick to find a way to end a standoff. Not everyone is good at negotiation. You need someone organized, someone who can think on her feet under pressure, someone who can communicate your messages succinctly, and who has the patience to wait for the right moment to make demands. You don't want a deal done fast. You want your deal done your way, sometimes no matter how long it takes. Did you think about that?"

She held One's gaze unblinkingly, glad he couldn't hear her heart rapping against her breastbone or see the cold sweat that slithered down her spine.

"And you expect me to pay for this service?"

Gemma let a cynical laugh break free. "I'm not an idiot. Negotiations are transactional. I give something, you give something." She nailed One with a piercing stare. "I negotiate for you for free; you let me go when you get your deal. You're holding my life in your hands. Seems like a fair deal to me."

"Isn't that my leverage? To release the hostages in exchange for what I want? What do you get out of this?"

"A chance to make sure the negotiation is successful. That means a chance at life. Otherwise, the deck may not be stacked in our favor."

"And you can do that?"

"Yes." Short and simple, Gemma let her confidence fill the single word and then backed off, not wanting to crowd One while he made his decision.

Two finished tying Logan's ankles and then moved toward Gemma. He paused momentarily, then glanced back at One, as if unsure if Gemma was to be treated differently at this point.

One stared at Gemma for a long moment. "Do her ankles. Leave her hands free. For now. If she gives us any trouble, bind them."

Two was none too gentle as he wrapped Gemma's ankles with the zip tie and yanked it tight. Tight enough her shield dug sharply into her ankle. But in some ways, she didn't mind; it was a constant reminder of who she was and what she could do here.

Two moved on to the man beside Gemma and she sat back against the marble base of the information booth. She sat straight, her eyes coolly watching Two tie the man's hands, even though she wanted to sag in relief that she'd been able to pull off the bravado of making the offer convincingly when she'd been quaking inside.

Located roughly in the middle of the hostages, it allowed her to see the whole group on either side of her, seated with their backs against the curved wall of the information booth, from the mother-and-son pairing farthest to the right, to the older woman Logan had rescued farthest to the left. They appeared scared and shaken, but at least the blond teenager had settled into a terrified silence, punctuated only by an occasional shuddering sniff.

One needed some quiet to consider her offer, and if there was constant chaos in the ranks of the hostages, he'd never be able to work out the logic of her argument. She needed him on her side—only then could she control the negotiation, could speak to her team, and secretly pass them information.

If he didn't allow her to step in, there was no telling how short—and how fatally final—the negotiations might be.

Chapter 8

For one brief moment, Logan thought their game was up. Now, minutes later, after watching Gemma talk her way into a seat at the negotiating table, he understood her gamble.

It was a good one.

Marking herself as a business negotiator would give her a reason to discuss the situation with the suspects, to hopefully insert herself into the actual negotiations. It was the single angle to this situation with the best chance of saving their lives, and a cool head to ensure frustrations and fury didn't override the upcoming conversations. One had yet to make a decision on it, but Gemma's blatant what's-in-it-for-me attitude screamed typical American capitalist. Perfectly convincing, even to his ears, though he knew what she was really doing.

If she pulled this off, it was going to be a hell of a shock to her commanding officer, Lieutenant Tomás Garcia, when he found out one of his best hostage negotiators was one of the taken. It would put a different spin on this negotiation from any other they'd likely had to manage—to have an officer inside the crisis working both sides of the conversation.

If she could tilt the negotiation in their favor, then it might be up to him to bring down the suspects.

Logan casually looked down at his zip-tied wrists. Gemma had timed her disruption just right, distracting Two from his task of making sure Logan was trussed like a Christmas turkey. Two had done a great job with the business jerk beside him, the one who'd manhandled a terrified teenage girl into compliance. Logan wasn't sure what he was expecting for his assistance but didn't think brutally tied hands and feet were it from the guy's muttered comments and the way he kept trying to find a comfortable position for his hands to keep the zip tie from biting into the soft flesh of his wrists.

Because of Gemma's precisely timed interruption and conversation with One, Two had been careless when he'd tied Logan's hands, allowing Logan to gain extra space by clenching his fists, which shortened and expanded his wrists, as well as holding them side by side instead of front to front. Now, with his fists relaxed, he could turn his wrists in to face each other and there was a definite gap in the tie's girth. Besides keeping his skin from getting sliced by the tight bonds, it meant if he could get his hands on it, there would be space to slide the blade of his knife between his wrists to cut through the tie.

Unfortunately, the suspects weren't idiots and had used zip ties thick enough even he wasn't sure he could break them. He'd broken thinner ties before as part of his training—it could be done efficiently by snapping the wrists in toward the chest while jerking the elbows out. He could try that technique on these ties, but success wasn't guaranteed and the time lost might be a fatal mistake. He had the knife; he just needed to free it from his boot and then bide his time to use it—no point in freeing his hands now, just to get shot for his trouble—but then he would have the advantage.

He wished he could communicate his plan to Gemma, but that kind of conversation was out of the question. As it was, staying detached from her, as if she were a stranger, was crucial. The gunmen had come out of the upper train shed shooting when he and Gemma had been in the middle of the concourse. There was no way they'd been spotted together, and they'd separated the moment bullets flew. The key to their being able to get out of this might rest in the suspects not knowing they were working together toward a common goal, knowing each other's strengths and using them to their combined advantage. Both had considerable hand-to-hand skills, but additionally Gemma had the ability to read people, pivot on the fly when negotiations went to hell, and communicate effectively to get results, while he excelled at crisis strategy, weapons, and specialized tactical skills. They could be a formidable team, but it was crucial that teamwork wasn't overtly identified.

Twenty feet in front of him, One's head swiveled sideways, a grin spreading inside the mouth hole of the balaclava.

Logan followed One's gaze, up to the massive trio of windows on the east side of the building, and realized what had attracted his attention— dark figures were running along the walkways sheltered between the heavy glass panels of the windows. A glance at the west windows showed a second team getting into position.

Logan couldn't identify the men at this distance, but he could discern they were A-Team officers based on their shape—wearing Kevlar vests, their pockets stuffed with all the ammunition they might need for the siege, helmets, and heavy utility belts. Logan knew each officer would have a pistol strapped to their thigh, but it was the M4A1 carbine they carried that was the weapon of choice in this situation. Logan could shoot 1,000 yards with the M4A1, even farther with his M21 sniper rifle. But in this case, the M4A1 would be more than sufficient to manage this abbreviated distance.

He watched as men entered from both sides on each of the five levels, sprinting to their places behind the wide marble dividers between the tall curving windows, with more out of sight at the edges, he was sure.

He wasn't certain who was commanding this op—it could be Lieutenant Sanders or Cartwright or one of several other officers—but if it was him, he'd have duplicate setups on each side, with men staggered on every other floor in each vertical position and window. Ten or twelve shooters on each side would more than cover any possible angle. It was early in the op, so numbers might fill out later. He wondered if the balcony, behind him and out of sight, already had men in place.

"NYPD!" One's bellow filled the space. "Do *not* shoot. If you take out any of the three of us, I'll release the dead man's switch, detonating the vest and the extra bags of C-4. You'll all die and you'll lose this city block. You want the hostages to live? You want to live? Stand down. *Now!*"

Logan knew one thing was for sure. It didn't matter who was running the op, standing down wasn't an option. Holding, however, was.

The cavalry had arrived, only to find their hands tied.

I know how you feel...

One seemed pleased with the standoff. He had the attention of the NYPD, and, as far as he was concerned, they were dancing to his tune.

The other two suspects had also spotted the A-Team officers getting into position and both moved to discuss the issue with One, standing with their P90s facing the hostages, ready to react if anyone attempted escape or an attack.

Time to take advantage of their temporary distraction. If he could reach his knife and transfer it to a higher pocket, then it would be available to his bound hands if he was on his feet, whereas its current placement in his boot only worked when he was seated. Logan dropped his hands between his spread knees so the backs of his fingers rested against the tops of his boots, his gaze locked on the suspects, noting their distraction as they tried to identify all the officers stationed around them. When he was sure everyone's eyes were off the hostages, he slipped the fingers of his right hand into his left boot. The space was small, the zip tie yanked tight, locking his boots together, but his folded tactical knife was a solid bar digging into his inner left ankle. With his index and middle finger, he tried to clasp the end of the knife handle but he couldn't get a grip on it. A second attempt, his eyes locked on the suspects, was equally fruitless. What he really needed was to be able to rotate his hands so he could get his thumb and index finger inside to grab it as a pincer, but even with his wrists tied a little loose, he didn't have that kind of flexibility.

He slipped his fingers inside again. Failed again.

Gemma's cool fingers slid over his, freezing him in place. Without a word, she tapped his hand away, then shifted her bound feet so her right boot pressed against his left, forming a partial barrier to the movement of her unbound hand. She slipped her right hand between his lower shins, tapping one, then the other a few times in quick succession.

Give me as much space as you can.

Without taking his eyes off the suspects, Logan pulled his feet as far apart as he could, feeling the cut of the tie digging into his boot right down to his skin, still not sure he was giving her enough space to work.

Apparently, it was sufficient, as she slipped her thumb and index finger inside his boot, found the knife, and slowly drew it out, only losing hold of it once. Then the pressure of the bulk of the weapon was gone as the knife mostly disappeared into her closed fist and she drew her hand back, keeping it pressed to her outer thigh.

Three's eyes suddenly broke off from the west window to scan the group, and Gemma froze, her hand near her hip. Logan let his left leg fall slightly toward her, blocking her hand from Three's line of sight. His gaze passed over them to hold with a sneer of disgust on the teenage blonde.

Logan didn't like the man's attention on the girl, but there was nothing he could do about it for now. And it gave them the cover they needed.

Gemma nudged his leg away, freeing her hand, and then carefully slid her elbow behind her enough that she could get her hand into the left front pocket of his cargo pants. He slid his boots forward a little, trying to buy her more space as she forced her hand deep, as deep as she could reach, then released the knife, pushing it down as far as possible before sliding her flat hand free. A last glide down the front of his pants to make sure the knife lay flat and wouldn't be a noticeable bulge if they had him stand, then her hand was gone.

Only once her hands were again neatly folded in her own lap did he turn his head enough to give her a sideways glance. Blue eyes met brown, and he gave her a small smile of thanks. Then he couldn't resist a single raised eyebrow as if to recognize where her hand had been.

She turned away from him, not wanting to risk any chance of their being seen, but he saw a flash of her satisfied smile before she wiped her face into neutral lines.

Her smile held a promise, the kind that made him even more determined to get out of this situation. He wanted to live, no question about that, but now he also wanted to know what that smile foretold.

Chapter 9

As much as Gemma would have enjoyed a little light flirtation with Logan, now was definitely not the time. Turning her mind back to the current situation, Gemma knew she had to make the next push. She'd given One the idea to use her; now she had to be proactive. Useful. *Invaluable*.

That meant actual negotiations, and to open those negotiations, they needed a channel. There would likely be phones inside the glass confines of the information booth, but the single door on this level—installed following 9/11, so there was more than one method of egress—would be locked, and anyone who had survived the initial attack would have fled down the circular staircase and out through the original door in the middle of the lower Dining Concourse. Same with the ticket booths—all doors into the space across from them would be locked. The hostages had phones, but the NYPD didn't know the identities of the hostages or their phone numbers.

Except for herself and Logan. But their superiors would never dream they'd have detectives literally caught in the crossfire. And while One had so far used bellowing into an empty, cavernous hall to get his message across, that wouldn't work long-term. They needed a dedicated phone for this.

More than that, somehow, Gemma needed to get the message to the NYPD that she and Logan were among the hostages. They couldn't help either the negotiation process or a tactical breach, if it came to that, if the department wasn't aware of their presence.

Or her presence, specifically. Once that was known, it would have significant ramifications, as her father would be pulled out of the Special

Operations line of command, but it would allow Garcia to put together a very specific negotiation team, one with Gemma's fellow negotiators, especially the ones who knew her best and who would be trying to hear any hidden message in her conversation with them.

Equally as important, once word rocketed through the Capello family, Alex would bring the last crucial piece of information to the table—Logan's presence with her this evening. If she was one of the hostages, then unless someone had heard from Logan—and they wouldn't have—he was either dead or also part of the mix. That would be useful information for whoever was commanding the A-Team officers.

But how to get that information out? She knew there wouldn't be a single word of contact with the outside world unsupervised by the hostage takers, so she couldn't simply call her father and fake a 911 call reporting the hostage taking. And if she called 911, whoever she ended up with wouldn't necessarily know her voice.

Everything rested on her being recognized.

The idea came to her with the precision of a lightning strike. She could think of one person she could sell to the hostage takers who they'd see as an opportunity. One person who would be like a rabid dog in his enthusiasm to have a role in this crisis, even if she personally saw it as a potential detriment. Mostly because she disliked him so intensely.

Greg Coulter from ABC7.

The man who looked so coiffed and perfect in every headshot with his sparkling eyes and snow-white teeth, you'd swear he was an AI hallucination, except he always had the right number of fingers.

He might not recognize Gemma's voice on the phone, but if she could get him in here, he'd recognize her on sight and would carry that information back to the NYPD, where it would move at the speed of light through the department. Dominoes would fall in succession—her father's role in the op being the first of them—but the end result of the game could free them all.

She took a full five minutes to consider any other option but couldn't come up with one that would work as well as Coulter.

Dannazione. No help for it.

Gemma studied the three men for a moment. They still stood in a group, watching the space around them—not just the hostages but the NYPD officers, briefly visible through the glass, now in position, hidden from view. Gemma couldn't see the balcony directly behind them, but she imagined officers had slithered across the floor there and had taken up position, their rifle barrels braced on the lower edge of the marble balustrade between the decorative spindles. More men would surely be stationed on the 42nd Street sidewalk just outside the doors leading into the Onassis Foyer, with more inside the foyer, tucked into the walled recesses on either side of the doors leading into Vanderbilt Hall. She doubted there was anyone inside Vanderbilt Hall, as the hallway leading to that space was a direct and unprotected line of fire from where the gunmen stood.

The two gunmen held their P90s ready to take out any hostage who stepped out of line—unlikely, as they all had their feet bound—or any cop who encroached on their space, each exuding the confidence of someone in complete control.

She studied the bomber. How long could he hold the dead man's switch? From her police training, she knew the basics about bombs and how a dead man's switch worked. She'd worked a hostage situation early on where a man in a homemade vest threatened to blow himself up unless the hostage negotiators could get his soon-to-be ex-wife on the phone because he wanted her back. In the end, his wife hadn't wanted to talk to him—possibly thinking if he took himself out, her life would be easier in the long run—and in his despair, he'd released the dead man's switch...and nothing had happened. The bomb squad had moved in then, only to report later the vest had been so poorly constructed, it was never going to blow.

She'd received a lesson in explosive vests and dead man's switches from Sergeant Hamill, the supervising bomb technician that day. Based on what he'd taught her and from the very little she could see, the bomber most likely used a simple circuit held open with some sort of spring-loaded switch. As long as he kept the switch depressed in his fist, the circuit stayed open. When the switch was released, it would spring out, closing the circuit, detonating the vest, and taking the rest of the C-4, the hostages, Grand Central Terminal, and too much of midtown Manhattan with it.

The bomber himself might be the weakest link in this whole scenario—how long could one man hold a spring-loaded switch in position? If the spring had relatively light pressure, it would extend the time, but from the moment he'd armed the bomb, the clock had started to tick. Given enough time, the muscles holding the switch depressed would begin to cramp. At some point, the man might not have any choice but to let go. He might attempt to pass the switch off to his other hand, or to another man, but depending on the sensitivity of the switch, that could end in disaster. Hopefully, they were hours away from that, but it was an issue they needed to keep in mind.

Time to move things along, no matter how much she didn't want to do what she now felt was her only choice.

"I have an idea."

The three men swung to look at Gemma. One stayed silent, simply staring at her with cold, flat eyes.

"We need to get your message out," Gemma continued. "You must have demands or you wouldn't have gone to this extent. But right now, there's no communication and we need to establish that so you can get what you want." She let confidence in their position fill her tone. Now was not the time to bring any doubt into the equation. "We could call 911, tell them who you are, and get a conversation started. But I have a better idea—one more likely to grab their attention. Greg Coulter from ABC7."

Beside her, she heard Logan's quick catch of surprised breath.

I hear you. You of all people know I wouldn't be doing this if I thought we had any better options.

"Why Coulter?" One asked.

"Because he could get the ball rolling for us. Ever seen his 1-800-TIPSTER billboards? It's a direct line to him. We call him, he'll show up with bells on, ready to take your demands to the NYPD. He'd be like a dog with a bone, making sure your story gets told. Making sure the city and possibly the world know about it. Not just what's going on here, but *why.*"

Interest bloomed in One's eyes, exactly as Gemma expected. Every hostage taker wanted his story told; if he'd wanted anonymity, he wouldn't have attracted attention by taking hostages. And, in this case, these men had taken hostages and closed down midtown Manhattan and one of the city's major travel hubs. They weren't looking to remain in the dark. She knew the idea of Coulter's broadcast reach would appeal to them.

Little did they know the NYPD would bar Coulter from bringing cameras into the space, or at least from releasing whatever footage he filmed. But Gemma knew very well, seeing as she'd been the one to block him only a few months earlier at the standoff on Rikers Island.

One nodded in agreement. "I like this idea."

"I can call him directly from one of the phones we have here." When One's eyes narrowed in suspicion, she quickly added, "I don't have to be the one to dial the number. I don't have to hold the phone. One of you can, and the phone can be on speaker so all three of you can hear the conversation." Her gaze dropped to the switch in One's hand. "We want to move this along, right?"

One pointed at Two with his free hand. "Grab one of the phones."

Gemma relaxed slightly when Two selected a phone in a pink sparkly case that had to belong to one of the two teenage girls. She didn't want either her phone or Logan's to end up in their hands because of any information there that might lead to their identification as law enforcement. However, she'd seen Logan place his phone into his zipped jacket pocket while she'd buried hers at the bottom of her bag, minimizing the chance they'd be selected when they were simply looking for a phone easily at hand. Two walked over and held the phone in front of the blond girl's face, but nothing happened, so he moved on to the brunette. Her face unlocked the phone.

"Keep your distance but toss her the phone," One ordered, piercing Gemma with a hard stare. "Call this one number. You call anyone else, the blond girl dies."

In response, Three pivoted to level his P90 at the blond teenager, who gave a small shriek.

Two lobbed the phone to Gemma, which she caught in her unbound hands. Holding the phone in both hands, she leaned forward to look past Logan and down to where the two girls sat. "It's okay, honey. Hang in there. They won't have any cause to hurt you." She aimed a hard stare back at One. "You don't have to terrify her. I'm on your side. I'm going to do what needs doing without you using a child as leverage."

"Keep doing it and there'll be no issues. Tell Coulter not to bring a crew with him. Just him. No cameras. No phones. No recording devices of any kind or the hostages will pay."

That direction avoided an argument between Coulter and the NYPD. The hostage takers were doing everything they could to keep their identities hidden, which meant one thing only—they fully intended to return to their own lives once they got what they wanted here at Grand Central Terminal. They didn't intend to die here.

That gave her hope.

She disabled the lock screen on the phone to minimize interactions with the girls. Then she dialed the phone's volume to maximum, opened the phone app, entered Coulter's 1-800 number, connected the call, and put it on speaker.

It rang twice before it was answered. "1-800-TIPSTER," said a female voice. "Helping you do your part to balance the scales. How can I help you?"

Of course he has a fully staffed phone line. "I need Greg Coulter."

"Mr. Coulter is out on a story. If you give me your full information, I'll—"

"I'm calling from the hostage situation at Grand Central Terminal. I'd like to speak to Mr. Coulter. *Now.*"

"Let me get him for you. Hold, please."

Gemma glanced up to see One's smile of pleasure as Coulter's lackey scurried off the call to find Coulter. The line was only silent for about fifteen seconds, then, "Greg Coulter speaking. You're calling from Grand Central Terminal?"

"Yes. The individuals holding hostages in the concourse would like to express their demands to you. They need you to come down here to meet with them. You can then carry those demands to the NYPD."

"I'm happy to do that, but the NYPD may not allow it."

"You're a smart guy, you'll figure it out. But no cameras or recording devices, or the hostages will pay the price."

"How will I bring back their demands?"

Gemma fought the urge to roll her eyes. "Kick it old school, Coulter. Paper and pen. Get down here. You have twenty minutes."

"Twenty minutes?" Outrage edged his tone now, a man used to calling his own shots. "What if I can't get there in time?"

"This is the only story in town today. If you're not here already, you're on your way. Make it happen." She disconnected the call and met One's eyes. "That's how it's done. We're in a position of power now." She purposely included herself in her statement, using the beginning of negotiation to start to build the bond between herself and One. Letting her knees fall open over her bound ankles, she stretched forward to set the phone on the floor about a foot from her boots, where she could still reach it again, if needed, but the hostage takers could see she had no plans to use it for any other outside contact.

See how trustworthy I am?

"And if he can't make it here in twenty minutes?" Two asked.

"We'll give him a little grace. I'm sure he's here by now, or he's close by. His bigger issue will be getting past the NYPD, who may not believe he got a call to go in. They may call to confirm, because now they have a number. Guaranteed they record every number calling into the tip line."

The group settled into silence for the next ten minutes as they waited.

Then, as Gemma expected, the phone on the floor rang, the screen lighting up with "NYPD."

Gemma didn't reach for it but looked to One for direction. Only when he nodded did she pick up the phone. "Hello?"

"This is the NYPD. Am I speaking to someone inside Grand Central Terminal?"

Gemma didn't recognize the voice; it was definitely not one of the hostage negotiators she knew. She imagined they were still incoming this early in the event.

"Yes."

"You asked for Greg Coulter?"

"Yes. Just him, no camera crew, no electronics. Send him in through Vanderbilt Hall so we can see it's just him." Gemma terminated the call and set the phone down again. "I expect he'll arrive shortly."

"Good."

The men rearranged themselves, One pulling back so he wasn't in a direct line of sight from the Onassis Foyer entrance, while Two and Three stood back-to-back, Three covering the hostages, and Two covering the 42nd Street entrance.

They didn't have long to wait. From Gemma's position, she could see the outer door open as Coulter stepped into the Onassis Foyer.

This was it. It all depended on Coulter. If he didn't see her during his short visit, the rest of the plan would fall apart. Of course, if it became obvious to the hostage takers that Coulter recognized her personally, it might be over for her quickly. For both of them.

Considering the alternative, it was a risk she was willing to take.

Chapter 10

The wood-and-glass door closed behind Coulter with a thump as he stepped into Vanderbilt Hall.

Even from a distance, he presented a polished persona with his neatly trimmed hair, a body he clearly put time into working on—not bulky but fit—a snowy-white shirt, and bright blue tie to complement the same tone in his ABC7 station jacket. Gemma was sure she could see his teeth gleam from over one hundred feet away.

Just the sight of the reporter set Gemma's own teeth on edge. The thought of so much riding on him alone left her with a sick feeling in the pit of her stomach, but it was where they needed to be at this point.

Coulter moved cautiously through Vanderbilt Hall, his hands out at his sides in full view, a pad of paper clutched in his left hand.

When he was halfway through Vanderbilt Hall, he called out, "I'm Greg Coulter. I'm unarmed and I have no recording devices."

Gemma could see he had no eyes for the hostages, simply for the masked man with the submachine gun pointed at his chest. In all honesty, she couldn't blame him for that; she would have done the same. She was impressed he was walking so calmly into a building that could explode at any moment. Sure, it was because he was after a story, confirming her belief that he'd do anything to get the story for which every journalist was currently competing; but there were a lot of journalists who wouldn't have the sheer guts, or bravado, as the case may be, to walk into this building.

Score one for Coulter, she thought grudgingly.

It took Coulter about thirty seconds to enter the concourse. He faltered slightly at the sight of bodies on the floor; then he pushed himself through the last few steps. His gaze finally left the P90, moving up to take in the man actually holding the weapon—his attitude and his masked identity—before moving on to scan the area. He managed to keep his expression neutral, but Gemma could see his jolt of fear when he spotted One standing off to the side. The NYPD had to have told him what he was walking into, but it was different to actually see the blocks of C-4 and the dead man's switch gripped in One's hand.

Gemma followed as his gaze moved on, circling the nearly deserted space, from the scattered dead on the west side of the concourse, to the bags and coats dropped in the panic to get away, back to the deserted MTA desk and the blood-spattered wall behind it, to the windows and balconies, where surely sharpshooters lay, to the grotesquely splashed blood against one of the information booth windows.

After taking in one of the duffel bags full of C-4, his gaze started at one end of the hostages and scanned the group. Gemma could imagine him trying to not only count the hostages but remember everything he could about them to fill out the human aspect of his story. From where he stood, she deduced the jackass business guy and Logan were hidden from his view, but he should be able to see most of her behind the legs of Two and Three. She didn't want to be obvious, but leaned slightly to her left, making sure he could see her whole face.

Coulter's gaze ran across the hostages, touched on Gemma, and moved past. He froze, blinked twice, then his gaze backtracked, his eyes flaring ever so slightly.

Mission accomplished.

In the second before Gemma dropped her gaze to the floor in front of her boots, a silent message to him to break his stare and move on, she could see the connections flaring in his eyes: She'd been the voice on the other end of the call. She'd been the one to deliver his marching orders.

Her gambit had worked. He'd seen her, recognized her; now she could move forward knowing that, given a little time, she'd be talking to her own HNT colleagues.

He finally stopped about twenty feet away from the hostage takers. Gemma could see his glossy Italian leather oxfords halt and calculated she'd be safe raising her gaze. Coulter's attention would be 100 percent locked on the hostage takers.

He couldn't get his story without them.

His Adam's apple bobbed once as he swallowed, then he seemed to steel himself. "I'm Greg Coulter from ABC7. I'm happy to hear your demands and take them back to the NYPD." He raised the pad of paper, slipping a pen out from the ring binding, and flipped open the cover. "Go ahead."

One moved to stand with his men. "One moment."

He leaned into Two, who set his P90 down at One's feet, the barrel pointing harmlessly across the length of the concourse floor, and stalked over to Coulter, circling him to come up behind him and roughly pat him down. Coulter's lips tightened, but he held still and silent, his arms extended out from his body, the pen fisted in one hand, the ring pad of paper in the other. Satisfied, Two returned to pick up his weapon, pointing it again at Coulter.

"You'll take this information to the top men in the NYPD," One ordered.

"Yes."

"You'll tell them the hostages are unharmed. For now."

Coulter's gaze shot sideways to one of the fallen, then back again, clearly having thought better of his initial reaction. "Yes."

"Then we'll share our demands with you."

Coulter brought pen to paper again and then looked up at One. "I'm ready. Let's start with who you are." His eyes bulged slightly as he realized his misstep. "Not who you are personally," he hurriedly added. "Your group or organization."

"We're members of Sinister 13."

Logan's quiet huff of breath told Gemma he recognized the name, but it was unfamiliar to her.

"The paramilitary group?" Apparently, it wasn't unfamiliar to Coulter.

"Yes."

"There are thirteen of you?" It appeared the name was all Coulter knew.

Even from Gemma's oblique angle, she could see One's derogatory lip curl. "No. It's a reference to the thirteen arrows on the Great Seal of the United States held in the eagle's talon on the sinister side. It's a symbol of war. Of might. Of power."

Coulter was scribbling fast on his notepad. "And you're representatives of the greater group."

"Yes."

State and federal law enforcement kept tabs on paramilitary groups that sprang up around the country, so Gemma knew simply naming the group would give the NYPD and any federal agencies assisting a starting place to identify these men.

"This was clearly a well-organized incursion." Coulter stopped writing to look up. "You've been planning this for a while."

"Yes."

Coulter's expression flashed irritation at One's monosyllabic answer. They'd brought him in to tell their story—a juicy one, he was no doubt hoping—but he was having to drag it out of them a point at a time. "You have demands for which you're willing to exchange these hostages?"

"Yes. We want the pardon and release of Jon Cortes, Craig Hulland, Shawn Lee, and Buck Wale."

The room had been still before, but there had been the odd movement from the hostages. Now the tableau was frozen, no one seemingly breathing.

Including Coulter, who hadn't actually noted any of the four names, he'd been so stunned. "Jon..." He started to repeat and then pulled himself together. "The four men responsible for the bombing of the William J. Green Federal Building in Philadelphia."

"Yes."

"But they're in federal prison. They were found guilty of killing one hundred twenty-nine people. The proof was irrefutable."

"They were patriots doing their patriotic duty."

"Their—" Outrage built in Coulter's single word before he cut himself off, visibly sucked in a breath, and tried to settle himself.

He knew his role here, and it wasn't to be judge and jury of the situation. It was to get every detail he could and then take that message back to the NYPD.

Gemma fully understood his struggle and outrage, because that same feeling was burning through her like an out-of-control forest fire.

She remembered the morning three years before. She'd been off duty that day and had enjoyed a slow start with her cat, Mia, curled on the couch with a book and an extra cup of coffee. It had been a warm, late fall day, possibly the last one of the year, and she'd had the balcony door open, letting in both morning sun and temperate breeze. Balmy and perfect, a moment of calm in her often-crazy life.

Until Alex had texted and told her to turn on her TV.

She'd spent the next few hours staring at talking heads, her coffee gone cold in her preoccupation with the unfolding horror.

Someone had parked a van full of explosives on N 7th Street, directly adjacent to the William J. Green Federal Building, a ten-story glass-and-steel structure at the corner of Arch and N 6th Streets in Philadelphia that housed the FBI, IRS, DEA, US Secret Service, the State Department, Treasury Inspector General, and the US Attorney's Office. They'd walked away, leaving the bomb on a delay timer and had been blocks distant when the explosives detonated, devastating the building, killing one hundred twenty-two immediately—ninety-eight inside the federal building and twenty-four as collateral damage in the federal detention center on the other side of N 7th Street—with seven more succumbing to their injuries over the next weeks. The building itself was condemned and had to be brought down, while parts of the federal detention center were closed for more than a year.

The miracle that day was the daycare center that normally operated in the Green Federal Building had closed for renovations a few weeks earlier, and the children who should have been there—would have lost their lives there—were in a church basement blocks away at the time of the attack.

It hadn't taken the FBI long to find the men responsible for the bombing—the four men One wanted released—and they had been tried together, their court case blessedly swift and definitive. All four had been recommended for the federal death penalty, which, while rarely used, might be considered appropriate in this case. Many Americans felt it would be a just ending for them.

Gemma was one of them, considering the circumstances.

Fury whipped through her, leaving her helpless in its wake. The thought of these men—who'd caused so much devastation, ripping families apart, orphaning children, and giving PTSD to the good people of Philadelphia—getting off, essentially getting away with their crimes, filled her with rage. How dare they discount the agony they'd caused? And how dare they put the good people of New York City in a similar position? New York had weathered a crisis worse than this once before. The thought of what was essentially another terrorist attack killing citizens and changing the cityscape forever so guilty men could go scot-free was unbearable.

From Logan's clenched fists, he felt the same way.

Gemma let her right hand fall to the outside of her leg, where she could press the back of her hand to Logan's thigh. He pressed back lightly against it, a tiny bit of solidarity when none should have been allowed, an understanding of the rage they were both feeling.

Somehow, knowing she wasn't alone in the storm of emotion, frustrated by forced inactivity, gave a tiny bit of solace.

Coulter was similarly struggling but had the much harder job of trying not to anger the men with the guns in front of him. "Let me read this back to you to make sure I have everything correctly." He proceeded to read out the four names, followed by their request. "And for the full pardon and release of all four men, you're willing to release all the hostages."

"Yes."

"And then turn yourself in?"

"No. We want an unmarked, untracked car for safe transport out of the city. We won't be followed by ground or air and we'll be allowed to leave the city with our C-4. The roads won't be closed; we expect normal traffic to flow. If we're followed, if we're at risk of being captured, I'll detonate the bomb, taking any cops and surrounding civilians with us."

It was insanity to think they'd be able to simply drive out of New York City and return to their lives, so Gemma knew the car had to be part of a larger plan of disappearing, likely using multiple vehicles or possibly splitting up to increase their chances of getting away.

Logan's leg vibrated against the back of her hand. Blocked from Three's eyes by the close press of hostage bodies, she flipped her hand over, pressing her palm against his thigh and gripping the muscle.

I know. Me too. We'll figure this out. Take a breath.

Words she needed to take to heart herself. It was more important than ever they figure a way out of this mess.

Logan wasn't just considering the men in this room; she knew his tactical brain was steps ahead, figuring out every roadblock. The biggest of which was the president of the United States.

Only the president had the clemency power to pardon federal criminal offenses. This wouldn't be an applied presidential pardon, the kind that could take years to navigate through administrative application hell, but one that would have to be granted under the pressure of a time limit.

What if the president didn't agree? Were there any other options at that point?

This situation kept sinking into worse and worse possibilities every minute. Coulter made a few more notes, then looked up from his pad. "Okay, I have it all. I can take this back to—"

"Not yet. You're missing one very important point." One held out the hand clenched around the dead man's switch, the sagging wire that connected the switch to his suicide vest swaying with the movement. "I've now been holding this for about ninety minutes. At some point, my hand is going to cramp. I could try to pass the switch off to my other hand, but that would be extremely dangerous, as it's a very sensitive switch."

Coulter's horrified gaze was locked on One's fist and the dangling wire.

"I could set a time and then tell you we are going to execute hostages one at a time starting then, but that will be overly dramatic and messy. We'll use this time limit instead and kill them all at once instead of one at a time. How much longer can I hold it?" He didn't give Coulter time to guess, but steamrolled on. "I'd guess maybe three more hours. Who knows? Maybe more." He leveled a flat stare at Coulter. "Maybe less. Tell them I need their answer within three hours, starting now. Could be less if I can't make it, so make sure they don't drag their feet. Clock's ticking. Make sure they know that. Now go."

Coulter didn't hesitate, turning without another glance at any of the hostages and sprinting for the 42nd Street exit doors.

Gemma pulled her hand back into her lap, knowing all attention would be back on the hostages shortly.

The echoing thud of the door out to the Onassis Foyer and then a second, quieter thump marked Coulter's exit from the Terminal.

One and Three turned to face the hostages again, both smiling at the horror they found on the faces there.

Gemma met One's gaze, carefully banking the fury still spinning in her gut. She needed all the calm she could muster in order to get them out of this situation.

Because she and the HNT had a problem—time. Normally in a hostage situation, the goal was to stretch out the negotiation to allow tempers to cool, to build a rapport with the hostage taker, and to gather intel crucial to a successful resolution.

Three hours was so little time. Even if it were a negotiation where there was a good chance of success—and this decidedly wasn't that scenario—it would take hours to bring a hostage taker around. In this case, the dead man's switch was a ticking clock they couldn't fight.

She needed to temper their expectations in case One's muscle fatigue could be managed. Her team was going to need every second they could scrounge.

"You realize it's Friday night." Gemma was impressed her voice could be so calm externally when she was a roiling mess inside. "Everyone at the Justice Department will have gone home for the weekend. It will take time to get them in. Three hours isn't enough time."

"I don't need the Justice Department. Just the president."

"But he can't do it alone. He—"

"*Enough!*" The single word lashed out, echoing repeatedly against the cold marble surfaces surrounding them even as Three brought his P90 around to aim directly at her skull.

Gemma jerked once and then forced herself to hold absolutely still, her nails digging into her thighs.

"We're calling the shots," One thundered. "If you speak for us, you do so because we can use you. Never mistake that we're in charge."

Gemma jerked her head in the affirmative once, then dropped her gaze, reading herself the riot act. She knew better. Never *ever* negotiate when your emotions weren't under control, and hers most certainly weren't right now. Understandably, perhaps, but that didn't matter.

She had overstepped, possibly decreasing their chances of survival.

The deck was stacked even further against them now.

Chapter 11

Lieutenant Tomás Garcia only gave the soaring recessed entry and the stunning Art Deco touches of the entrance to the Chrysler Building a scant glance, then he pushed through the right-hand rotating door to the first-floor lobby.

His eyes scanned the space, a cop's gaze, dispassionately traveling over red Moroccan marble walls and pillars, the yellow Sienna travertine floor with its diagonal patterning, elements of chrome accents spread through the space, and the hand-painted mural above, stretching across the ceiling.

Word had spread rapidly as the perimeters went up around Grand Central Terminal. The NYPD had called for a full evacuation of all buildings within two city blocks of the Terminal—a significant goal considering the surrounding skyscrapers. Inside that external perimeter, only NYPD personnel were allowed, with an internal perimeter encompassing a full city block, which included the Chrysler Building. All trains terminating at Grand Central Terminal and Grand Central Madison had been stopped at the preceding station, each over four miles distant. Only A-Team specialists were permitted closer to Grand Central Terminal itself.

The NYPD had worked fast, using every available officer to clear the outer perimeter. Walking toward the Chrysler Building had been eerily quiet, as if an apocalyptic event had occurred. New York was a vibrant city; this kind of quiet was beyond unsettling and carried too many memories of 9/11.

Turning, Garcia found the twin silver doors to his left, their glass panes filled with a poster of a twinkling nightscape of New York City, the long window to the left of the door showing the brilliantly lit tower of the Chrysler Building sparkling against the midnight-blue night sky.

He pushed open the right-hand door and stepped into a room only about ten by twenty feet, though one wall was angled to follow the triangular floor plan of the main lobby. Unlike the main lobby, softly glowing with its 1930s design, this room was modernized, a room that could be rented out for limited group or business use with its plain white walls and bright fluorescent lighting.

Or, in this case, had been usurped for a high-stakes NYPD operation. Keeping in mind the rest of the building had been evacuated due to the risk of explosion, it wasn't like anyone was using the space.

A long conference table filled the middle of the room, and Trevor McFarland was crouched over equipment spread across its surface—laptops, recording devices, headsets both with and without a microphone, cables, and connectors. McFarland—slight of build, wearing an off-the-rack, pond-scum greenish-brown suit that might have actually fit someone two inches taller with an extra twenty pounds—wasn't officially a tech person but was such a whiz with technology that he was often in high demand. For a high-stress negotiation, he was at the top of Garcia's handpicked list, especially when McFarland often arrived well ahead of TARU—the department's dedicated tech unit.

"McFarland. Just about ready?"

"Give me another three or four minutes and I will be, sir." McFarland's buzz-cut blond head stayed bent over the tech as he kept working. "Who else is coming?"

"Dyer, Shelby, and Alven. Taylor's on standby. I would have pulled him in, but he's not close enough. He said he'd come in, just in case, but we can't wait for him. Everyone else can be here inside of twenty. I would have called in Capello, but she's off today."

"She's a Capello. If you need her for an op like this, she'll come."

"I have a B team in mind. If this goes to alternating shifts, I'm calling her in no matter what. She can complain to her father if she doesn't like it."

McFarland snorted a laugh as he stretched across the table, laying out a headset.

"*Garcia?*" A shout came from out in the lobby.

Garcia strode across the room, pushed open the door, and leaned out. "Here."

He pulled back in, only to be followed by an A-Team officer in full body armor wearing an M4A1 carbine on a single-point sling, his hand on the pistol grip, holding it close to his chest, the barrel pointed at the floor. The name stitched into his uniform read "Kirkpatrick." "Sir, Lieutenant Cartwright wanted me to pass on a message."

Irritation snapped along Garcia's nerve endings. *Command...always keeping its thumb on the scale.* "He couldn't call? Or radio?"

"Considering the intel? No. Word will travel and he doesn't want it to move that fast."

The term "intel" stopped Garcia, and in his peripheral vision, he could see McFarland pause. "What do you mean 'intel'?"

"Apparently the suspects wanted Greg Coulter from ABC7 to go in so they could lay out their demands."

"I heard they wanted that pompous son-of-a-bitch specifically." Garcia practically spit the words.

He didn't like media types much in general, but his loathing for Coulter was a well-known fact within his unit. And likely, out of it. Coulter had tried one time too many to insert himself into one of Garcia's teams' negotiation processes and was inclined not to take no for an answer. When Coulter had been shot four months earlier during the City Hall crisis, Garcia had hoped he'd get the message he was an impediment to police procedure and could damn well wait on the sidelines like every other journalist. So far, that hadn't happened.

"He just came out after meeting with the suspects."

"What are we negotiating for?" Garcia tossed a look at McFarland, who grabbed a pad of paper from the pile on the table as well as a pen.

"That's not the issue."

"That's always the issue. We need full details."

"You'll get them. They're interviewing Coulter now and transcribing his notes. But there's something else just as important. Detective Capello is one of the hostages."

Garcia felt like he'd been poleaxed, the mental blow was so intensely physical. Surely he'd heard wrong. Or they meant the wrong person. "Detective Alex Capello?"

"No. Detective Gemma Capello. Your negotiator."

"What the f—"

"You're sure?" Garcia cut McFarland off. "There's no mistake?"

"A couple of the tactical guys high in the windows are checking out the hostages through their scopes. Some of them know Detective Capello from previous ops. If the hostages are spread out enough, and if they're in a position to see individual faces, they'll let us know. But Coulter was definite. It's her."

"He would be. He just had a face-to-face with her last week." Garcia turned away, running a meaty hand through his salt-and-pepper hair. "*Fuck.*"

"My thoughts exactly," McFarland said.

"Coulter said to tell you specifically one other thing," Kirkpatrick said. "When they called him asking for a meet, she was the person on the phone. Somehow, she's convinced them to let her speak for them."

Hope bloomed fierce in Garcia's chest—they had an officer inside the scene. "If she's managed it once—"

"She'll do it again," McFarland finished for him. "We'll be speaking directly with her."

"We have to assume they'll be listening in. We can't let it slip in any way we know her, that she's NYPD, or she's dead."

Kirkpatrick took a step toward the door. "You'll get a call from ESU command soon with their demands and the number of the phone used to make contact with Coulter." Kirkpatrick gripped his carbine, spun on his heel, and was gone through the door.

As the door thumped closed, Garcia locked gazes with McFarland. The younger man had lost several shades in a complexion normally so pale he now almost looked waxy. "We've never negotiated with one of our own people inside."

"First time for everything."

"In any other situation, this kind of conflict of interest would get us kicked off the team."

"We *are* the team. You kick off everyone who's worked with Capello, including yourself, and you have no team, period. We'd have to go up a level and request state negotiators. Or FBI."

"Over my dead body. We can do this."

"I thought that would be your opinion."

Garcia stared at the equipment partially organized on the table and realized he needed a different strategy. "I need to change the team."

McFarland took a step back, his eyes going icy and his mouth stubborn. "Sir, I want to be part of this. I need to be. It's Capello."

Garcia waved his concern away like he was wafting away an insect. "No, no, not you. We need you. *She* needs you. But she doesn't need Dyer or Alven." He met McFarland's gaze. "We need the people who've worked most closely with Capello. Those who will be able to interpret anything she says to us that has a double meaning. You and Shelby are perfect."

"We need Taylor."

"Absolutely. And..."

"Williams." McFarland's tone was sure. "He's worked a lot with Capello, and as our most senior team member, he's the right call for this."

"Agreed. I'll call Taylor, you call Williams. We'll send patrol cars for them if needed to get them here with lights and sirens." Garcia made himself stop, draw in a breath, and lock down his rising emotion. Negotiation was always a stressful process, but this one was going to have layers on top of layers because everyone in this room was going to have a personal stake in the case. "Capello's going to try to negotiate her way out from inside the crisis. She's putting herself in an incredibly dangerous position where one wrong word could mean a bullet to the brain." He jerked as another thought occurred. "Jesus. A bullet to the brain."

"Sir?"

"Her mother, McFarland." He didn't need to say more. Every negotiator who was close to Capello knew her family history. "That adds another layer of difficulty for her because she has to be seeing the similarities."

"So will Chief Capello. They'll have to pull him because Capello's inside."

"It's probably already done. They won't shut him out, but he won't be in a command position for this incident." Garcia turned to look back toward the doors that led toward 42nd Street and the Terminal more than a full city block away. "Let's get those calls made. We have to do everything in our power to help Capello. We have to keep her alive."

Chapter 12

Alex Capello's phone rang in his back pocket as he walked down the hallway of NYPD Headquarters at One Police Plaza. He checked the screen. *Dad.* He answered. "Hey."

"Where are you?"

The whip-sharp delivery paired with a harsh edge of tension ran like a knife down Alex's spine. He jerked to a halt, nearly causing two detectives to run into him from behind. He waved his apology. "Headquarters still. I needed to finish a report. I'm just heading home now. Why?"

"You need to get up to Grand Central Terminal."

It was clearly an order from the Chief of Special Operations, but there was too much emotion in the request for strictly a police operation. "What's going on?"

"There's an ongoing incident in the Main Concourse. Three men stormed the place. Multiple fatalities, including MTA officers. Now they've taken hostages. Two men with P90s; one has a suicide-bomb vest with a dead man's switch. They brought in several extra bags of C-4." If Tony Capello heard his son's sharp catch of breath, he didn't stop for it. "Enough to take out the full city block. Maybe more."

"You'll need all hands on deck to evacuate the area."

"Yes, but that's not why you're needed. Greg Coulter from ABC7 met with the hostage takers to get their demands." When Tony paused to take a breath, there was an audible hitch. "He reported Gemma as one of the hostages. He had that interview with her last week and has worked several of her negotiations. He's sure it's her."

Alex's knees went to water and he sagged against the corridor wall as details shot through his mind at lightning speed.

Gemma had the day off and was out to dinner with Logan. She'd told Alex the plan was to go first to La Cassatella for coffee and then up to Midtown for dinner at some Irish pub. They were going to take the 6 train from the Bleecker Street Station to Grand Central Terminal and walk from there.

They'd walked into a bloodbath.

"Logan." The word came out as a croak, so he cleared his throat and tried again. "Is Logan with her?"

"I don't know. Should he be?"

"They were going out to dinner together tonight. You know how they've been dancing around each other. They were finally going to see where things went and were headed to some Irish pub after hitting La Cassatella. If she's one of the hostages, there's a good chance he is, too."

"Unless he's one of the fatalities. The A-Team guys stationed high in the windows say there are two officers and nine civilians down."

"He'd be in street clothes and wouldn't necessarily stand out. You said they're up high. Can they see the hostages?"

"We're trying to identify Gemma."

"Get them to identify Logan as well. If they're both inside, we need to know. It could be to our advantage."

"And their detriment. Coulter says Gemma has talked her way into speaking for the hostages."

Pride filled Alex for Gemma's quick thinking and strategy, but at the same time, her courage filled him with fear. "That could be a good way to get herself killed."

"Or to communicate with her own team without the hostage takers knowing."

"Are you on scene?"

"I was already on the way when I heard. ETA about five minutes."

"I'm right behind you. Have you called Joe, Mark, and Teo?"

"Joe and Mark know. Teo is out on a call but will hear as soon as he and his crew are back at the fire station. Everyone will come." For the first time, Tony's words took on a slight quaver and Alex knew he was thinking of his murdered wife, in a situation not so very different from this one. "This is going to hit every one of us the same way. Get up here. Have someone bring you in a cruiser, if need be, but get here. *Now.*" Tony ended the call.

Alex jammed his phone in his pocket and sprinted for the elevators.

Chapter 13

His negotiators had moved heaven and earth to get there, and his team was ready to go.

Garcia scanned the faces around the table, seeing the same soul-deep determination he felt. One of their own was in trouble, and they were going to do everything in their power to get her back.

McFarland sat at the head of the table, under the digital clock mounted high on the wall so he could stay on track based on the time the hostage takers had already set. As the primary negotiator, McFarland would be the one person talking for the team unless there was a breakdown in communications. While everyone around the table knew Gemma, McFarland knew her best and Garcia hoped he'd be able to roll with the flow of the conversation quickest. His laptop monitor displayed the details of the hostage takers' conversation with Coulter.

Beside him sat Gina Shelby in a dark plum, single-button suit layered over a white V-neck blouse. She'd come in with her blond hair down over her shoulders but had pulled an elastic out of a pocket and had bundled it into a low knot at the nape of her neck; she was focused and didn't want anything to distract her. As the coach, she sat to McFarland's right and, like the others, had a pad of paper and a pen in front of her for rapid note-taking; she would also be the one to give McFarland written suggestions while he was talking. Sometimes the coach had the space to hear things in the background the negotiator missed due to their exclusive focus on the suspect, or could concentrate on the communication in different ways. In this case, her job would be more important than ever. Shelby would also stand as the secondary negotiator if for some reason McFarland couldn't continue in his role.

Elijah Taylor sat across the table from McFarland. Tall and broad, with a dark umber complexion, Taylor was, as always, impeccably dressed, this time in a dark suit, charcoal shirt, and luminous silver tie. He was set up as scribe, the team member who took exacting, verbatim notes about the conversation in case the negotiator needed to review the exact wording as expressed by the hostage taker. The scribe was, in effect, the historian of the negotiation, a crucial member of the team, because even though they'd all take notes, Taylor's would be the verbatim record. All calls would be recorded, but when a rapid refresh of the conversation was needed, Taylor's notes would be instantly accessible for searching.

Beside Taylor sat Kurt Williams, the elder statesman of the hostage negotiation team. The longest running negotiator, even more than Garcia, Williams was the institutional memory of the group. He loved his position in the field too much to want to move into a command position like Garcia—too much paperwork, he always said. But his experience was invaluable for the negotiation itself as well as for his current position as team liaison. It would be Williams who would work with the other aspects of the operation—primarily the ESU—allowing the rest of the team to focus on the negotiator.

Normally, the hostage negotiation team would only need four officers, but Garcia made five, pulling up a chair at the end of the table. He would be the one standing between his team and the department brass. When Chief Phillips, the head of the NYPD, or Deputy Chief Harrison—who had stepped in to replace Chief of Operations Tony Capello, given the clear conflict of interest—came looking for details, they'd be talking to Garcia. He could absent himself from this room if need be; he knew this team was the best in the department. They'd stay on task if he was needed for some sort of dog and pony show for the department or the media.

Garcia's phone dinged and he pulled it out, read the text, and then typed a one-word reply—**Now**—before turning to his team. "Cartwright and Sanders are on their way in with an update. Then we need to call and get the negotiation started." He glanced upward. "Clock's ticking."

The doors to the conference room swung open in unison and two men stepped in. Both were dressed in unrelieved black—boots, cargo pants, shirt, Kevlar vest, helmet—and both wore transparent safety glasses. They each held their M4A1 carbines pointed at the floor.

"Garcia." Sanders's eyes took in the room, the equipment, the personnel. "You haven't called yet?"

"We're about to begin. We're almost fifteen minutes into the three hours, so we need to move."

"We won't take long," Cartwright said, "but you need an update first."

"Confirmation Capello is one of the hostages?" McFarland asked, a thread of hope in his words that maybe, just maybe, Coulter had been wrong.

"Capello is there. Johnson is on the fifth floor and reported a clear identification. But it gets worse."

"How?" Garcia demanded.

"She's not alone. Detective Sean Logan is with her."

Shelby's head whipped sideways to stare at Cartwright in shock. "Logan?"

"Yes." The set of Sanders's mouth spoke volumes about how unhappy he was about the situation. "It looks like they were together. They're seated side by side in the middle of the concourse, their backs against the base of the information booth, facing south, toward Vanderbilt Hall. Neither appear to be harmed. The rest of the hostages are lined up on either side of them. There are fourteen hostages in total, then the three suspects. Two have P90 submachine guns—"

"*Shit*," McFarland murmured.

"One has the suicide vest. There are two duffel bags about thirty feet apart, each about fifteen feet from the hostages."

"So the guy calling out to the NYPD was giving us the straight facts?" Williams asked. "The suicide vest is wired?"

"Yes," Cartwright replied. "A few of the guys have been able to get a good view of it through their scopes as the bomber has walked around. Doesn't look complicated, but looks real. And deadly."

"What about the bags?" Taylor asked. "Can they see inside to prove the extra explosives?"

"Not from their angle. We're going to have to assume he's telling the truth."

"He's been truthful about everything else," Garcia said. "No reason to think he isn't now. Anything else we need to know?"

"The hostages are bound. Zip-tied wrists and ankles."

"Capello and Logan as well?"

"Logan, yes. Capello, only her ankles."

"She's already ahead of them," McFarland stated. "She's sold herself to them as someone who can help them get what they want. They left her hands untied so she can make calls for them."

"That's our take on it."

"Logan being bound is a problem though."

Sanders made a noise expressing his disgust. "Only for as long as he wants to make himself look helpless. You think our guys can't get out of a zip tie if they need to? Also, Logan goes nowhere without his tactical knife, whether he's on duty or not. My money is on his having found a way to hold on to it. But the knife won't be his focus if he can figure out a way to get his hands on one of their weapons."

"He could be useful either way if things start to move." McFarland made a note on his pad of paper. "What else can your guys see?"

"Nine bodies on the concourse floor. We assume already dead, as no one has moved since they arrived." Cartwright met Garcia's gaze. "Two officers are down behind the MTA desk. One is a headshot. The other isn't clear because of body positioning."

"Probably more of the same," Garcia finished. "This whole op has been planned from start to finish. There's no reason to think they didn't take those officers into account and terminate them in the first seconds of the attack."

"Especially considering their weapon of choice." Taylor's expression was closed, but Garcia's own dread was reflected in his eyes. "Eleven down in total seems like a low body count for a weapon that can empty fifty rounds in a matter of seconds."

"That's what we know so far," Cartwright said. "Other victims got out of the concourse and then collapsed. Multiple GSWs taken to the hospital. Eleven isn't going to be it. Those were the ones who died instantly or who had no one to drag them out in an attempt to save their lives. We've already lost more; we just don't have a concrete count yet. It's chaos out there."

"I bet." Shelby looked around the table. "One thing is for sure—if at any point Capello or Logan are discovered to be NYPD, they're finished. They think they have a bunch of scared civilians in there who can be easily controlled. If they find out they have two cops, especially one of them a tactical officer, they're not going to have a discussion about it.

They've already killed two cops we know of; they'll take them out without a second thought."

"Agreed," Garcia said. "But they haven't been found out so far. Either they weren't searched or they managed to hide or discard their badges, but they likely had them on them when they entered the Terminal. As long as they haven't said or done anything to let their law enforcement training slip, they may be safe." His gaze shot to the clock. "For now."

"We'll update you as we learn more," said Cartwright. "For now, we have men in position at multiple levels from multiple angles in the concourse. They're also stationed at every external egress location. There's a lot of space inside the Terminal, but limited exits. We have them all covered. The area is contained."

"You're covering a lot of ground," McFarland said. "Any chance you can get us visuals? If we could see what's going on, it would be a huge help. Something up in the windows to give us as clear a view of everyone as possible."

"We can do that. One of the two south corners would work best. Unit 5 is here and they'll have what we need in the truck as well as Boone to set it up. He'll make it happen. It would be good for you to see what they've done. It's a smart use of the space, one that ties our hands. If it was just guns, we'd already have taken them o—" He cut off as a knock sounded on the door to the foyer.

The door opened an inch, paused, then opened fully as Alex Capello stepped into the room, his gaze falling first on Sanders and Cartwright and then on the team gathered around the table.

Garcia stood. "Detective Capello."

Alex stepped around Sanders to get closer to the table. A quick glance took in the negotiators and equipment; then he focused on Garcia. "I know Gemma's in there. They say she's negotiating for the hostage takers."

"That's our understanding. We're just about to find out."

"I want in on it."

"What skills does an IAB rat have in a hostage negotiation?" Sanders growled.

Garcia could see Alex fighting for calm. He knew from Gemma's occasional comments that many other cops perceived Alex's role as part of the NYPD Internal Affairs Bureau as nothing more than a snitch, rather than his actual job of fighting corruption and preserving the integrity of the NYPD, and as a result, safeguarding the public's trust in them overall as a law enforcement body.

Instead of cutting Sanders down, Alex simply turned his back on him, dismissing him and his poisonous attitude. "You guys need me. You know her, but not like I do. Think about the Boyle case. She had three seconds of silent communication to indicate who she needed and to tell me where she was going. And that's exactly where I found her. No one else would have been able to pull that off, likely not even one of our brothers. I'm not going to talk to her, that's not my skill set. But I can help translate. Maybe together we can save her, Logan, and the rest of the hostages."

"You knew about Logan?" Cartwright asked.

"I'm who clued in Chief Capello so you knew to look for him in the first place." Alex spun back to Garcia. "That's why you need me. You want to get in her head. I'm already there."

Garcia gave him a curt nod before turning to the A-Team commanders. "We're going to open communications to the concourse. Have all communications to us sent via text, as we'll be running silent except for the line into the Terminal. Williams is your contact." Garcia turned his back on the tactical officers as if they'd already left, and dragged over another chair to sit at the end of the table beside him. He looked up when a set of unmic'd headphones thumped onto the table in front of the new chair. Raising his eyes, he found McFarland on his feet, connecting the headphones into the master panel. It was the clearest tacit acceptance of Alex and his IAB credentials he could get from one of his negotiators. Shelby pushing a pad of paper and a pen toward Alex only strengthened that opinion.

Garcia laid a hand on the back of the chair. "Detective Capello, have a seat. Welcome to the HNT."

Chapter 14

Tinny music with a heavy backbeat exploded from the cell phone still lying on the marble floor in front of Gemma's boots.

She sat with her back straight against the information booth, her head tipped against cool marble, her eyes constantly moving. While One, Two, and Three had been keeping an eye on the hostages, Gemma had been trying to size up the NYPD response to the crisis. She knew Logan was making the same evaluation, both aware that when things moved—if they moved—they'd have one chance at success, and they needed to know where their backup might be.

Hopefully Coulter had passed on the message she was in the hostage group so word would filter through the NYPD. If so, every officer in the building would be focused on helping them.

She'd seen officers in the windows on both ends of the concourse and a transient shadow in the 42nd Street Passage that had to be an A-Team officer getting into position. She hadn't seen anyone else but knew command had to be weighing the risk of filling the Terminal with officers, all of whom would die if the bomb went off, against having someone in the right place at the right time if they managed to split the hostages up and someone could get off a clean shot.

Which could only happen if they could guarantee the bomb wouldn't go off. The NYPD would have to run on the assumption it was a live bomb with an active dead man's switch unless they learned otherwise. By this point, Gemma was sure the bomb was truly live after she'd seen One close his left fist over his right, allowing the muscles in his right hand to relax as his left hand took over.

His hand must be tiring or cramping from so long in the same position, exerting constant force for two hours. Either that or he anticipated muscular exhaustion was imminent and was trying to delay it. Either way, surely one of the sets of eyes around the concourse would have spotted One's actions and reported it for the NYPD brass to come to the same conclusion.

As music blared, Gemma sat forward to see the phone screen, where "NYPD" was displayed, but she didn't move farther than that and didn't reach for the phone. She wasn't sure what damage she'd done in her last conversation with One, so she wanted to make it clear he was in charge and she was following his lead. She looked over to where he stood with Two and Three, their weapons pointed toward the group of hostages.

One took two steps toward the phone and then stopped, as if realizing that would put him too close to the hostages. "Who's calling?"

"Caller ID reads 'NYPD'," Gemma said.

The phone went quiet, likely going to voicemail. After about ten seconds of silence, it rang again.

"Can I trust you to convey our requirements?"

"Yes. I understand what you need. That's all that matters."

A smile curved one corner of One's lips. "Decided your opinion was wrong?"

"You're calling the shots; it doesn't matter what I think. All I want is for them to give you what you want, so you'll let us go. It's pretty simple."

The phone stopped ringing again. Behind One, Two's hands repeatedly clenched white-knuckled around the frame of the P90, then released, as if he were worried they might have missed their chance at getting their demands met. Gemma knew better—whoever was on the other end of the line would keep calling until someone picked up.

Nothing but death could happen without conversation.

The phone rang again and Two relaxed.

"Answer it," One ordered, "and put it on speaker."

Reaching forward, Gemma scooped up the phone, hit the talk button, and changed the call to speaker. "Hello?"

"This is Detective Trevor McFarland of the NYPD Hostage Negotiation Team. Who am I speaking with?"

Warm relief flowed through Gemma at the sound of McFarland's voice. It was possible McFarland just happened to be the one Garcia selected as the negotiator for this negotiation, but her gut told her it wasn't a random selection. Garcia had chosen McFarland as primary because he knew Gemma best.

Now they were in business.

"I'm one of the hostages. I'm speaking for the men in charge."

"They're nearby? They can hear this conversation and give you information, if needed?"

"Yes."

"Good. Now, before we start, you know I'm Trevor. What can I call you?"

"Elena." Gemma used her middle name, wanting anything related to her more common name out of the conversation. "Elena Vella."

"Thank you, Elena."

The space behind McFarland was quiet as his fellow negotiators let him speak for them, but in the background, she could hear the wail of a siren. *No other street traffic. They must be close. Within a block or two.*

It was standard procedure for the negotiation team to avoid harm to the negotiators by never coming face-to-face with a hostage taker, but they'd be nearby, rather than down at One Police Plaza. It allowed for flexibility, for faster, in-person interaction with the on-site A-Team, and for greater control over what went in and what came out of the incident.

"The first thing I need to do, Elena, is ask if anyone requires medical care," McFarland continued.

The gazes of the three hostage takers snapped to the German man, who sat with his left hand still stained with his blood, the winter scarf wrapped around his right biceps.

Gemma's gaze stayed fixed on One, waiting until he looked back at her and shook his head.

"We're fine. No major injuries." She knew McFarland would read from that there were injuries, but the A-Team snipers should have already reported it. They'd be using regular scopes, not night-vision scopes that washed everything in an eerie green glow. They wouldn't have been able to miss the blood.

"I'm glad to hear that. Next, we want you to be comfortable. I'm not sure how long this will take, and you may have missed dinner. Can we send in something for you? We could bring in fast food. Or pizzas. Or there's an Irish pub down the street. Whatever you like. Food, drink...just tell us what you need."

Gemma had to take a moment to make sure that when she took her eyes off the phone to look up to One, none of the hope that exploded through her showed in her expression. *Or there's an Irish pub down the street.* McFarland was sending her a message. Only two people besides Logan knew where she was that evening and who she was with—Alex and Frankie. And there was no reason for Frankie to be brought into this incident. That meant one of two things—either they'd talked to Alex and he'd told them of her plans for the evening and who she was with, or McFarland was telling her Alex was in the room with the negotiators and she had another ally to depend on.

She bet it was the second.

When she raised her head, her face was set in interested though neutral lines. Just someone looking for direction to answer a question.

One shook his head.

"No, thank you," Gemma replied. *Time to look proactive before One decides you're not an advantage.* "We don't want to waste time. We want to discuss our demands." She made sure to couch her statement as "we" so the hostage takers would mentally start to think of her as one of the team, even if one only in it for the end goal of freedom. It was still a goal that made sense to them.

"I have a record of those demands. Let me explain how this process will work. Our conversation is a give and take. You tell me what you need and I'll do my best to do that for you. In return, we'll ask something of you. That give and take is how we're successful—you give me something, then I give you something. And here's an important point, Elena—I'm always going to be totally honest with you. You need to know when I say something, it's the truth. I'm not going to fool you or put one over on you. I'm not going to lie. The only way to solve this is to be straight with you."

"The only way to solve this is to give us what we want. Four lives for seventeen. That seems like a fair trade to me."

"There are seventeen hostages?"

Gemma had to admire how McFarland was trying to seem slightly out of the loop, as if the gunmen overhead weren't communicating any details to the ESU and therefore to the HNT. She could use that to her advantage. She let out a derisive laugh. "No. There are fourteen hostages.

Do you think we're stupid? We'll deal fairly with you if you'll deal fairly with us. We can see the officers stationed up in the windows—they must be telling you what's going on down here. How many people there are, and how many are hostages. Are you trying to get us all killed? The guys in the windows, too? They have a bomb. A real bomb. And extra explosives in bags." She let some of her real fear for everything that could go wrong in the next few hours color her tone.

"The goal is to bring you out alive."

"You bring us out, you bring them out. It's all of us or none of us. So, it's time for you to start dealing with us as a whole. The clock is ticking." She took a deep breath, then settled herself. "Let me reiterate the demands. We want the immediate full pardon and release of Shawn Lee, Buck Wale, Craig Hulland, and Jon Cortes. From..." Gemma snapped her gaze up to One. She knew very well where those men were incarcerated, but Elena wouldn't.

"Lewisburg," One stated.

"Lewisburg," Gemma repeated.

"Are you familiar with the pardon process?" McFarland asked.

"No."

"We explored it as soon as we got your demands. It's a complex and lengthy process. Normally what happens in the case of a federal crime is a petition for pardon is submitted to the Office of the Pardon Attorney at the Department of Justice. In the petition, the specific purpose for desiring a pardon must be laid out in copious detail and usually takes into account the applicant's admission of responsibility for the act. The applicant includes their arrest record, credit status, and if they're involved in any civil lawsuits. They add character references. Most importantly, there is a five-year waiting period."

"Not true. Just ask anyone who's ever been pardoned by an outgoing president. If you grew up in our school system, you know your American history. Look at Nixon. He wasn't even charged. He was pardoned of any crimes he *might* have committed as president." Gemma made a point of meeting One's gaze, to be sure he knew she was giving her all, desperately hoping she was completely hiding her disdain. "That took less than a month. The president has it in his power to waive the application and the waiting period. That's our demand."

"We've already contacted the Department of Justice."

"That's not who you need to talk to."

"That's where we need to start. But rest assured, it's going up the chain. *Fast.* Now, keeping in mind we're doing something for you, you need to do something for us."

"Which is?"

"We need proof of life. Hand the phone to each hostage. All they need to do is say their name."

Three's face clouded and he took one step toward Gemma. She raised an index finger in his direction but said into the phone, "I need instructions. Hang on." She put the phone on mute and looked up at the three hostage takers.

"We don't want to give them any information," Three snapped.

"That's a mistake," Gemma advised.

"Why?"

"Remember, this is what I do for a living. No, we're not fighting for a living wage, but the same concepts are in play. He said it himself—we give them something, they give us something. This is something we can do to look reasonable. What are they going to do with those names? When I told them my name is Elena Vella, how did that give them an advantage? It didn't. We want them to work for us, we need to make it look like we're working with them. Giving up something for no cost is the best way to achieve that. You don't even need to get near the hostages to do this. We can start the phone at one end and then pass it along to the other."

"No." Two was shaking his head. "What if the phone gets dropped and breaks? Or one of them disconnects? That phone is our only outside connection." His eyes shot sideways to one of the bags of C-4. "We could use another phone, but that would waste time getting patched through to the right person."

He's scared. He's afraid to die, which makes him the weakest link in the chain.

"I could do it," Gemma offered. "If you don't want to get that close again, I can move down the line, holding the phone for each of them so they don't touch it. All you'd have to do is cut this zip tie." She looked down at her bound feet. "Then I'd come back here." She stared hard at Three's P90. "If I do anything stupid, you have the power to stop me permanently. Let me assure you, I'm not interested in dying today."

One stared at her unblinkingly as the seconds ticked by, weighing his options. "Fine."

"That's a mistake." Three partially turned toward One, the barrel of his submachine gun moving away from the hostages as he pivoted. "You're playing into—"

"*I say it's fine.*" One's words weren't loud but cut like a knife. "And point that fucking gun somewhere else."

Instead of obeying, Three turned fully toward One, his P90 pointed directly at him in a full challenge of his authority.

From twenty feet away, Gemma knew there was nothing she could do to prevent a fight from breaking out between the men. Heart pounding, all she could do was watch.

Was this entire incident going to end here and now without a chance to save their lives?

Chapter 15

For a full fifteen seconds, tense silence filled the concourse as Three seemed ready to go toe-to-toe with a man in an explosive vest, an act which would be nothing short of absolute insanity. Then he seemed to realize what was at stake and backed off, wordlessly turning away and pulling back into position covering the hostages.

Gemma took the phone off mute, hoping her voice would be steady and her alarm at the last few moments didn't show. "We consent to proof of life. You need to give us a minute though."

"I'm happy to wait," said McFarland.

Gemma muted the phone again. "Who's cutting me loose?"

One indicated to Two to do it. Not willing to risk a hostage going for his weapon in close quarters, Two left his P90 on the ground by One, pulled a folded knife from his pants pocket—good to know he had a knife and where he was keeping it—and came only close enough to quickly sever the zip tie. The plastic parted easily under the extremely sharp blade... also good to know.

Relief flowed as the pressure around her ankles disappeared, the unyielding brass of her detective badge no longer biting into bone.

Gemma unmuted the phone. "I'm getting up now." She rolled onto one knee and pushed off the floor to stand, keeping both hands in view in the air, the phone clasped in her left fist. "I'm going to start down here." Gemma indicated the west side of the group. "I'm going to come to each of you from the front, and I'll hold the phone out toward you. Don't touch it, just speak your name. That's all." She raised the phone toward her own mouth. "Trevor, we're about to begin."

"Thank you, Elena. I'll let you know if someone isn't clear."

Gemma walked to the end of the line of hostages until she stopped in front of the teenage boy wearing a black Brooklyn Nets hoodie and jeans. He stared up at her, his blue eyes huge in his pale face under a flop of dirty-blond hair. She held his gaze and smiled warmly, giving as much encouragement as she could with nothing more than a facial expression. She flipped the phone around so the microphone pointed away from her and held it toward him. "Go ahead."

The young man cleared his throat, then said, "Dameon Chance."

"Trevor, did you get that?" Gemma asked.

"We did. Thanks for checking."

Gemma leaned sideways, holding the phone out to the middle-aged woman in jeans and a sweater beside him. Her auburn hair was shot through liberally with gray, and her bound hands were clutched together in her lap. Gemma nodded for her to speak.

"Margerie Chance."

"Thank you, Margerie."

Gemma stepped back, then moved to the adjacent men. Upon closer appraisal, Gemma realized they must be family, likely brothers from their similar ages. But the physical resemblance was as striking as could be without them being twins. Minus the fact, of course, that one of them had been shot and his shirtsleeve was saturated with blood.

Gemma was close enough to get a good look at his arm, which Margerie had bound tightly with a wool scarf. The scarf was wrapped twice around his right biceps and tied off tightly, but Gemma was relieved to see that while his sleeve was soaked, the scarf, while stained, hadn't absorbed excessive blood. Margerie had done a good job of getting the bleeding to stop. It gave her some room to not have to negotiate to release one hostage who was on the brink of death. He could hold on in the short term.

Gemma suspected that was all they had.

She held the phone between the two men, tilting it toward the injured man.

"Erdmann Schäfer." His deep voice carried the slightly harsh edges of a German accent.

"Gregor Schäfer," said the man beside him when Gemma angled the phone toward him.

From their comfortable traveling clothes to the strength of their accents, Gemma had to wonder if they'd recently flown into LaGuardia and trained into Grand Central Terminal to start a Manhattan vacation.

This was definitely *not* the way to see New York City.

The two teenage girls were next. The brunette leaned forward as if eager to be proactive, to contribute, or just to get her name out there so those missing her would know where she was. "Holly Fabb."

"Thank you, Holly." Gemma turned to the blonde. "And you, honey?"

The blonde stared up at her, her lower lip caught between her teeth, her legs curled tight into her chest, trapping her bound hands. But she didn't speak; Gemma wasn't sure she was even processing what was going on around her.

Holly leaned sideways. "Come on, Suz. Just say your name."

"Suzette Pannell," the girl whispered, her eyes dropped down to the floor.

"That's great, Suzette, very helpful. Thank you."

Gemma hadn't straightened when the man beside Suzette spoke. "Elliott Redmond." It was the impatient businessman, still in his dark suit for his day at the office, though the hunter-green tie was slightly loosened and the top button of his shirt was undone.

She threw him a look that said *Stay cool*. "Trevor, did you get that last one?"

"We heard a male voice but didn't get the name."

"Hang on. We'll try again." Gemma moved closer to extend the phone and mouthed *Now*.

"Elliott Redmond."

"Got it," said McFarland.

Gemma stepped in front of Logan, finally able to make eye contact with him safely. What she saw there—confidence, support, approval— settled some of her ragged edges. She knew he'd follow her lead in not giving his real name—in her case, using her middle name and her mother's maiden name—to safeguard his identity. They obviously had Alex in the loop, and once the ESU heard one of their men was in the mix, they'd be visually identifying Logan to confirm. They'd know this was the one name to ignore. Not to mention several people in the room would be able to identify Logan's voice. "Go ahead."

"Isaac Lyford."

Gemma covered the rest of the group fairly quickly. Marek Czarna, the man beside her in the sweatshirt; Liza Grimes, the young woman who looked like she was on her way home from college classes; Deborah Cowell, the older woman who had just lost her husband; Luke Hoyle, the man with the camera; and Bethany Heffernan, the older woman Logan had carried to safety.

"Trevor, that's all the hostages."

"Thank you. Now let's work on your demands. We'll provide half hour updates at the very least, if not sooner."

"Understood." Gemma looked up to find One's gaze locked on her and she forced herself to maintain contact. "Don't forget, we have a deadline. He can't hold on to that dead man's switch forever."

"We remember."

Gemma ended the call and sat down, pleased the first call had gone so well. She'd shown the three men she was on their side and was willing to push boundaries to get them what they wanted, but knew when to give a little to keep the other side happy. That was the good news.

The bad news was her unease about the cracks showing between the hostage takers. She didn't know if the tension was getting to these men, with Two starting to waver and Three having an issue with One's control, or if those disconnects had existed before they set foot in the Terminal.

Either way, that discord could sow the seeds of a chance to break free. Or it could spell death for them all.

Chapter 16

The clock ticked as the minutes slipped by.

Her ankles zip-tied once again, Gemma settled into her spot on the floor, knowing they were in a temporary lull. Many hours spent on the other end of the phone line made her familiar with the strategies used at this point in the negotiation. Some of which, in this case, might be short-circuited somewhat due to the added pressure of an unusually abbreviated time frame.

Job number one for her once things started to move was to stall for time, to find a way to stretch out the deadline as far as possible without putting them in lethal jeopardy from the bomb going off when One couldn't hold the trigger down any longer.

Her gaze slid to where One stood propped against the ticket booths under the HARLEM LINE DEPARTURES sign. He had his back to the short edge of the counter with his right hand resting on it, knuckles down, letting the weight of his arm keep his fist pressed closed around the detonator. Gemma's nerves kicked at the thought that he was already beginning to experience muscle fatigue, the strain of which could be deadly for all of them. He was probably wishing for a place to sit down, to cradle his hands together in his lap, but the main level of Grand Central Terminal was designed for motion. The concourse floor had never had seating, and even the long benches that had once filled Vanderbilt Hall in its original role as the waiting room were long gone. The Terminal wasn't meant for sitting and resting while you waited for your train; it was meant as the area you passed through between the city and your transportation. The modern Terminal now had multiple dining options where travelers could be seated, but none of those were close and would necessitate the hostage takers splitting up. That didn't appear to be part of their plan.

Behind the scenes, she knew her team had to be coming up with contingency plans. Word would travel through to the Justice Department and up the chain to the president, but Gemma didn't have any confidence the Powers That Be would bow to pressure and release the four imprisoned men. In fact, it was national policy that the United States would not negotiate with terrorists who held American citizens captive. Doing so would only legitimize their actions and encourage more of the same. Then when would it end?

She'd known from the beginning that unless she could talk their way out of this, or she and Logan could somehow act from within the group, they were doomed. Worse, she knew her family would also realize the same brutal truth—there was an extremely good chance she would die in the coming hours.

I'm sorry, Joe, Mark, Teo. But I'm especially sorry, Dad. You too, Alex. If I don't come home tonight, everyone will suffer, but you most of all. Dad, everyone will close ranks around you. Alex, you need to lean on Frankie. You'll go on like there isn't a giant hole in your world. She'll know there is, because she'll have one, too.

A ragged sigh slipped from her on a whisper of breath. What her family was going through, might go through, ate at her, crowding her every thought and action. She knew when things started moving again shortly, she'd need to compartmentalize, to rip out her heart and lock it away. Hopefully, she'd have the chance to free it again when the time was right. When they'd all be together again.

But she gave herself a moment to sink, to feel the grief and agony she knew they were all feeling, standing on the outskirts, so close, only a few blocks away, but essentially miles distant. To share that pain somehow made her feel closer to them.

Warm pressure against her right side made her realize Logan had watched for a moment when all three hostage takers were looking elsewhere to sidle a little closer to her. To make contact with her from shoulder to hip.

He tipped his head down to partially hide his face. "Hanging in?" he asked quietly.

Gemma did the same. "Yes. You?"

"Yeah." He paused for a moment. "Boone's here."

"Detective Boone?"

"Yeah. Got a brief glimpse of him in the east window. Fourth floor."

Detective Orin Boone, one of the A-Team officers from Unit 5. Shorter and stockier in stature than the rest of the guys, he would be easily identifiable. But Gemma understood Logan's true point—Boone was the A-Team's prime boots-on-the-ground tech guy. They had sound already through the phone calls. So that meant—

"You think he has visuals set up?"

"I'd bet a year's pay on it. Look up to your left. Southeast corner. Your family's watching."

She couldn't help the hitch in her breath, knew he'd feel it through their connected bodies, even if he couldn't hear it. She shouldn't have been surprised he'd be able to read her so well. The truth was he always had...until she'd walked away from him and, much later, frozen him out.

You know, when we stop arguing and work together, we make a hell of a team. Her own words from a few weeks ago rang in her head. She wasn't wrong then; it held true now.

Raising her head, she scanned the space, panning casually, as if seeing the concourse for the first time and not wanting to miss a single aspect. Then her gaze rose to where she judged the camera might be. Knowing at least two of the family would be in a position to watch. Maybe more.

I'm here, Dad. Have faith. I'll do everything in my power to get back to you.

Alex, I need you. I need our connection. Help us.

Not taking her eyes off where she thought the camera might be, she slipped her hand across Logan's hip to find his hands held against his belly, sheltered by his bent knees. She slipped her hand around his, intertwining their fingers, and answered the intensity of his grip with her own.

For now, they held on. Resting. Waiting. Each knowing every passing second might be their last. Each knowing when the hostage takers' demand was denied, it *would* be their last.

If this was the end, they'd spend it together.

Chapter 17

The sound of furious whispers coming from past Logan attracted Gemma's attention. She pulled her hand from his loosened hold, sliding it into her own lap before scooting forward slightly to look down the hostages.

Suz and Holly had their heads together, whispering. Gemma couldn't hear the words, but Suz seemed upset about something and Holly was trying to calm her down. They were getting a look of annoyance from Three as their volume built.

She tapped Logan's left knee, and he straightened his legs, expanding her view. The two girls were sitting with their heads together, with Suz's hands in her lap and Holly's resting on top, her little finger hooked around Suz's index finger. Their voices were low, but as Suz wiggled her butt against the slick floor, Gemma heard "Can't wait..." as a low whisper.

It appeared they were going to be getting to practicalities earlier than she had hoped. It was a flat-out truth of long hostage negotiations that certain biological functions had to be managed—from food to bathroom trips. She'd hoped they'd have longer here. Even the class taken hostage a few weeks ago had done better than this, which was good because with two A-Team units outside the door, there was no way Russ Shea, the hostage taker, was going to open the door to let someone out to hit the bathroom.

But as the whispers rose in pitch, Gemma knew they weren't going to be so lucky this time. She needed to solve this issue before the hostage takers decided silence was golden and this one young woman was more trouble than she was worth.

Bracing her hand on Logan's thigh, she leaned over him, catching Redmond's disgusted expression where he sat on Logan's other side. The businessman seemed to have a knee-jerk reaction to teenage girls, or at least *this* teenage girl. "Suz." She got Holly's attention, but not Suz's. She didn't want to push her tone much further but needed the girl's attention. "*Suz!*"

Another furious whisper from Holly, and Suz looked up. Her pale face was splotchy and her eyes were red, as if she'd been quietly crying. The blue eyes that met Gemma's were wide and terrified.

"You okay?" Gemma asked.

"Clearly not," Redmond said, "or she wouldn't be carrying on like a toddler."

Gemma opened her mouth to snap back at Redmond when Logan beat her to it.

"Shut it." Logan's voice was low, but there was no mistaking the authority in it. "Or try some compassion for a change. You pick. But making this worse isn't an option. Understand?"

Redmond threw a poisonous glare Logan's way but pulled his elbows in tighter so as not to touch the man to his left he now felt was a threat or the teenager to his right he wanted to throttle. He simply stared straight in front of him, color rising high on his cheeks.

Gemma wondered if it was shame or fury. She was willing to bet it was the latter.

She gave Logan's thigh a gentle squeeze—*Thank you*—knowing he'd understand the message.

She met Suz's damp eyes and repeated her question.

The girl only shrugged.

"I can't help you if you don't talk to me. What do you need?"

Suz mumbled something and for the first time Holly looked annoyed, like her patience was running thin.

You and Redmond both.

"She has to go to the bathroom," Holly hissed as Suz's face flamed. "Bad."

The hostage takers had set a time limit, but they were hours away from it. This girl simply wasn't going to last that long. Worse, she could cause a real problem and was out of Gemma's reach to try to calm her. This needed to be dealt with.

Gemma did a quick review of the station structure as she knew it. Because the Terminal was built as a rapid thoroughfare, the large public bathrooms were all down a level in what was now the Dining Concourse. She didn't believe the hostage takers would allow someone to go to a separate level.

But there were both a ladies' and a family restroom inside the Station Master's Office, where the only waiting space on the main floor still existed for ticketed travelers. She'd used the space herself once when she was traveling on Metro-North, and had been surprised to find several of the century-old wooden benches from the original waiting room installed for use. The location was only about two hundred feet from where they now sat. Maybe she could talk them into sparing one man for that.

More than just a bathroom trip, it could be a way to separate the men. If one gunman took a hostage to the bathroom, that only left one gunman and the bomber.

However, the bomb was the sticking point. There could be no rushing him, no trying to overpower him. It would be over in milliseconds. The possibility of separating the men still had promise, but if they were going to pull that off, this very first attempt at it had to go perfectly.

"Suz, look at me." Gemma waited until the girl met her eyes. "If I can get one of them to take you to the bathroom, do you swear to go and come back without causing any trouble? It's crucial you do what needs doing and then come back. No fussing, no cajoling. Just do as they say." She decided to couch it with a little fear to ensure compliance, as their lives might depend on it. "Otherwise, I can't guarantee your safety."

The girl simply nodded rapidly, her eyes huge in her pale face.

"Let me see what I can do." Gemma pulled back to sit against the wall. "Excuse me," she called.

Three sets of male eyes focused on her and she forced herself not to shrink back under the combined force of their cold stares. Especially Three, who looked like he'd cheerfully kill her for the imposition of his attention.

"We need to take care of something," she said, her voice entirely calm, hoping some of that calm would trickle toward Suz. "Suz needs to use the bathroom."

"She can wait." Three turned back toward One.

She wasn't only negotiating with her team outside the concourse; she was negotiating with the hostage takers inside, as well. "She could, but I think you'll find that's a disruption. Better to let her take care of it. You don't want to take action against her that could be seen by the NYPD sharpshooters watching us."

"Why would I care? What are they going to do if I kill one of you?" Three taunted, his voice rising in pitch and echoing around the empty space. "They can't shoot us. Not without risking all of you and their men."

"No, but I'm negotiating for you with them in good faith. If you kill someone—especially if it's just because they needed a bathroom—you may find you don't get what you want. We all die, but so do those four men." Gemma met One's gaze, knowing he was in charge and could make the call. "One of you takes her, two of you stay here with us. She's promised to do what she needs to do and immediately come back. She's not going to give you any trouble. Right, Suz?" Gemma pinned the girl with a pointed look.

The girl nodded.

"She goes, she comes back. That's the end of it. The Station Master's Office is just behind those stairs." She pointed to the West Balcony. "Go through the glass double doors into the office and there's a waiting room with benches and the bathrooms. It's a few hundred feet away and you'll be back inside of five minutes. You wouldn't need to unbind her hands, just cut her ankle tie. She's already terrified; she's not going to run, because she knows you'll kill her before she gets away."

One held her gaze for an extended moment, then studied the girl. "Fine." He turned to Two. "Take her. Anything seems off, she tries anything, shoot her. No questions asked."

"Sure." Two pulled his knife from his pocket, let the blade spring free, and then strode to Suz, who shrank back against the marble wall. He slit her ankle bindings with a single flick of the blade.

Two stepped back a couple of paces and motioned with his P90 for the girl to rise. Suz scrambled awkwardly to her feet, then hesitated, staring at the gun, her terror shining bright in the rapid rise and fall of her chest and the spasmodic twitch in her left index finger.

"Suz." Gemma waited until she tore her eyes from the P90 and her gaze slid to Gemma. Gemma held it, trying to convey strength and calm in a single look, to give her the confidence to do this. And to set the stage for others to follow in her footsteps. Including herself or Logan. "Do you know where to go?"

Suz shook her head.

"Go past that staircase, through the arch on the far side." She pointed to the northwest exit from the concourse, near the track entrances, picturing the way in her mind. "Go down the hallway. Past the bakery on your left, the coffee shop on your right. In front of you will be double glass doors with 'Station Master's Office' on them. Go into the office, the bathrooms are clearly marked. Take your time and don't rush while you're walking. Take care of things and then come straight back. Okay?"

"Okay." The girl's voice was barely audible, but she stepped away from the row of hostages and walked across the floor slowly, Two stalking behind her.

Three stepped forward, an imposing figure, his expression unreadable behind the balaclava, but his stance made it clear he was in charge of the hostages now.

Gemma watched Suz disappear behind the staircase and sat back again.

She kept her gaze on Three, watching for any warning sign of trouble. The man made her uncomfortable. All three men were threatening, but she was getting a feel for the individual personalities. One was in charge, though Gemma wasn't sure how rock solid that leadership position was for him. Two seemed the most reasonable of the group, invested in the cause, but perhaps not in the excessive violence once the initial attack required to gain control was complete. But Three...he was the one who truly frightened her. The one who seemed to ride the line, always teetering on the edge of rage. She sensed his rage was wrapped tight, but the threads were stretching thin under pressure, and a little weight might be enough to blow it apart.

And, if it did, someone would die. Possibly all of them.

Three would bear watching. She could tell from the way Logan sat, motionless, his eyes constantly tracking, but most often returning to Three, he also felt Three was the unpredictable one.

In less than five minutes, Gemma caught movement in her peripheral vision and found Suz walking slowly back to them, her eyes fixed on the hostages, relief in her expression that the scene was just as she left it. That Holly was just as she left her.

She crossed the floor, circled mother and son and the German tourists, then sat down with her back against the wall and her feet together so Two could bind them again. Then she collapsed in on herself as Two stood and walked back to the other hostage takers.

Sara Driscoll

Gemma tracked his movements across the floor. With Suz's help, she'd done it—she'd shown the hostage takers a hostage could be trusted on a short trip.

Now it was up to Gemma and Logan to figure out if they could use that to their advantage.

Chapter 18

An uneasy silence filled the concourse once again.

McFarland's third call a few minutes ago had gone very much like the second—a brief update to tell them things were progressing. Gemma could tell he wanted to stay on the phone longer, wanted to do what would normally be done during a negotiation—to start to build a bond with the hostage takers—but when he could only report they'd reached out to the Department of Justice and the White House with no response back yet, One told her he didn't want her on the phone, and Gemma had ended the call.

Ending the call had carried the pain of chopping off a limb. Just hearing McFarland's voice made her feel closer to her team; the silence that now strung between them felt like a chasm. But she knew things were moving behind the scenes and patience was required at their end.

In the meantime, she needed to use this lull to stretch the next conversation. She had more information now but hadn't had enough time to solidify her plan around how to use it. Part of the HNT's strategy of breaks between calls would be to leave the hostage takers to stew. To think about how what they'd done could go wrong in so many ways. She'd take advantage of that time.

After the third time Three scowled at the phone, she caught his eye. "Negotiations can take time and we have to give them some space to give you what you want. They'll call on schedule, as you instructed. They know you're in charge."

Sara Driscoll

Three's stiff stance reflected his impatience, but more dangerous was the rage brewing behind his eyes. "Or they're buying time between calls to figure out how to smoke us out of here."

Gemma kept her tone light. "Only if they're idiots, and I don't think they are. Trust me, with a deal this important, they've sent their best. You guys hold all the cards, but we have to give them time to do what you asked. Or at least to start the request." She paused momentarily, hoping what she aimed for as a thoughtful look carried through. "There's something we could do as we wait, though."

Three didn't take the bait, and simply stared at her.

It's like talking to a brick wall, except the wall might have more personality. "I could speak for you better," she continued as if invited to speak, "if I know more about you. About what you're fighting for."

Three walked away from her to stand twenty feet away from Two.

Staring down at her knees, she blew out a frustrated breath.

"How would that help?"

Gemma looked up at the sound of One's voice from across the empty floor to the ticket booths. "You need me to talk them into seeing your side, see why you're making the request. In all the deals I've negotiated, making a connection with the person on the other side of the table is the first strategy to getting what you want. They see you as a person, not just a business contract with numbers. This isn't a business deal, but the same strategy applies. The human connection is everything."

That much was true. There were several guiding principles in hostage negotiation: Develop a rapport with the person you negotiate with, be it hostage taker or someone on the verge of taking their own life. Listen much more than you talk. Be empathetic and make sure the person understood they were being heard. Never lie to a hostage taker, as your credibility could take a hit from which you'd never recover. No matter how distasteful you find the suspect, no matter how you dislike them, never, ever let it show. And, most importantly, never negotiate face-to-face with a hostage taker because that was the only way a negotiator could die during the dialogue.

Gemma had blown the last out of the water the moment she'd offered to negotiate for them with the HNT, when she was really negotiating *for* the HNT inside the concourse. But not revealing her dislike for the hostage takers, making it look like she was on their side for the purpose of winning her own survival, was paramount.

It was also true, because it *was* a fight for survival.

"They're talking to me because you want to keep your identities secret," Gemma continued. "But they don't care about my background. I'm here because I'd just come off the subway. It's you they want to get to know. More importantly, *you* want them to get to know you. And I can help you with that, but you need to help me do it. I told you—you've essentially bought my services in exchange for my being able to walk out of this place alive. You want your guys free; I want to live to see my family. We can help each other." Gemma kept her gaze fixed on One. He was the one calling the shots; without his approval—even if there was dissent in the ranks—nothing would happen. She let a touch of her desperation show on her face. She wasn't lying—she *did* want to live to see her family.

"You want us to spill our guts to you? To use against us?"

Gemma's laugh had a sharp edge to it. "That would be a stupid thing to do. Using anything against you is using it against all of us." *Or at least the plan is for you to think so. The NYPD needs to figure out a way to save us and not create a second Ground Zero in an already scarred city.* "And there's something you might not have thought of."

One's silence gave her permission to continue.

"About fifteen years ago, I briefly dated a cop. Well, cop-wannabe—he was in the academy. He used to tell me about what was going on at the academy, what he was learning from the cops training them. And you might be surprised, but some of those guys shared a number of your views. Assuming you have similar views to the four men jailed for the attack, there are cops who have similar feelings about the Second Amendment. They approved of citizens arming themselves, said they were seeing violent crime significantly decreased because of it. A lot of cops are pro-gun rights. You might find that plays into a connection on the other end of the line."

Gemma knew her argument was largely correct for the majority of cops who approved of the right to self-protection, but knew the cops sitting around the negotiation table had a different view of it, a largely negative view. They'd seen too many times when a domestic situation got out of hand simply because a firearm was easily at hand. Worse than that, they'd seen what happened to the weak and small when confronted with that power.

They'd seen the bodies following occurrences when a negotiation had failed. Often in circumstances when they'd suspected from the outset they'd never had a chance to make a difference.

"Talk to me about what makes you tick. I can use it to your advantage." Gemma let her gaze roam across all three men before returning to One. "Unless you've changed your mind and decided you don't intend to live."

"That's not the goal."

"Then talk to me. Give me all the influence I can swing. It doesn't have to be here; I understand you'd consider that a security threat. I can sit on the floor where they are and talk to them there." She glanced down at the fitness tracker on her wrist. "We have a little more than twenty minutes before they call again. We could make the next call as short as the first, but that doesn't do anything for you. Let's use the time, then use the call to our advantage. You're in charge. *Be* in charge."

One stared at her as seconds ticked by, then turned away and walked back toward the ticket counters, spun, and strode back. "Fine. Start with that one." He motioned to Two. "But I'm going to listen to every word. I don't like what you're asking, it's over."

"Fair enough." Gemma didn't give them time to change their minds. Digging in with her bootheels and pushing with her unbound hands, she inch-wormed across the slick floor, headed directly for Two.

Two shot a sideways glance at One but got a sharp nod, the order to comply unmistakable.

Let's see if you're as willing to talk.

Gemma purposely steered herself to the outside of Two, so she could turn around to face him but could keep One, Three, and the hostages in view. A number of hostages watched her, but the sharpness in Logan's gaze said he'd be keeping his eye on the proceedings. She appreciated the support, even if across a distance, but knew if he needed to act—to pull his knife, free himself, and enter the fight—it would already be too late.

Facing the east windows, she glanced at where they thought the camera was placed, knowing her team would be following her movement. *Good. They'll know I'll have information to pass along.*

Gemma was familiar with Stockholm Syndrome, and also how it was misconstrued. Contrary to the generally held belief that some hostages who spent enough time with their captors fell in love with them, it actually referred to the bond formed during the power imbalance of hostage taker/ hostage interactions that led to a psychological bond, most often one of compassion. That was the emotional bond she intended to portray for Two.

She looked up at Two, who appeared even taller from this angle as he towered over her, his eyes on the hostages, his barrel pointed mid-crowd. "Thanks for talking to me."

Two shot her a quick glance, confusion clouding his eyes; evidently, she wasn't what he expected. He stayed silent.

"Can you tell me why you're doing this?"

"To free them."

"I realize that, but I need something to tell that cop on the line. I need you to be a real person to him. Why is this important to you?"

"Because they did what they had to do."

"The attack on the building, you mean? They were forced to do it?"

"No."

Gemma gave him to a count of ten to expand, not wanting to feed him his lines. Not wanting to reveal that as a cop herself, she knew a few things about the kind of people who would stage an attack of that magnitude. "'Had to do...' Do you mean they had a duty to do it?"

"Yeah."

"A patriotic duty?"

"What else?"

Gemma had to fight to keep her face absolutely neutral. Two might be looking at the hostages, but in her peripheral vision, she could see One was watching her closely. This man and his version of patriotism—the kind that killed 129 innocent people without a second thought—made her feel simultaneously physically ill and enraged, but she couldn't let it show without risking their lives. "Can you explain why that was their patriotic duty? Shouldn't we support the government?"

"We would, if it supported the Constitution."

"This one doesn't?"

"No. This one is trying to throw us into chaos. Then it will suspend the Constitution, call for martial law, and put a new constitution in place. *Their* constitution. We're the three percenters. We take action when it's needed."

Three percenters—Gemma was familiar with the term. Most anti-government or militia group members talked the talk but rarely walked the walk. The war is coming...next week, so they better be ready for it. But next week never came. However, a small percentage of those militia members were prepared to act *now*—these were the so-called three percenters.

These hostage takers as well as the four men who plotted and carried out the William J. Green Federal Building bombing were among their number.

"Our men were just protecting us from an overbearing government," Two continued. "Slowing them down. Keeping them distracted from their main goal."

"Which is?"

"Coming for our freedom. Our guns. Us, when they force us into concentration camps so they can replace us with illegal immigrants who will vote to keep them in power."

Gemma forced an image of her nine-month-old nephew, Nate, into her head, something good and pure to balance out the hatred coming from this man. The last time she'd seen him was at Thanksgiving at her father's. They were a family of first responders, so not everyone could be there—this was the reason they kept August *Ferragosto* celebrations as the one everyone booked off—and while Teo couldn't be there, his wife, Rachel, and their son attended. Nate had recently started cruising and had his family in stitches as he made his way around the family room from couch to table to chair.

Gemma saw once again the joy in his eyes at his newfound independence, heard the trill of his laugh in her mind. Used it to cool the fury whipping through her and to keep her face absolutely neutral.

Nothing could excuse what those men had done in Philadelphia, but Gemma needed to do everything in her power to keep her cool and to not let one flicker of her bone-deep disgust show. All was lost if she couldn't.

"Tell me more about your group. The Sinister 13. You're from New York City?" She knew very well they weren't, but wanted to look uninformed.

Two's laugh was heavy with derision. "See? Typical big city type. You don't know anything about how real Americans live."

"We're not real Americans?"

"Hardly."

"Because we don't know how hard it is out there?"

"Have you had to go without? Had your government fail you, so your factory closed, then you couldn't find work?" His eyes roved over the opulent marble surrounding them. "You're a big business type. You're the kind of person who built *this*."

For the first time, it struck Gemma that their plan to bomb Grand Central Terminal wasn't just to cripple New York City; it was also to destroy a piece of architecture they saw as elitist and a wasteful use of money that could have gone to others in the Vanderbilts' care—their employees, the regular folks who worked day in and day out for those who held unimaginable wealth, especially back then before the advent of income tax.

Gemma knew she had to stay true to the persona she'd created to get to where she now sat at Two's feet. "Yes, I'm a business type. But I'm not as wealthy as you think I am. I play with other people's wealth. They pay me a salary, but the millions of dollars I throw around during contract negotiations isn't my money. I'm not so different from you." Gemma didn't want to dwell on their differences, so she pushed on. "I'm sorry you lost your job. I know many areas have had a hard time with industrial losses, with many steel mills and car assembly plants closing."

"As long as the shareholders are making money, that's all that matters to them." His jaw tight, Two stared off toward the East Balcony. "Sometimes you do what you need to do to provide for your families, even if it's goddamn steak sauce for those fancy shareholders, because God knows I haven't had steak in years. I lost my job and haven't been able to find anything since. And if I was lucky enough to find work, it would be twelve-hour shifts for less than half of what I made before. A man wants the ability to work, to provide. To survive. But the government gives to the coastal elites and lets the Rust Belt starve."

Steak sauce. That wasn't something he simply pulled out of the air; that was a real-life experience. Which meant one thing—the closure of the Kraft Heinz plant in Allentown, Pennsylvania, from a few years back. He'd just told her where he was from.

"I'm sorry about that. Everyone should have the dignity of work." Gemma's gaze rose to One, then slid to Three. "I'm sorry if it's affected you all."

"Not all. Just me. Didn't have the skills to transfer to a big important energy project like some of us." Two's words were a sour mutter as his gaze flicked toward One.

Clearly there was some jealousy and resentment between these men. In an unfair world, those feelings even surfaced within the group that should have had a united front if they hoped for success. But the cracks were definitely forming and it appeared Two felt he was the least of them.

A quick glance at One showed growing impatience. She needed to get as much as she could from him before she was cut off. "I understand more now and am able to speak to it better. This is about fairness and equality. About the dignity of self-reliance. It's not just about violence. Your hand was forced to have to go to that extent." Gemma hoped she was putting on a performance worthy of a Tony or an Oscar, because these men made her want to vomit.

As a negotiator, she always had to put on a good front. But never like this, directly in front of the threat where one false move could mean a bullet to the brain.

One Capello dying like that was enough. Her family wouldn't survive a second, similar death.

"What can you tell me about—"

"That's enough." One's voice cracked out to cut Gemma off, the sharp tone echoing off the bare walls. "Get back."

Gemma didn't like the look in One's eyes, as if unsure if he'd let things go too far, and she didn't want to further antagonize him. She'd only learned something about two of the three men, but it would have to do for now. Not that she was sure she'd ever learn anything useful from Three. "Okay."

She slid back along the floor, conscious that every hostage had their eyes fixed on her, keeping hers down so as to not accentuate her connection with Logan.

She wiggled back into place, sitting back against cool marble, and checked the time on her tracker again. Just over ten minutes to go.

She closed her eyes and reviewed everything Two had told her, trying to figure out how to convey information to her team without alerting the hostage takers to her plan. She knew what would be going on behind the scenes in the negotiation room—by this time, they'd have taken the information given to them by Coulter and would have made contact with the Feds to supply them with an up-to-date list of Sinister 13.

These men were working hard to keep their identities hidden. But those identities could be key to figuring out how to end this and it was up to her to help her team with that problem.

If they were lucky, something in this information would help them identify the hostage takers and acquire the leverage required to finish this without further loss of life.

Chapter 19

"Are we ready?" McFarland checked the clock on the wall. "We're on in one minute." He turned to look directly at Alex. "I'm going to try to keep her talking this time. The last two calls have been too short for her to get us any information."

The fear that Gemma might not ever be given enough time to help them save her was a twist of barbed wire in Alex's gut. "It's out of her hands. They're not giving her that time."

"I know. But if they try to cut things short, I'm going to talk around her to convince the hostage takers we need additional information. She's been pumping them for info. It's why she spent ten minutes sitting with one of the gunmen."

Alex's gaze rose to the monitor sitting at the head of the table so the HNT could have visuals of the hostages during the negotiation. Being able to see the hostage takers was a critical advantage in managing the negotiation, but in this case, it also reassured the team their officers were safe...for now. With the exception of Gemma, the hostages hadn't moved since the last time they'd called. When she'd slid across the floor to sit with one of the gunmen, everyone in the room had stopped what they were doing to watch. Alex wished he could read lips, because for the first time, Gemma was actually facing the camera. Though he wasn't sure if the downward angle of the camera or the clarity of the feed—shot through glass and only zoomed in enough to capture the entire group of hostages and hostage takers so nothing was missed—would be sufficient to actually understand her words. However, no one in the room had that skill. Shelby, whose brother was born deaf, had been their best shot, but while she could read American Sign Language, she'd never learned lip reading. Garcia had put in a request for anyone who could read lips to watch the recorded feed and see if they could discern the conversation. Everyone thought it was a long shot, but it was worth the attempt, as it could give them an edge.

Everything was on the table.

At that moment, Gemma turned her face up to stare at the camera for what felt like a long moment. For Alex, it felt like he was making eye contact with her. Her fear, stress, and exhaustion screamed at him in both her expression and body language, as if she were letting her guard down for him only for a moment—then the walls slammed back into place, her face went stoically neutral, and her spine snapped straight.

I'm here, Gem. Hang in there, we won't give up on you. Don't give up on us.

She turned toward the phone on the floor, but Alex still felt the contact as if it were ongoing. They could do this.

Alex looked down at the piece of paper in front of each of the negotiators and himself that Garcia had brought in a few minutes before with an update. He'd taken point with the FBI, who was providing information they'd gathered about Sinister 13. Only formed a few years prior, the paramilitary group had a currently known roster of 117 members and was centered in Pennsylvania. The list in front of him comprised the active members of the group, so the names of the four imprisoned men were not included. Alex had scanned the list when it was handed to him, but there wasn't a single name that meant anything to him. If even one of these men listed was inside, let alone all three, they might be able to find a way to convince him to stand down.

Alex lifted his head to meet McFarland's gaze and gave him a nod. "If anything she says strikes me as a double meaning, I'll let you know."

"If they let her talk, she'll get us something." McFarland's gaze swept everyone in the room. "It may take all of us to decipher what she means." He checked the clock again. "Calling in now." He grabbed his pen, pulled his pad of paper closer, and placed the call.

It rang three times before it was answered. "Hello?"

Relief flooded through Alex at the sound of Gemma's voice. He knew a crucial part of her training was to always be calm and collected, no matter how badly the situation might be falling apart, so they weren't hearing her true emotional state. Still, it eased him slightly.

"Elena?"

"Yes."

"Before we begin, can I get an update on the hostages?" McFarland asked.

"We're fine. We haven't been harmed. There's been no abuse. They're even allowing bathroom breaks, if needed."

"Does anyone need any food or drink?"

On screen, Gemma looked to the man wearing the suicide vest. He shook his head. "We're fine."

"You let us know if you need something."

"We will. We'd like to know the status of our request."

Our request. Reinforcing her alignment with the hostage takers.

"It's moving along. The president has been informed and discussions are ongoing."

"You know we've given you a deadline. It feels to me like you're not trying to meet it." Gemma's words were clipped and carried an edge of frost.

"That's not true. You have to understand you've asked for something complicated."

"And you have to understand these men would simply like to see their government stand up for them for once."

There it is. She's opening the door.

McFarland flicked a glance across the table at Taylor, whose head was down, writing as fast as possible, but paused for a moment to give him a chance to catch up. "I think we'd all like to see that. Do they feel that hasn't happened for them?"

"It hasn't. And they're not alone in feeling like that. Look at how many in the Rust Belt feel they've been abandoned by a government that bails out the banks but not the little guys." A snort of disgust came down the line. "It's like you assume they're the type to use red sauce at every meal and spend their days standing in the unemployment line because it's the easy way. You're wrong. They're normal folk, just trying to get by."

A bolt of electricity shot through Alex and he jerked upright. McFarland's gaze shot to him briefly as if he registered Alex had heard something no one else did, but then he turned his attention back to the call.

Alex made a couple of notes on his pad of paper, then pulled out his phone, opened his browser, and started searching, while still keeping his attention on the conversation.

Beside Alex, Shelby wrote down the words "Rust Belt," underlined it twice, and then listed states below it—Ohio, Michigan, Wisconsin, Indiana, Pennsylvania, West Virginia.

"Normal folk is who the government tries to help."

"By doing what? Letting crime get out of control and then working to take away Second Amendment rights?"

"They have an issue with the Second Amendment?"

"They don't have an issue with the Second Amendment. They have an issue with the government riding roughshod over it. They just want to be able to defend their families. That can't happen if the government takes their guns. But who has the energy to constantly fight the government?"

"Maybe we could find a way for them to meet with their representatives."

Sharp, cynical laughter from at least one of the hostage takers was clearly audible to the negotiation team.

McFarland's gaze rolled up to the ceiling as if asking for strength, but when he spoke, his tone was smooth as glass. "They wouldn't be willing to let their representatives know their opinions? How can those people help if they don't know?"

"I'm sure those congresscritters have time and energy to burn, but even if you were lucky enough to get one who understood specific difficulties, how would you effect change? It would be like trying to turn the *Titanic* with the power of a paddleboat."

In the background, a male voice gave a short, sharp command.

"You're wasting time," Gemma said, her tone icy. "We expect progress in the next call."

A click sounded as the line went dead.

"Damn, that wasn't long enough. Though she was definitely trying." McFarland immediately turned to Alex. "You heard something we didn't. What was it?"

"She mentioned red sauce."

"As in marinara?"

"That's what most people would think. And that's certainly what she was trying to express, so what those guys heard was someone talking about plain cooking from an Italian perspective. Nothing fancy. A spaghetti and meatballs kind of basic meal."

"And that's not what she meant?"

"We're assuming your clue about the Irish pub got through and she knows I'm here. Me, the only person besides her best friend who knew where she was going for dinner. In which case, 'red sauce' has a different meaning in my family. Well, two meanings. Yes, marinara, but more importantly, it's a slang term in our family for ketchup."

"Ketchup?" Confusion creased Shelby's brow. "Why would she mention that? You think it's a clue?"

"I think so." He turned to Taylor. "Can you read the exact wording of the red sauce line back to us?"

"Sure." Taylor turned back a page, scanned down the lines of text. "Here it is. 'It's like you think they're the type to use red sauce at every meal and spend their days standing in the unemployment line because it's the easy way.'"

Alex scrolled down the page he had open on his phone, sure now of his direction. "I think she worked a couple of clues in there so we knew they were connected. She could have stated it more clearly, but we know they're listening. If they get any hint she's feeding us information, it's over. Not just cut off from communication, but dead. So she did an end run. When he was a kid, my brother Mark was a ketchup fiend. Put it on *everything* at any meal. We're a Sicilian family, so we used to tease him and call it his 'red sauce.' So 'red sauce at every meal' is definitely ketchup. And when you tie it into her comment about the unemployment line, especially when you consider the earlier Rust Belt qualification, you get this." He turned his phone around so everyone could see the title—*Heinz Plant Closes 6 Years After 3G Capital Buyout.* "That factory was in Allentown, Pennsylvania, one of the most devastated areas of the Rust Belt. Four hundred workers lost their jobs and hit the unemployment line. They didn't make ketchup there, they made other products like steak sauce, but Gemma was pointing us at that facility because she knew I'd connect ketchup to Heinz."

"She's trying to steer us to one of their identities," Williams stated. He picked up the list of Sinister 13 members and scanned it. "This is very bare-bones, but before he left to get updated, Garcia said this came from the Feds. They'll have more details. Especially governmental details—places of work, unemployment claims, taxes filed. If they have social security numbers, we can track them."

"If they can figure out if one of them worked at that Heinz plant, then we can start making connections," McFarland said. "If there's no connection there, then we need to rethink it, but I think you're onto something, Capello."

"Thanks."

"Did anyone else notice Gemma used the term energy a few times? And power?" Shelby asked. "It's like she was attempting to circle around to something but couldn't make it work when the time got cut short."

"She used it mostly in terms of human energy, but you think she was implying some aspect of the energy industry? Some form of power generation?" Taylor clarified. "Even if we're sticking with the Rust Belt, we'd be looking at multiple aspects of production. Like natural gas in Ohio."

"Gas and oil in Pennsylvania," Williams said.

"Coal in West Virginia," Shelby added.

"Don't forget renewable energy," Alex chimed in. "Solar. Geothermal and hydro. Wind farms out in Indiana and Illinois." He tapped the end of his pen on Shelby's pad of paper. "You left Illinois off your list."

"Good catch." Shelby added the state to her Rust Belt list.

"And almost all those states have nuclear power plants." McFarland shook his head. "She's going to need to take another swing at it next time. We'll just have to string clues together." He glanced at the closed door. "I wish Garcia would get back here with an update on the request."

"What are you going to do when they refuse to release the prisoners?" Taylor asked. "They're not going to suddenly begin negotiating with terrorists or it will open the floodgates."

McFarland sighed and sank down in his chair. "I know. I guess I just want that confirmed."

"And when they do?" Alex asked.

"Then we'll continue to 'wait.' If we tell them they've been refused, we're going to immediately lose control of the whole situation. As soon as they know nothing will come of their efforts, they'll well and truly have nothing to lose. They're killers. More than that, they're cop killers. They know how this will end if they're taken into custody when there's no chance of them escaping the city. They'll want to end this their way at that point." McFarland met Alex's gaze head-on. "If that's where we end up, they'll all be dead instantly."

Chapter 20

During the call, Logan had spent equal time watching Gemma and the hostage takers, but his gaze settled on her as she set the phone down in front of her boots. While One called Two and Three over, likely to discuss the call, she tipped her face up to the camera for a long moment, as if imploring her team to read between the lines of her statements. To make the connections needed to end the crisis. To bring them home. Then she sagged back against the wall.

Her reaction wasn't overt, but his experienced eye could tell from her discouraged stance she wasn't happy about the call. He could only assume she hadn't been able to get out all the details she wanted. Disappointing, but she was walking a razor-thin line with the ultimate stake—her life.

Logan flicked a glance at the hostage takers standing about thirty feet away. Two and Three stood sideways, ready to swivel to face the hostages at any moment, but their faces were turned away, their attention firmly on One, who spoke in low tones.

"Take a breath," he murmured, his lips barely moving. They had to keep the volume down or risk the sound echoing off what seemed like miles of hard, slick surfaces. "You did well."

"It wasn't enough." Her words matched his volume. "We're going to run out of time." She sucked in air through clenched teeth. "I couldn't find a way to clearly pass on some of the info."

"What info?"

Gemma glanced at the hostage takers as their voices rose, but they stayed focused on each other, not the hostages. "Two let it slip One got a job at a new energy project. I tried to seed the idea but couldn't figure out a way to pass it on clearly. It's too specific. That would have earned me a bullet between the eyes."

"Where's the project?"

"Pennsylvania, I think. Two's from Pennsylvania and most of these paramilitary groups are local."

"Maybe the Tripoli project?"

"The what?"

Another glance at the hostage takers told Logan the stress of the ongoing situation was testing the relationship of the three men. Their stiff stances spoke of the tension between them. Now Two had a phone out—probably a burner phone so he couldn't be traced—and was looking for something with his left hand while holding the P90 with his right. *Media reports? Looking for updates not filtered through the NYPD?*

"Was in the *Times*," he murmured. "Big new solar energy project going up in eastern Pennsylvania. In Tripoli."

"You're sure of the location?"

"I remembered the name because it's the same as a major World War Two battle." Another lightning-fast check of the gunmen. "The company bought open farmland because it was already cleared and it's close to Philly."

"If I could figure out how to get that info out, they might be able to find a connection." She sighed, her shoulders collapsing in and down as she pulled her knees in tighter. "I overestimated how much I could secretly leak to the HNT." Restrained nervous energy burst from its confines as she tapped her middle finger repeatedly against her knee.

Tap tap tap tap...

The idea came in a flash. "Wait." Logan's voice was low but backed with a restrained intensity that stilled her movements. He casually scanned the concourse from the west windows, past the ticket booths, over the hostage takers who seemed focused on the burner phone, then up to the east windows. He stared directly at where Boone and his camera must be, stared for a stretch of seconds, and gave a single nod. Then he turned his gaze down to where he shifted his bound hands to the side of his left knee, curled his fingers in except for his left index finger, and tapped out a pattern.

Keeping his head up, he kept his eyes on the gunmen, especially Three, who stood at an angle to see Logan's left side. As Three scanned down the group, Logan's fingers stilled. He waited until he was sure his attention was elsewhere, then he started again.

He heard Gemma's tiny indrawn breath when she realized what he was doing.

NYPD officers weren't required to learn Morse code, but A-Team officers often trained in additional tactics. For instance, how to speak to your sergeant through radio clicks when you weren't tactically able to talk. Morse code was perfect for that.

When you worked the department's most dangerous job, when you were called in for the highest impact situations with the greatest possibility of fatalities, you made sure you had every arrow in your quiver available at all times. Logan knew Morse code. So did Boone. But Boone wasn't the only person watching the feed. Someone would see, someone would understand the message. Someone would pass on that message, so he'd keep repeating it.

S-O-L-A-R E-N-E-R-G-Y T-R-I-P-O-L-I P-A

He got through the message at least six times, tapping his finger once for a dot, leaving the finger in place for several seconds for a dash, and curling his hand into a fist to hold for seven seconds to represent the space between words. At the end of the string, he rapped his fist twice against his knee before pausing and starting again. Morse was supposed to be an audible message, not a visual one, but he was sure if someone was paying attention, his message would get through. He knew his teammates were watching like hawks, watching *him* like hawks, waiting for a way to help. This was a way.

Garcia would be digging into the Sinister 13 roll call. This detail might narrow down a suspect identity. Could give them the leverage they needed.

Three rolled his shoulders, adjusting his hold on his P90, and stepped a little closer.

Logan let his fists slide out of sight. Another few seconds of silence and he knew his communication had gone unnoticed.

"Thank you." Gemma's muted whisper was just a thread of sound.

"Welcome." His murmur was barely audible.

They'd done everything they could for now to get inside information to their teams. Now it was up to them to pick up the ball and carry it into the end zone.

Chapter 21

Logan was used to waiting. Was used to the patience required in a sniper's nest until the perfect angle, the perfect timing, all came together in the perfect shot. But he was also used to being in charge of a situation. This enforced pause was gnawing at his patience with razor-sharp teeth. He was used to *doing,* used to waiting for the right moment, and then taking decisive action. Being forced to sit here, like a docile lapdog, grated on him.

He suspected Gemma felt the same way. She was used to the flurry of activity that happened in the negotiation room even when they weren't on a call, so having nothing to do but sit quietly until the next time the phone rang would feel uncomfortably restrictive. Logan understood her desire to keep the conversation flowing to maintain the bond with her team—he felt that same connection anytime there was a brief view of one of his teammates up in the windows. Their brothers and sisters in blue had their backs; they just needed to get them into a position where they could more safely assist them.

The hostage takers seemed content to let the wheels turn, having the NYPD manage their request, wanting nothing more than the barest communication. Essentially, they wanted their demands met and didn't want to hear much more. Logan was familiar with the beginning of hostage situations and how hard it was sometimes to get the hostage takers to talk to the negotiators. In this case, it was a bit different, as Gemma was the one speaking, but she was speaking at their behest. If they wanted space while the NYPD figured out what was possible, she would have to comply.

At this point in the process, everyone needed patience.

It didn't take long for Logan to realize the man beside him—Elliott Redmond—wasn't settling in like the rest of the hostages. More than that, he wasn't bonding with anyone around him. While most of the group were in pairs—mother and son, teenage besties, German tourists, he and Gemma—a few of the hostages were solo. But of those, most were making a connection with the person beside them. Hoyle, the camera guy, was between the two older women, and Logan had seen him checking in with both of them, making sure they were both as comfortable as they could be and consoling the woman who'd just lost her husband. On the far side of Gemma, the young guy with the backpack, Marek Czarna, had been whispering with Liza Grimes, the university student.

Everyone had been careful to keep their voices low and only took the chance to do so when it looked like the hostage takers were otherwise distracted. As time crawled on, the hostage takers didn't seem to be watching with the same intensity as a few hours previously, giving the hostages a tiny bit of freedom.

If exhaustion was setting in with the hostage takers, it would give them an advantage.

Redmond, however, had isolated himself with his piss-poor attitude from the start, showing he wasn't a team player. Whether it was his aggressive business attitude or he was a self-centered egomaniac, Logan couldn't be sure. But the guy hadn't made himself any friends.

Now he seemed like he wanted to pop. He was restless and constantly in motion, from bouncing the heel of one foot up and down, to tapping his fingers together, or patting his thigh—he couldn't sit still. Logan didn't think it was a neurodivergent personality not able to still itself; he saw it as the force of a personality who couldn't contain its importance or control. He'd been subtle so far—muttering under his breath or glancing furiously, not only at the suspects but at the hostages themselves—but it was most definitely growing in intensity.

Logan had intercepted that glance once; it hadn't stayed on him for long, but it had been enough time for him to read rage simmering below the surface.

Logan had met men like this before, had clashed with them in his role as an A-Team officer. There were some people—mostly men, but not always—who felt their opinion carried more weight than anyone else's, even if that other person was an authority figure like a police officer. He'd seen how that kind of personality could spin out—often those were the people he arrested after a violent situation—or if the individual learned how to shape it, camouflaging it from those in authority above him, while letting it loose on those below him; those were the people who used the power of that personality to climb the business world. He'd heard an unusually high number of CEOs could be clinically categorized as psychopaths. They were self-centered, entitled, and craved recognition from others. They were often also risk-takers, something viewed as sharp and courageous... as long as that risk was successful.

If that was Redmond, while many of the other hostages were terrified, he'd be outraged his rights were being stepped on.

All their rights were being stepped on...that was the point of the men who held them hostage. Redmond wasn't a special case to them. But he could make all their lives hell.

Gemma's elbow tapping his twice drew his attention, but she wasn't looking at him. Instead, her eyes were fixed on the suspects.

He'd been watching the suspects, too, keeping an eye out for any signs of weakness to exploit as well as for any additional signs of interpersonal discontent they could use as leverage or that could become deadly as they were caught in literal crossfire.

The three men were standing together, their voices low, but their tones had taken on an uncomfortable sharpness. Logan couldn't hear their words, but he watched the little of their expressions he could see—he wished they were unmasked, so he could better read their emotions—as well as their body language. Three had the most to say, and it was his voice that rose the loudest, carried the most insistence and outrage.

A few hours in and things were definitely getting rocky, something he wouldn't have expected this soon. Granted, who knew what had happened between these men in the days and hours leading to the actual attack? From the pinched corners of Gemma's mouth, she also wasn't happy about the growing discord.

"Hey!"

Logan was concentrating so hard on the three suspects that Redmond's shout from beside him gave him a jolt. He turned to find Redmond staring directly at the three men. *What is he doing?*

They turned to stare at him but didn't say anything, as if letting him make the next move.

"This is getting us nowhere," Redmond said. "This one"—he tossed a look in Gemma's direction—"isn't doing shit for us."

To his left, Gemma pulled in, muscles bunching, as if bracing to protect herself.

"Let me speak for us in the next call," Redmond continued. "I'll get the job done."

One broke away from the other two men, striding forward to stand within fifteen feet of the hostages. "Why do you think you can convince them to do what we want?"

Coming considerably closer than ever before, One's proximity gave Logan a chance to study him. Like the gunmen, he'd carefully removed his heavy jacket, revealing the full vest Logan now had a chance to see from all sides as One moved around their section of the concourse. A double line of pockets covered the vest as it wrapped around One's torso, each filled with a half block of C-4. Each chunk of explosive was individually wired in serial, each feeding from the previous block, each connected to an electric blasting cap. All it would take was one small charge to generate a mechanical shock from the detonator and it was over. They might have been able to detonate one block to blow them all, but they'd covered their bases to ensure their success.

Logan's bigger concern was the tremors he was seeing more often in One's right hand as muscular strain became a significant problem—shaking and an occasional jerking twitch. How much longer would he need to hang on? These men must have foreseen this and were using it as a pressure point for the negotiations, but what if he couldn't even make the initial time frame? And then what if they needed an extension to pull off what the suspects wanted? Had they thought of that?

"Because I'm a stock trader. I work on Wall Street," Redmond boasted. "I handle high-risk situations every day. She deals with unions. I deal with millions of dollars in a single transaction on a regular basis. She doesn't know stress; *I* know stress. I have to deal with people depending on me to get their deals done or else they could be wiped out financially. I'm a winner and I make those deals. I can make *this* deal."

One's gaze flicked to Gemma, who stared back at him, unblinking.

"He has no idea what he's talking about." Gemma's voice was calm, though Logan knew she had to be furious. And alarmed—Redmond had no idea what was going on behind the scenes. If he took over the negotiations, their only chance of coordinating with their teams would evaporate. And they all could die.

Logan wasn't actually sure if Redmond would care. If he was the egotistical type, he might not think anyone else could do the job. If he was a misogynist—and nothing Logan had seen from him so far today told him he was anything but—then he might not feel a mere woman could do the job.

Buddy, you have no idea.

"He deals with dollars," Gemma continued. "No, scratch that, he doesn't even deal in real money. He deals in bits and electrons. He watches numbers. Crunches numbers." She glanced sidelong toward Redmond. "He may be very good at that. But he's not good with people. That's clear to all of us." She turned back to One, as if Redmond was below her notice. "I'm very good with people. You've already seen what I can do for you. I'm here with you for the long haul. His kind of desperation for freedom won't get you what you want. He'll cut corners, which could get every one of us killed, including your four jailed patriots." The harsh finality in her tone left no doubt of her surety.

One stared at her for a moment longer, then turned his back on the hostages and strode back toward the ticket counter.

Gemma sagged back against the wall, the release of her breath a quiet sigh of relief.

But Redmond leaned forward, pushing into Logan's space, his face suffused with color. "You fucking c—" He stopped abruptly on a pained wheeze.

Logan pulled his elbow out of Redmond's ribs where his single shot had cut off the other man's vile invective as it stole his breath. "Sit back and shut up. If we survive, it's going to be because of her." Logan met defiant blue eyes, but ones now with an edge of fear in them. "Even bound like this, I can put you down. And I will, unless you keep your mouth shut and mind your own." He turned away from Redmond.

Gemma met his gaze, smiling her thanks, and he gave her a single nod in return.

The silence continued. Even the hostage takers seemed to recognize the stress was getting to them as well, and they gave each other space. One retreated to the ticket counters, where he once again rested his fist, while Two and Three stood nearer the hostages, though separated by a full twenty feet. Yet within mere minutes, Three seemed to have trouble keeping the lid on either his temper or his impatience and started to pace back and forth in front of the hostages. As he walked, he held the P90 ready to fire, the barrel angled so if he pulled the trigger, the bullets would catch a hostage mid-chest. The kind of shot guaranteed to seriously maim or, more likely, kill.

Logan was sure Three was doing it purposely to terrorize the hostages, who couldn't relax or take their eyes off him as the danger from him ramped up and down with his movements. His amusement might be cooling his temper, but it was tormenting the innocent civilians in his sights.

What made Logan most uncomfortable was each gunman's habit of threading a finger through the trigger guard to lie against the trigger, instead of along the guard, as Logan himself did when he held a killing weapon in his hands. One jostle, one twitch, and the P90's bullets would fly at a rate of fifteen rounds per second. The thought of the magazine emptying into a human body—or bodies—in just over three seconds sent fear arrowing through his gut.

Just because he was A-Team didn't mean he didn't have the capacity to feel fear when his life could end in a split second. His own words to Gemma's nephew Sam rang in his head: *Smart guys know that only stupid guys aren't scared when their lives are on the line. It's what you do with the fear that matters.*

Three passed by, walking down to the west end of the hostages, creeping closer to their extended feet to stay inside of where Two stood unmoving fifteen feet away. He turned and Logan tracked his progress as he approached them. Three was clearly enjoying watching the hostages react as the barrel of his gun passed over them. Holly and Suz shrank back, ducking their heads, Suz clenching her eyelids shut, only opening one eye when she thought she'd given him enough time to pass her. Some hostages didn't give him the satisfaction of seeing their fear—the man on the other side of Gemma simply stared straight ahead—while others, like Gemma and himself, watched his every move.

Three hit the east end of the hostages, turned, and paced back. Like the hostages themselves, Logan guessed from the set of his shoulders he was wound tight with nervous energy with nowhere to go. Thus the pacing, the only energy expenditure allowed; definitely not enough to even take the edge off that kind of tension. But apparently it gave the guy some jollies to terrify the hostages. As long as that was where it stopped.

Back and forth one more time. Logan turned his attention back to Two, who still stood motionless watching the hostages, but Logan noticed he glanced cautiously at Three every so often, as if nervous of Three's control of his emotions. As if nervous of what Three might do.

It didn't make Logan feel better.

He turned his attention to One, where he stood separated from the rest with his left hand once again cupping his right to give it some ease.

One's hand strength might have been a miscalculation on their part, possibly a fatal one for all of them. They had to hope he could hold on or else—

The hit came from his right, knocking him sideways into Gemma. With his hands bound and his attention focused on One, he careened sideways, his automatic reaction being to try to free his hands in the fraction of a second before his brain kicked in to have his hands working in concert rather than against each other. He slammed into Gemma's shoulder, but she was already reacting, throwing up an arm to block him.

"*No!*" Her shout exploded in his ear even as he pushed off her bracing arm with his forearms, righting himself so he could take in the disaster about to take place.

Redmond had taken advantage of Three's pacing to catch him when his back was turned and while he blocked Two's line of sight. He'd inched forward about a half foot with his knees bent and his shoes flat on the floor, but this time as Three passed by him, his gleeful eyes locked on the two teenage girls and the terror he was inflicting, Redmond shot his feet out, tripping Three at the last second so he went down hard like a toppling monolith. Bullets burst from the P90, barely missing Two's feet as Three twisted as he landed. Two leaped away, and before he could turn back, Redmond had thrown himself on top of Three and was scrabbling for the P90 with his bound hands. He had his left hand clamped over the top of the frame, attempting to wrest it up and away.

A second earsplitting blast of bullets flew, glass shattering as they pierced the windows of the information booth behind them.

Hostages screamed and ducked for cover, trying to disappear into the floor.

"Get down!" Logan threw himself sideways, half covering Gemma as she cried out, her hands flying to her face.

The ejected casings landed on the floor in a musical shimmer and one bounced off the back of Logan's right hand, a brief blaze of heat from the rapid-fire spray of bullets. Then silence.

Logan's head snapped up, recognizing the break in the shooting for what it was—an empty magazine, even as the two men still wrestled for the gun. The thought of the empty magazine must have penetrated Three's rage because he released the P90, rolled clear, and then climbed to his feet. Redmond was left clutching the P90, which he shuffled in his bound hands, finally getting his finger on the trigger.

Don't you realize it's useless?

His eyes going wide with horror, Redmond also realized the weapon was empty. He dropped it and pushed to his knees, his bound hands half extended in entreaty.

There would be no mercy.

Three strode to Two, issued a short, sharp order, and roughly grabbed Two's weapon even as Two still held it fixed on Redmond. Then he turned back to Redmond.

Logan braced himself, knowing what was about to happen, knowing there was nothing he or anyone else could do without risking the same fate. Gemma seemed to sense it, too, as she pulled in tighter under him, shying away from what was coming in horrified anticipation.

This had to be hitting too close to home for her. She'd watched her mother die, standing within a group of hostages, trying to negotiate for a lost cause.

More than that, Logan was sure Gemma could see the killing rage in Three's eyes as well as he could. Right now, their biggest danger was being so close to Redmond. What were the chances his rage would overflow onto other hostages?

"No, don't!" Redmond begged. "I was just—"

Stopping six feet away, Three raised Two's P90 and squeezed the trigger in one short, sharp motion, driving a single bullet straight into Redmond's forehead. A red mist exploded outward as his body jerked with the force of the impact, driving him backward into the wall of the information booth.

Logan couldn't see Redmond's face, but he didn't have to. Under his commander's order, he'd made that same shot himself enough times to know how the face simply lost all animation, as death was instantaneous. A small-caliber bullet like that didn't have enough force after the initial penetration to shatter the skull, but instead would bounce around inside the brain cavity, ripping the tissue to shreds. It would be like putting a brain into a blender.

The teenage girls screamed at the sound of that final, echoing gunshot, then lay on the cold marble sobbing, and all around was the sound of terrified breathing and a moan or two as the hostages waited to die.

Then...silence for long seconds.

Logan looked up from where he half lay across Gemma in time to see Three stepping back, still sweeping Two's P90 over the hostages as Two grabbed Redmond by one foot and dragged his lifeless body toward the New Haven Line ticket booths.

A long smear of blood marked the trail of the body as Redmond's head lolled to one side.

Three waited until Two returned to hand him back his P90, then grabbed his own discarded weapon before stalking to one of the duffel bags. He dispassionately ejected the empty magazine, tossing it with a clatter to the marble tiles, pulled a new one from the bag and loaded it, then returned to his previous position, his expression blank, as if nothing had happened.

Gemma squirmed under Logan, and he lifted his weight from her. As he straightened, he noted the distinct forms of his fellow A-Team officers standing in clear view in the windows, all in a shooting stance, but they'd held fire, knowing no good could come from it. They remained visible and in place, but the crisis had passed. For now.

The phone rang, the noise echoing off the walls, the upbeat tune a grotesque melody following the brutal death. The HNT had no doubt watched Redmond's attempt and were checking in.

Gemma stared at the phone, which had been kicked several feet away during the struggle, but didn't lunge for it, letting it ring. Instead, she turned her gaze up to One.

"Leave it," One snapped as Two and Three pulled back to stand closer to him. "We don't have anything to say to them."

With a shaky breath, Gemma pulled up to sit beside Logan. A trail of blood ran from a gash near her hairline over her right eye to trickle down her cheek.

"You're bleeding." Logan reached up with his bound hands as if to touch the wound, then pulled back.

She touched the wound on her forehead. Her fingers came away wet with blood. "Hurts a bit. How bad is it?"

"About an inch long. Shallow. Might need stitches. Flying glass?"

She nodded as her eyes searched his face. "You're okay?"

"Didn't get touched." His gaze shot to the blood-splattered floor. "We got off lucky."

Logan's gaze followed the bloody path to the sprawled corpse rolled against the wall of the ticket booth. Redmond had been infuriated that no one was listening to what he had to say. The man had come across to Logan as an egotistical control freak who didn't like his opinion being discounted. Maybe he thought he'd be a hero, taking control, saving the day. He'd gotten his hands on the P90, but he'd really never had a chance.

Even Logan, with all his tactical skills and training, never would have attempted it.

Redmond hadn't only lost his life in his bid for freedom, he'd also made things much harder for them. The suspects would now be on edge, waiting and watching for the next attack. Redmond's death would be the ultimate deterrent for the civilians, but now negotiations could be harder for Gemma, and any aggressive move he made would be met with more resistance.

One wrong word, one wrong action, and they'd end up like Redmond. The suspects would only move faster next time.

Logan looked away from the crumpled form. But it was a reminder they still had so much to lose.

Chapter 22

Garcia pushed back into the negotiation room to find his people head down over their electronics. A glance at the wall clock told him they still had fifteen minutes until the next check-in.

This entire negotiation had been unusual, and not just because they were talking to one of their own officers. Normally, they'd aim for longer stretches of conversation with the hostage taker to build rapport. Sometimes it took time to figure out what a hostage taker wanted; sometimes they were so desperate, they didn't even know themselves.

But these men had entered Grand Central Terminal with an agenda that had been stated at the very outset as part of their demands. They had no interest in conversation, only in an answer from the president.

Heads, life. Tails, death and destruction. For them, it was a binary choice. And their unwillingness to let Gemma talk to them for any extended period of time meant she and Logan struggled to get out any information that might be helpful.

One glance at the monitor told them the short conversations weren't her choice. But with the bomber standing about twenty feet away and one of the gunmen aiming directly at her to insist on compliance, it was clear who was calling the shots. Garcia had the distinct impression the details she'd been able to sneak out to them so far would be the sum total of the help she could give them.

Hopefully it would be enough.

It certainly hadn't been in time to save the one hostage who'd made a try for one of the gunmen. Garcia had no idea what he'd been thinking, but it was pure insanity to go after one of them like that. Capello and Logan would know not to attempt it—the ratio of failure to success was simply too great to overcome. But that man had somehow thought he could gain the upper hand and had died for his arrogance.

Capello and Logan knew killing one of the hostages would be easy after the eleven lying on the concourse floor or behind the MTA desk. Not that he thought eleven would be the final count. There hadn't been time for updates, so Garcia didn't know the status of anyone taken to neighboring hospitals. Many had been treated on scene—or as close to on-scene as the NYPD would allow as they evacuated the area after the bomb threat was revealed—but sixteen had been taken to the hospital with severe or critical injuries. They were a long way from any kind of final kill count. Or a resolution to this incident.

Especially with what he now knew.

Taylor looked up from his laptop. "News?"

"Not the kind we want, but what we expected." Garcia pulled out the empty chair next to Alex and sat down heavily, feeling like an enormous weight was dragging him to the floor. He set a thick file folder on the table in front of him. "The president has been fully briefed and has discussed the situation with his senior staff. We just heard back from the attorney general's office. They won't negotiate with terrorists."

Beside him, Alex lost what little color he'd had since this incident began. "So that's it? They're doomed?"

"Not at all. But we have to figure out how to work around this. In a normal situation, this might be when we switched to discussing a tactical breach, but that's not possible. We have to find another way." He flipped open the file folder. "The Feds came through with the full information we requested on Sinister 13 personnel. You'll find a copy in your email, but I also have a paper copy here for quick scanning. Where are we with the information Capello and Logan provided?"

"We have the details on the Heinz plant closure," said Williams. "It happened in 2016. We had a couple of detectives reach out to the company, and they provided a list of the employees who were there up to the last day. Of the one hundred seventeen names in Sinister 13, we have a single match—Wyatt Lockwood. He was a line technician there for nearly twenty-five years and then *poof*—out of work. Government records say he's been in and out of temp jobs since then, though nothing for the last two years. Lockwood is divorced, no kids, no living parents or siblings, last known address was in Pottsville, about fifty miles west of Allentown, an area known as the cheapest place to live in Pennsylvania."

"He lost his job, can't find reliable work, if any work at all, can't afford to live in one of the biggest cities in the state, and had to uproot to somewhere more affordable," said Shelby. "Has no family support. Blames much of his misfortune on the government, when he'd be better blaming it on company investors driving the need for higher and higher profits. He'd be perfect pickings for a group using anger and outrage to fuel its efforts."

"Found family," said Taylor. "The kind that comes without the baggage of growing up in their midst."

"Exactly. As a result, they'd be more attractive. There's no obvious string to pull with him as a result." Shelby studied Garcia's file folder. "But we might find something in this new info. It's broken down by participants?"

"Yes." Garcia extended the folder to her. "Alphabetical by surname. Take a look."

Shelby took the folder, flipped it open, and sorted through the names.

"We've hit a bit of a wall on the energy project," said McFarland, "so that might help us there, too. Logan's message—solar energy Tripoli, Pennsylvania—led us to a brand-new project. Bachman Solar has a new build actively under construction in New Tripoli, also outside of Allentown. They bought approximately four hundred acres of farmland there and are opening an eighty-megawatt facility. Construction started four weeks ago and they're working as fast as they can knowing they may have to pause when the snow flies. The area isn't known to get excessive snowfall, but they can get hit by some significant nor'easters."

"That sounds promising. What's the wall?"

"No one at the company will talk to us. Detectives have made contact, but they say they won't release any names without a warrant. They've started the process, but you know that takes time. We might get an answer in the next hour, but I don't know it'll be in time. Still, those wheels are turning. We've made another connection there though. A good one." McFarland turned back to his laptop. "Because of Pennsylvania regulations, they had to apply for a license to use explosives as part of the project." He looked up and met Garcia's eyes. "In this case, C-4."

Garcia heard the imaginary click of a piece falling into place in the puzzle they were trying to solve. "That's the linchpin. Without the C-4, this incident would be a standard hostage situation with loss of life—though not catastrophic loss—with no risk of destruction of a large part of the region's transportation system. What are the explosives for in this new build? If they bought farmland, then it's already cleared and not likely in a mountainous area."

"Apparently it's for bedrock. They'll excavate and grade the site, and will have to build a substation and bury the posts of the array itself, but it's really the buried 34.5 kV collection circuit they need the explosives for. The plan was to use standard excavation equipment, but apparently that proved insufficient, so they applied for a license to blast. Capello was only able to get us information about two of the three hostage takers, but that might have been because it was all she learned. My money is on the fact one of them worked for Bachman Solar and either does the blasting or has access to the supplies."

"It doesn't necessarily have to be the guy in the bomb vest," Williams pointed out. "But it would be more likely it is. Especially if he's the one who built it. Who has the experience with blasting cord and caps."

"The one who wants to maintain control," Garcia said. "He could be just the one wearing it, but I suspect he's also the expert. No expert in explosives would want to trust them to someone who isn't. That gives us somewhere to go. McFarland?"

McFarland had a document open on his laptop and was running a search. "Already into that file. Give me a second." A few clicks, then some scrolling. A glance at the clock on the wall, more scrolling, then he scanned the document.

The tension banding Garcia's shoulders wound tighter with each second that ticked by.

McFarland scrolled back a few paragraphs. "I've got him."

Some of the tension released with a snap. "Who is he?"

"Owen McCadden. Born in Bath, Pennsylvania, in 1979. Student at George Wolf Elementary in Bath and then shipped off to Northampton High School after that. Started his career in fracking, which is where he trained in explosives. Currently employed at Bachman Solar as an explosives technician. He might not be the main explosives engineer, but he'd still be hands-on."

"That puts him in a position to access the C-4," Shelby stated. "To steal it."

"I'd think so."

"Aren't they required by law to track every last ounce of materials like that?" asked Taylor.

"Yeah. But what if he walked out of the place yesterday with it? Or over the past couple of days in smaller amounts? Depending on how much they had on hand, unless someone took that moment to inventory, it might not have been noticed on the short-term."

"Or whatever term it's been so far," Alex said. "If they knew C-4 had been stolen and didn't report it and it was used to kill people or destroy property, they'd be liable."

"They may still be liable," stated Williams. "If they don't know it's gone, then there's something wrong with their processes."

"True enough."

Shelby had opened her copy of the file and was reading through McCadden's information. "He lives in Kutztown, about fifteen miles from New Tripoli. Married to Ruth McCadden. One child, Silas, thirteen."

"Could we use those as leverage?" Garcia was thinking out loud. "Tell McCadden we know who he is and that we have his family?"

"We could threaten to charge his wife as an accessory to the murder of the victims killed in the initial attack," Taylor said.

"That won't be enough." Williams braced his elbow on the tabletop and rested his chin on his fist as he stared at his laptop monitor.

Garcia gave him a few seconds before prodding. "What are you thinking?"

"That there won't be time for discussions. We have to hit this guy and hit him hard."

"Him?" Alex asked. "Meaning the bomber as opposed to the gunmen?"

"Yes. He's the only one with the power to take everyone out all at once. The gunmen could open fire and we might lose everyone, but we won't lose two city blocks and anyone missed in the evacuation or who refused to go. But the bomber is a different story. We attempt an incursion. *Boom.* We fire a shot at him. *Boom.* At one of the gunmen. *Boom.* Someone rushes him. *Boom.* He has all the advantage; we have none."

Garcia could see where Williams was going. "You're saying we need to neutralize the bomber specifically, not the bomb. If the bomber is taken out of this scenario, and therefore the bomb, we have a scenario we've dealt with many times before. And we have twenty or thirty A-Team officers ready to take out either gunman the moment they're unprotected. They've already killed two cops and ten civilians. They won't need any provocation to take the shot."

"Absolutely," Shelby agreed. "But you don't want to use his wife as leverage?"

"I didn't say that. I think we have to," said Williams. "And I wonder if we can use the kid, too."

"We can't charge the kid with anything," McFarland argued. "He's too young, and it's doubtful he had anything to do with it." He shrugged. "Granted, we could threaten it."

Williams shook his head. "It's not enough. Only one thing will work here."

As Williams met his eyes, Garcia felt the gut punch of what he was implying. *Can we pull it off?* "You want to bring them here. Bring them into Grand Central Terminal." He heard Alex's quick intake of breath, but ignored it. "Make it so blowing up Grand Central Terminal means not only his death, but his wife's."

"And his son's." Shelby sat back in her chair and crossed her arms under her breasts, her calculating gaze settling on Williams. "In fact, unless he has a terrible relationship with his son, that might have more impact. He might love his wife, but she's lived thirty, forty years, just as he has. It would be awful, but she had a chance to live. But his thirteen-year-old son..."

"As a father myself, I can tell you that would shut me down," said Taylor. "Especially if it was my only child. My ongoing line, cut short along with my own life. But what parent would allow their child into that kind of situation? Into that kind of danger? I certainly wouldn't allow it. Why would Ruth McCadden?"

For the first time during this incident, Garcia felt the warmth of hope quench a little of the jagged ball of terror rolling in his gut for every innocent life inside the Terminal, but especially for Capello. Every life was important, but he recognized his own humanity in a lot of his drive in this incident being specifically for her. Whatever incentive worked, and whatever saved her, saved them all. "I can talk a good game, as can any of you. At the very least, we'll give it a try." He checked the time. "There's no way to get them here before the three-hour limit. I'm not sure we can get them here inside of a few hours."

"Chopper."

Garcia turned to look at Alex. "What?"

"It's going to take too long to drive them. The bomber will either lose patience or his grip on the switch. Get an NYPD chopper in the air from Floyd Bennett Field in Brooklyn and headed for Kutztown. Get in touch with Ruth while they're already on the way there. If we wait to send it, we're wasting time. Helicopters can fly between one hundred fifty and two hundred miles per hour as the crow flies. No traffic, no circuitous routes. If we have her and the boy ready to leave, they could be here in a little under an hour. I bet we could get Gemma to stall for that much time if we tell her we need more time for the president. *We* know he's already given his answer, but they don't."

"Then, when it's time to take them in, tell them the attorney general is here and needs to talk to them directly," said Shelby. "No one would believe the Secret Service would let the president go in there, but they'd believe he'd send the attorney general as the head of the Justice Department. Then we send her, or them, in with one of the A-Team as an escort. They have men stationed all over the Terminal. Send one of them in."

"I like it. We just need contact info for the wife."

"It's here." McFarland shrugged. "We hate the Feds stepping on our toes, but they're damned efficient. One thing though—where's that bird going to put down once it's back in Midtown?"

"The East 34th Street Heliport is going to be closest," suggested Williams.

"Bryant Park is closer still," said Taylor. "The ice rink that's part of the Bryant Park Winter Village. It's only a block away and inside the outer perimeter, so it's been evacuated. A giant open space in the middle of the city. It's about fifteen thousand square feet."

"I think it's bigger than that, which is even better," Garcia said, pushing back his chair and standing.

Taylor held up a hand, palm out to forestall him. "Lieutenant, wait. I think I have a connection." He paused for a moment, his eyes scanning down his laptop monitor before he looked over the top to McFarland across the table. "You said McCadden went to Northampton High School?"

"Yes." McFarland scrolled up in his document. "From 1993 to 1997. Why?"

"Because Wyatt Lockwood attended Northampton High School from 1994 to 1998."

McFarland sat back in his chair. "And there's our connection. Lockwood is on his own." He looked back at Taylor. "As you said, he'd be perfect pickings for the kind of found family that Sinister 13 might offer. And Lockwood knew McCadden from their high school days, which might have been his entrée to the group. That's it, we've got two of the three."

"And we have a plan of action," said Garcia. "I'll get a helicopter in the air; then I'll talk to Ruth McCadden herself. Hopefully, she'll want to help us. McFarland, play for time when you call in a few minutes. Tell them we need at least another hour because we're making progress, but these things take time. At this point, you may have to play hardball. Walk all over Capello if needed—she'll know exactly what you're doing and will play along and then get them to buy in." He turned and headed for the door. He stopped with one hand on the door when Alex called his name.

"Garcia, what happens if she won't allow the kid to come? Or, worse, won't come herself?"

When Garcia met Alex's gaze, he saw his own fear reflected, as well as the same hopelessness he wouldn't let rise to the surface. Because the only answer was that there was a good chance everyone inside the blast radius would die. But he wouldn't allow himself to vocalize the fear, to give it life. "She's going to come. She has to. There's no other choice." He went through the door before Alex could contradict him.

She had to. Or all was lost.

Chapter 23

Gemma's heart rate kicked as the phone rang.

This was it, the three-hour mark. If the team didn't have anything for them, the situation could go to hell, fast. So fast, she wasn't sure she'd feel the pain of her own death.

When One nodded his consent, Gemma picked up the phone. "Trevor?"

"Elena. How's everyone doing?"

"Same as before." *Here we go.* "We're at the three-hour mark. Do you have our answer?"

"I have *an* answer. As you can imagine, the president is extremely concerned about this situation."

"As he should be. It's a very serious situation."

"And serious situations take time. We're aware of the three-hour time limit. We've been trying hard to resolve this for you that quickly. But you know the pace of government. It rarely moves fast."

Gemma kept her eyes on the hostage takers. As always, it was hard to read expressions, especially from this distance, but Three's fury was expressed in his rigid posture and narrowed eyes. One's stress was a little less obvious, but his left hand was wrapped around his right fist again, and some of his strain had to be muscular exhaustion. Gemma needed to find a way to impress upon McFarland that time stretching could only go so far without disastrous results.

"That can't be our concern," Gemma said. "We set a time limit. Are you saying you won't meet it?"

"Do you remember at the beginning when I said I would never lie to you?"

"Yes."

"I haven't so far and I won't start now. Doing so does neither of us any favors. We're fighting for you here, but the president is meeting with an adviser right now, a..." His voice trailed off as if he were searching for a name somewhere in his notes. "A Chris Galvin. Mr. Galvin is an expert in the case and is advising the president on how to manage the issue once the four men are released. You need to give him this time. He's coming through for you, but he has to manage the instantaneous fallout. He needs a little more time. I highly advise you to give it to them, because things are coming together for you as you requested."

Chris Galvin.

McFarland had done a masterful job of planting a name that would mean nothing to anyone in the concourse but Gemma.

Chris Galvin—the man who'd taken hostages at his workplace after he'd been unexpectedly fired for purported fraud. He'd been escorted from his workplace but had returned with a handgun hours later. When another employee saw him entering the building with the gun and had called 911, the police had arrived so fast he hadn't been able to put his plan into action and had taken hostages instead to protect himself.

Gemma and McFarland had worked that case together with two colleagues. The one person Galvin had wanted to talk to—his boss, Micah Huntley, so he could argue his innocence—had been out of the building at the time, and Galvin threatened to start shooting hostages unless he came in to talk to him face-to-face; not even a phone conversation would do. Based on his devolving emotional state, the negotiators felt there was a good chance Galvin would carry through with his threats. Involving outside civilians wasn't standard procedure, because there was simply too high a chance of someone saying the wrong thing, which could significantly worsen the situation. They tried to avoid using civilians, though there had been times when it had worked to their advantage. In this case, McFarland, primary negotiator for the incident, had promised to have an officer bring Huntley in to Galvin. And had instead sent him his father, who had been willing to do whatever was needed to avoid his son dying "in a hail of bullets when SWAT burst in," as he had put it. McFarland had assured him the A-Team wouldn't fire unless fired upon or unless they needed to save an innocent life. The father had thought his son would do something to provoke them, and felt only he could talk him down, so McFarland gambled on bringing father and son togther. In the end, it had seemed that the father had been correct and his presence had been instrumental in helping end the situation without bloodshed when Galvin surrendered. Galvin had lived, though he was still serving time.

In two words, McFarland had told her the plan. Something in her clues had led them to a useful connection, and they were going to use it, but they needed time to put everything into place. Her job would be to give them that time.

"How much time?" she asked.

"Another hour."

Three cursed viciously and stalked to where One stood.

Gemma knew she had to make it look like she was still firmly encamped with the hostage takers. "That's not what we agreed on."

"I know, and I'm sorry. But wheels are turning and it's looking like this can all be arranged. The attorney general is on her way to you. She wants to talk to the men in charge."

Gemma knew exactly how McFarland wanted her to steer this into a misunderstanding he could correct. "She could call from DC."

"She could. But to make this deal with you, she wants to talk to you face-to-face. An hour is what we need for those two things. For the president to give his final sign-off, and for Janet Garfield to arrive from DC. They're flying her in by helicopter because she's coming from out of state. That will get her here faster."

Message received. Whoever you're bringing is coming in by chopper, because otherwise it would take too long.

Across the concourse, Three had stalked toward One and was making his displeasure known. Gemma couldn't hear the words, but Three's tone said he was unhappy with the delay. *Are you in a rush to die when the bomb goes off because you couldn't wait?*

"Trevor, let me call you back. I think we need to discuss the delay." Gemma knew McFarland couldn't hear it, but he could see the discord brewing between the three men.

"Of course. At this number. I'll be waiting to hear from you."

Gemma ended the call. "I told him we'd call back with an answer," she called to the three men.

"The answer is no," Three snapped. "We gave them a time limit. They won't take us seriously if we don't stick with it."

Gemma had pushed back before and it hadn't gone well. But this was an all-or-nothing decision. If she couldn't talk them into this delay, it was all over. They were all over. "That's incorrect."

Three whirled toward her. "Shut the fuck up."

"You wanted me to speak for you because of my experience with negotiating. This is something I've seen before. When you begin a negotiation, you always ask for more than you know you're going to get because when you give a little, you get something in return. You lose nothing by giving a little more time." Gemma's gaze dropped to One's hands, clasped one over the other. *Unless...* "Did you think through how this is going to go? Were you expecting your men to be released, you to get word of it, and then get your escort out of town, all inside the three hours? Was it ever actually possible?"

"We thought so," said Two.

"I've never seen a negotiation move that fast."

"You don't negotiate for lives." One's voice was calm, but Gemma could hear a new and sharp edge behind it.

You have no idea. "But I do for livelihoods." She pinned Two with a steady stare. "People would lose their jobs if I didn't do mine to the best of my ability. Losing a job is soul-crushing, and sometimes you don't come back from that kind of loss." The way Two hunched slightly told her she'd scored a direct hit. "Lives are essentially on the line when I negotiate. I know what I'm talking about." She met One's gaze head-on, unblinking. "You need to take this offer. It's the only chance you have of getting everything you want. Freedom for your men. Freedom for yourself."

"Freedom for you."

"Freedom for us." Gemma made sure One's singular "you" instead reflected the whole group. "I've never hidden my desire to survive this. But you hold all the cards. I can bring my experience to the table, but it's your call." Instead of sitting back, taking herself out of the discussion, Gemma stayed sitting forward, upright and alert, her eyes locked on One.

He broke away from the group and strode back to the ticket booth to stand, his back to the group, staring through the brass bars to the deserted room behind it. A full thirty seconds passed before he turned and walked back. Slower this time.

Made his decision.

"Tell them we'll wait the hour. But that's it. No more delays." The finality of his tone told her there'd be no more negotiating on this point.

Hopefully, it would be enough.

"Tell them we don't want to hear from them again until they bring us the attorney general," One continued. "That's their last chance."

"I'll call them back now." Before anyone could change their mind, Gemma called McFarland back. "Trevor, it's Elena. You have the hour."

"I'm happy to hear that." McFarland's voice was neutral. "I'll get everything arranged."

"Good. And, Trevor?"

"Yes?"

Part of her wanted to draw out the conversation. If things went south, it would be the last time she'd ever speak with McFarland. It would be the last time Alex—all her family, really, because she knew her father would have arranged for them to have access to the feeds—would ever hear her voice. For her team to hear her voice and for her to feel their combined support behind McFarland's words. But she couldn't tarry. "This is our last communication until you let us know the attorney general is here. No more than one hour."

"I underst—"

Gemma cut him off by ending the call. Better to sever the tie quickly than drag it out. Elena the business negotiator didn't have the emotional connections of Gemma the hostage negotiator. *Be Elena.*

She set the phone down on the ground and sat back, her eyes on the three hostage takers.

"This is bullshit!" thundered Three. "You're making this call unilaterally. What happened to we all get a say?"

"We're not seeing eye to eye currently. Someone needs to make the call."

Three kept encroaching on One's space—as One took a step back, Three would crowd him farther, until One stopped moving, as if daring Three to jostle him, ending all their lives. Two was standing so he could keep both his eyes and the barrel of his P90 on the hostages, but at one point fully turned away so he could grab Three's arm, pulling him back from One, whispering furiously.

The truth of the matter was Three was putting all their lives at risk jostling One. Any slip of his hand on the detonator, and there'd be no need to wait that hour.

All that would be left would be a smoking ruin. They'd be nothing but molecules spread over several blocks of Manhattan.

"What if I decide to do this my way?" Three snarled. "How about we start executing one hostage every five minutes when they don't come through in an hour? Because you know they won't."

"That won't get us what we're here for. Dead hostages means no leverage."

"We have leverage. We could leave you here to die when you blow up the building. We'll just slip through police lines when they're not looking."

"Gem."

Gemma glanced sideways at Logan, whose eyes were fixed on the three men.

"This is going to hell. It's time to act before they won't allow any movement at all." Logan's voice was just barely above a whisper. "I'm going to ask them for a bathroom trip. Once it's only the two of us, I'll get my hands free and take him down."

Gemma's heart rate was already speeding, simply watching the men argue. Hearing that Logan wanted to make his move kicked it into overdrive, even though she understood his thinking. The alliance was shattering in real time before them. If they didn't act soon, they might not be able to act, period. But the danger involved in making a stand drove an icy blade into her gut.

Still, there was no help for it. Their duty to the city, to its citizens, had to come first. It was the oath they swore when they became cops; it was the mission statement of the NYPD.

Fidelis Ad Mortem.

Sitting in the group, surrounded by three hostage takers, was an impossible situation. Getting one of them alone would give them a chance. And while Gemma was good at hand-to-hand combat, Logan had a natural advantage in size and sheer muscular strength, as well as his advanced training. And he carried the knife.

It needed to be Logan. Her role was here, talking to the hostage takers, buying Logan time, if needed, or keeping One and Three distracted during his absence. His job was to tip the odds in their favor.

"McFarland told me between the lines that things are moving. They're going to send someone in, but it would be better if there's only two of them when that happens. You need to nail the timing on this. You and one of the gunmen need to be out of the concourse before McFarland calls, but you can't leave too far ahead or they'll come looking for you."

"Makes sense." He dragged his left sleeve along his abdomen enough to tug the cuff aside to reveal his watch. "In half an hour?"

"Go for forty minutes. McFarland seemed insistent on the hour. That gets you away with some leeway."

He nodded and sat back against the marble wall. She could practically see the dynamic mental preparations running in his head, so she sat quietly beside him, giving him the space he needed.

The argument between the men broke up when One walked to stand by the ticket counter, his isolated stance telling the other two men to keep their distance.

As the minutes ticked by, Logan seemed to calm, to still, as he got into the required headspace, whereas she wound tighter and tighter. Her role in this incident was coming to an end. Logan's, on the other hand, was just beginning, and she found only discomfort in her lack of a role. It wasn't a good feeling to sit by watching others carry the ball, even if it was the right play.

Forty minutes flew past, and the next thing Gemma knew, Logan was nudging her. "It's time."

Keeping her hand low so it stayed out of sight, she gripped his forearm tight enough he couldn't mistake her fear for him. She wanted him to feel it, to be reminded to temper his courage with rational sense. "You need to be careful. They won't hesitate to take you out. You're disposable to them." She paused, then took her eyes off the men to look directly at him, waited until he felt the weight of her gaze and turned to meet it. "Not to me."

Several long seconds passed under their locked gazes; then one corner of his lips tipped up. She saw it then—a flash of the A-Team cockiness he'd kept locked down since they'd sheltered behind the information booth until he could unleash it to gain the upper hand. "Hold that thought. We'll come back to it later."

She refused to consider they might never get that chance. "Yes, we will."

"Will you be safe here?"

Her gaze flicked to One. "None of us are truly safe. But McFarland has something up his sleeve. Let him worry about us. You worry about you. Head up." She gave him the first part of the mantra repeated to them daily as cadets.

"Eyes open." He completed the phrase, a promise to take care. "Let's do this." He gave his arm a bump as a cue for her to remove her hand, then faced forward when she did. "Hey!"

Three spun toward him, aiming his P90 directly mid-body, but Logan didn't flinch. "What?"

"I need to go to the bathroom."

"You can wait." Three's tone was dismissive.

"I've been waiting. But it doesn't look like we're getting out of here anytime soon." Logan shrugged carelessly. "I don't care if you make me wait. Some of the others might not like the smell—"

"For fuck's sake." Two threw Three a look of disgust. "I'll do it. Watch them." He pulled his knife from his pocket, the blade springing free as he clenched it in his fist, then stalked toward Logan.

All Gemma could think was they had a chance because it was Two. Neither man was going to be a cakewalk, but Two's aggression didn't ride as close to the surface. Three was ready to go off and might welcome the opportunity to get out some of his rage in a brutal hand-to-hand fight. Or another kill shot.

Her gaze flicked to Three, who watched Two approach Logan, and the harsh glint of hatred in his eyes was a revelation. Disorder was rampant in the ranks of the hostage takers; beyond their common cause, she wasn't sure there was anything else that bound them together. And if that cause fizzled because of the negotiation, it wasn't just the bomb that was going to be the problem.

Logan's plan was to take out Two. But that left Three here with Gemma and the hostages.

She wasn't sure that once Two disappeared, it wouldn't be Three's cue for an early start to the executions he'd threatened.

Chapter 24

Two used the switchblade to neatly slice through the zip tie binding Logan's ankles. He stepped back and used the barrel of his P90 to motion to him to stand. "Get up."

It was a relief to be able to change position after all this time, to get blood flowing freely into his feet. The pins and needles had started about an hour previously, his circulation slightly strangled by the extra thickness of his flip case in his boot. "Sorry," Logan murmured to Gemma as he bumped her, shifting his left foot back toward his hip to get the leverage he needed to brace his boot against the marble floor. He pushed himself up to a crouch and then stood. He paused briefly to stamp blood back into his feet and then stepped out from the hostages.

Knowing the odds of what he was about to attempt, he wanted to look back at Gemma again, to see her for what might be one last time, but didn't dare call attention to her. They'd kept their established connection under the radar thus far, trying to look like nothing more than strangers sharing a terrifying experience; he didn't want to highlight it now as he removed himself from the situation. She was good at hand-to-hand—as he'd learned the hard way himself—but none of her skills could withstand the killing power of the P90.

If he died in the next few minutes, he was going to be sorry he'd come back into her orbit to find their unresolved attraction from fifteen years ago still pulled at them both, only to lose the chance to see if they could make a go of it as mature adults. So much wasted time. They'd needed to go their separate ways after the academy—that separation had helped make them the cops they were today—but it was only in the last few months he'd begun to realize that in walking away from each other, they'd turned their backs on something potentially meaningful.

One more item in a long list of things to fight for.

He circled the hostages, giving them sufficient room so there was no chance he'd trip over anyone; then he was into the open space of the deserted concourse. The silence of the space, normally alive with people rushing to make trains while loudspeakers boomed departing train times and track numbers, was unnerving. Now, with only their quiet footfalls, the space felt otherworldly.

He cut diagonally past the double staircase leading down to the Dining Concourse and those leading up to the West Balcony. His gaze flicked to the doorway at the top of the balcony—the exit to Vanderbilt Avenue, the way they'd meant to exit the building. Two extra minutes was all they'd have needed; two minutes and they'd have been down the street and partway to O'Callaghan's before the call of a multitude of sirens would have told them something was wrong. Something big.

They never would have made dinner. They'd have turned around and come back to join their own teams even though they were off duty—Gemma would have been sitting at the table with McFarland, and Logan would have been up in the windows with his teammates. There would have been no question they'd try again to have an evening out together. Gemma had made that clear and he echoed the feeling.

Now he had to make sure they had that chance.

Logan and Two walked silently past the West Balcony and under the archway with its sparkling lights, marked TICKET MACHINES and TRACKS 31 TO 42 - LIRR. Past the alcove with the ticket machines and, opposite, the elevator, and then under a second archway leading to the SHUTTLE PASSAGE and WAITING ROOM.

The Station Master's Office—their final destination.

As if to remind him of his duty, of who he was, the badge in his boot rubbed against his anklebone. Not that the reminder was needed when his identity as a cop went bone-deep.

They walked past the bakery on one side and the coffee shop on the other. Both looked like someone had pulled the fire alarm, prompting a mass exodus—abandoned coats, dropped bags, spilled coffee, toppled chairs. Rapid-fire gunshots would certainly prompt an identical reaction.

The double glass doors of the Station Master's Office lay ahead of them, slightly recessed in the corridor, with a red-bowed wreath hanging on each of the flanking windows. Logan threw a quick glance over his shoulder to find Two about six feet behind him, the P90 barrel pointed directly at his back.

The P90 was going to be a problem. Logan was going to have to get close enough he could disarm Two, but in the amount of time it would take to close that distance, he would likely have at least a dozen rounds in him. Of course, to even have a chance at taking Two down, he had to get the zip tie off first.

He stopped at the doors to the Station Master's Office, waiting to see what Two would do.

Two maintained the six-foot gap between them. "Open the door."

Logan reached with his joined hands for the rightmost door handle, putting on a show of being clumsy with the door, his bound hands hampering his movements, forcing him to step back awkwardly to pull the door open, as he couldn't bend only one elbow to sweep the door past him. He braced his right boot against the door, which gave him enough time to step through, letting the door start to swing shut behind him, since he didn't have a hand free to continue to hold it open as he entered the office.

While Two was occupied with keeping the door from slamming in his face, Logan maneuvered both arms toward his left front pocket, snagged his knife, and clenched it upside-down inside his right fist.

Logan made sure to angle his body to see how Two negotiated the entrance and was gratified to see his right hand shoot out to hold open the door. He surreptitiously timed the movement and hope filled him as he realized he'd found the way to beat his opponent.

Two had taken his finger off the trigger for about a second and a half before it was back in place. More time than he'd need.

A doorway would be how he'd make his move. And due to the distance between the middle of the concourse and the inside of the Station Master's Office, it was extremely unlikely the sound of Logan's attack would be audible to the other two suspects. Which would give him the upper hand.

He stepped farther into the office, scanning the area. About twenty feet down on the right was the waiting room, a few of the Terminal's original wood benches visible. Opposite the waiting room was the open entrance to the women's bathroom. The family bathroom was located just to the right, behind a wood door.

Logan took a chance and angled for the women's bathroom in a calculated move because he didn't think Two would want a stall door in between himself and a hostage. If he didn't care, the privacy of a stall would allow Logan to cut the zip tie and emerge ready for a fight, weapon in hand. But he was willing to bet Two wouldn't go for it.

"Not there."

Logan stopped short, keeping his face carefully blank as he looked behind him. "It's a bathroom. That's why we're here."

"Not that one. Use the family bathroom."

Logan shrugged. "Okay. I'll be out in a minute."

"I don't think so. You're not going anywhere I can't see you."

Logan let a little horror crawl into his expression. "Did you do that with the girl?"

Two simply smiled.

Logan was going to enjoy taking this one down. For what he'd done to all of them, but further tormenting a terrified teenage girl was icing on the cake. His rage wanted to rise, but he tamped down most of it, just letting the edges of it float loose. Too much anger meant a loss of control; a little anger meant his attack would have some mean behind it. Not something he'd normally allow, but this time, he'd use it to his advantage.

This was it. Literally do or die. And from the pounding of his heart and the dampness of his palms, he knew his chances were fifty-fifty at best.

He turned away from Two and stepped to the door, curling his left hand over his right to make sure the knife wasn't visible before it made contact with the wood panel. He pushed the door open just enough to slide through, letting his fists run along the wood, maintaining a gap with just enough clearance for his shoulders, then pushed his hands forward and let the edge of the door bump off his shoulder as he stepped through into the bathroom.

A rapid check of his surroundings gave him the dimensions he had to work with to bring Two down. It wasn't much, only about eight feet by ten feet, with a sink, toilet, and a folded change table installed against one wall. Designed with an inward swinging door so no one in the outer corridor could be struck by anyone exiting the bathroom, it gave him a decent amount of floor space to work with.

He had to work fast. As the door started to close behind him, he hit the button on his tactical knife, the razor-sharp blade springing free. The zip tie bit viciously into his wrists as he rotated the knife toward himself, between his hands. Not having the luxury of time to take care, he twisted hard, slicing through both zip tie and the heel of his left hand.

Son of a—

The awkward position and uneven pressure torqued the knife from his grip and it clattered to the floor. The zip tie snapped off, flying off to hit the far wall by the toilet.

No time to go for the knife. Logan was already spinning as Two entered the bathroom with his left hand gripping the body of the P90, his right just dropping from the door. Everything depended on Two not being able to get his right hand back into place with his finger inside the trigger guard. The moment he did, it was game over for Logan. Possibly for everyone else as well, because the moment there was gunfire coming from the depths of the Station Master's Office—and Logan had no doubt the sound of a submachine gun shooting three rounds per second would penetrate every wall, door, and corridor leading back to the concourse—Three was going to lose it, likely on the remaining hostages. For the sake of everyone huddled on the floor of the concourse, he had to keep this as quiet as possible, which meant no gunfire, even if it was only pointed at the walls. As long as Two couldn't find the trigger again, the odds were in his favor.

There would be no negotiation. There couldn't be. This wasn't a street punk with a pistol coming for his wallet, giving Logan a chance to plead for his life. His only option was to move directly to an attack where his best defense would be a strong offense. Strike first, catch Two off guard, maintain control, take him down. Take him out if there was no other choice. There would be no second chance.

As Two stepped through the doorway, Logan was on him, going for control of both his arms to ensure his command of the weapon. Logan got a solid hold on both sleeves, twisting the material to tighten it, giving him more flexible restraint than a locked grip over his opponent's wrists, a hold that would be forced to change as Two fought back. Logan dragged Two's left arm up and against the P90, trapping the weapon in the crook of his elbow, and forced his right arm down, twisting him slightly so the door thumped closed behind them, and they crashed backward against the wall. Two bellowed and tried to wrench away while yanking his right arm free, but Logan twisted the material tighter, changed the angle to jam his movements, turning into him and bringing up his left elbow to brutally slam it into his right cheekbone.

Pain vibrated down Logan's arm, but he was already twisting to repeat the blow with his right elbow. Two's head snapped back and slammed into the wall, shattering the glossy tile behind them. Logan took advantage of Two's brief disorientation to move in, jamming Two's right arm under his left and threading his hand underneath to trap it there, while he switched his grip on Two's left sleeve, grabbing it with his left hand to free up his right, even as he rolled the arm outward, forcing Two to bend sideways with it. Both arms trapped, the submachine gun wedged between them, Logan went for the disarming blows—the heel of his hand to his temple, then an upward blow with his elbow, followed by another on the way down. Then, with one more vicious twist of his arm to bend Two low, he brought his knee up under Two's chin.

He felt the moment Two's body went loose, a mix of exultation and relief streaming through him with the knowledge he wasn't faking. Two was out cold, and likely would have a grade two or three concussion to show for it.

Logan had no regrets.

He lowered Two's limp form to the ground, then divested him of his weapon and rotated the dial of the P90's fire selector to the safe position. He unstrapped Two's Kevlar vest and dug into the pocket in his pants for the zip ties kept there. He made quick work of turning Two face down on the bathroom floor, and first binding his hands behind his back and then his ankles. He picked up his knife, wiped off the bloody blade, then folded it into the handle and jammed it back in his pocket.

Stepping back, he straightened and gave himself ten seconds to catch his breath and calm his pounding heart. He'd done it—in less than thirty seconds, he'd bought his own freedom, bought the chance they needed to end this.

Pain in his hand abruptly attracted his attention and he looked down at the blood welling from the heel of his left hand. He'd done a good job of shaving off a chunk of skin, but it didn't look any worse than that. Grabbing a few paper towels, he blotted off the worst of the blood and hoped it would clot soon, as slick hands didn't make for a secure hold on a high-capacity weapon as you ran through back hallways.

Speaking of running... He bent and quickly unlaced his boot, pulling out his flip case, which he slid into his back pocket before relacing his footwear. Now he'd be able to run without discomfort.

He picked up the vest, considering it. Solid construction and, based on the weight, fully armored. He didn't know the protection level, but if he wore it over his shirt and came under fire, whoever he opposed would simply avoid the vest and aim for a headshot, ending things quickly. However, if it was under his shirt, anyone aiming for him would most likely aim for center mass. If he was lucky, the vest would slow or stop the bullets, depending on the ammunition. It likely wouldn't protect either way from what the P90 was carrying, but it was his best chance at even minimal protection. He yanked his shirttails from under his belt, then unbuttoned his shirt and stripped it off. He donned the Kevlar vest directly against his skin, feeling the familiar weight settle on his shoulders as he pulled the heavy Velcro side straps tight and secured them to the front of the vest.

Perfect.

He shrugged back into his shirt, buttoning it and smoothing it down over the vest and his cargo pants. It fit a little snug, but it was a fair trade-off for the protection the vest provided. He picked up the P90, the firearm instantly feeling familiar in his hands. He checked the magazine, found it full. He'd have to watch his shots, as he had no extra magazine and he could blow every shot he had in only a handful of seconds on fully automatic. He rotated the fire selector to semiautomatic—maximizing each trigger pull to a single shot, thereby eliminating the immediate risk of being left with a useless weapon. He was known for his accuracy, even with a weapon he hadn't shot in a long time. If the optics were solid, he'd only need a bullet or two, as long as he could get off a shot that wouldn't put everyone at risk from a catastrophic explosion.

With one last glance at Two, who still lay motionless, Logan cracked the door open to find the Station Master's Office empty as expected, then slipped out of the bathroom. He was thankful for his rubber-soled boots as he silently crossed the floor and out into the corridor behind the West Balcony.

All was quiet. But it wouldn't be as soon as they missed Two. Then things might get dangerous fast.

He needed to get close, but he needed to stay out of sight. A scan of the deserted space showed him the way to go—down the corridor to his left, past the coffee shop, and directly into the upper train shed. It would keep him out of the line of sight of the suspects, giving him a hidden path to work his way back to the concourse.

He ghosted down the corridor and into the train shed by track 37.

After the brightly lit, wide-open space of the concourse and the surrounding corridors, the train shed felt dark and close. Thirty tracks ran in parallel lines into the upper train shed under a ceiling of weathered steel I-beams that looked like they had only mere feet of clearance over the trains. The platforms were brightly lit, but the spaces between were dim, and the ceiling above looked both grimy and gloomy. The floors, large slabs of utilitarian tile, were dirty and cracked, and the air was stale and uncirculated. This functional part of the Terminal was definitely a section the tourists saw less often. The train sheds were the reason for the Terminal and had much of the same history, but it was the grandeur of the concourse and the balconies everyone thought of at the mention of Grand Central Terminal.

The dark and quiet suited Logan's purpose perfectly. He needed to be invisible or this entire effort would be for nothing more than his own freedom. That wasn't his goal.

He stole silently through the main corridor of the upper train shed, padding past fenced entrance ramps down to the abandoned train platforms. In the illumination from the straight lines of suspended fluorescent strip lights hanging over both edges of the platform, Logan could see through the open doors of one of the deserted trains how complete the evacuation had been. At the sound of gunfire, travelers would have fled in one of several directions that would have led them both away from gunfire and out of the Terminal. Now there wasn't a soul around, which was a relief, as there was no one else to protect, leaving Logan to concentrate on the hostages inside the concourse.

Past the elevator to the lower train shed, he had to stop, his back to the wall, to peer out through the gap in the doorway leading out to the concourse. Paired steel-and-glass doors guarded every entrance to the upper train shed, but only one of the two doors was open, further hiding his presence. At his current angle, he couldn't see the suspects, so if he didn't have line of sight, neither did they. He slipped past the doorway as deep into the corridor as he could manage, and took shelter behind the wall at the edge of the entrance doors to track 29. The lighting was a little brighter here, so he took greater care not to be seen, and instead inched the P90 around the corner, only leaning out far enough to look down the integrated reflex sight.

On the far side of the concourse, One was partially out of sight while Three was fully visible, still holding his P90 on the hostages. But his head was turned away from the hostages, his eyes fixed on something down at the east end of the concourse, something at an angle Logan couldn't see from where he sheltered in the upper train shed.

The concourse was silent enough to hear a pin drop.

What had happened?

Chapter 25

Gemma tried to appear relaxed, keeping her face serene, patiently waiting for the next phone call, which would be in the next few minutes.

In reality, while exhaustion should have been setting in by this point in the incident, the constant rush of adrenaline through her veins kept her wired. Her heart rapped against her breastbone while cold sweat drenched the back of her neck. She had to force herself not to continually look in the direction of the West Balcony, though she occasionally closed her eyes, straining for any faint sound from that direction.

Have faith. Logan has the skills to carry this off and will have the advantage of surprise. Two won't know what hit him.

But she couldn't deny the power of the weapon Two carried; even in close quarters, it was a huge risk because it was so compact. As the silent minutes stretched on, Gemma dared to hope Logan had been successful. If so, was he biding his time in the Terminal? Had he slipped out to give better intel to the teams? Would he be nearby if things went to hell?

Would he be safe if One detonated the bomb?

The phone exploded with sound and Gemma jerked in reaction. Hours of stress were starting to get to her, so she took a deep breath, held it for a count of three, and released it as she reached for the phone. With One's nod of approval, she answered and put the call on speaker. "Hello?"

"Elena, we have good news."

Gemma's gaze shifted to One, who took a step closer to hear better. "We like good news."

"Then you'll like this. I have the attorney general here. She'd like to come in to talk to you about what you need from her. Then she has a call scheduled with the president. We'll have this settled shortly thereafter."

One shook his head. "No one comes in."

Gemma turned back to the phone. "I'm sorry, Trevor, that won't fly."

"Ask them to please think about it. We're not being given an option. If this is what they want—the release of their men and then their passage out of New York City—then this is the only way it's going to happen."

Three strode to One, and they had a furious, whispered conversation, their voices low but rising in pitch. Gemma knew this was a moment when she might have been able to feed McFarland a little more information, but she couldn't take her eyes off the two men and didn't dare to do anything to jeopardize whatever plan her team had in place, because it was clear to her they had one. But things could go seriously south any second. Conflict had been rising between One and Three for hours; if they couldn't come to a conclusion, whatever the HNT had up their collective sleeves would never happen.

Who were they sending in?

She took a breath to convince One and Three they needed to do this, but bit the words back at the last minute. She'd pushed things further than she thought she'd be able to, but this might be one step too far.

Let them try to come to a consensus. Don't put your oar in unless it looks like you have no other choice.

When you were staring death straight in the eye, there would be nothing lost in acting.

The tremor was back in One's right hand, and he slapped his left over it again.

Death might come sooner than anyone would hope if he couldn't maintain his grip on the switch.

One stepped around Three and strode forward, coming to within almost ten feet, the closest he'd ever come to the hostages. "Tell her to come. But she needs to come alone."

Gemma raised the phone toward her mouth. "Trevor, did you hear that? She can come, but she needs to come alone."

"The president won't allow that. He's not happy she's going to set foot in the Terminal at all, but said he'd only allow it with one of the officers.

And really, how different is it from the officers in the windows? The same rules apply. If he opened fire, the bomb would go off. No one wants that." Silence rode heavy for a long stretch of seconds.

Wait it out. Let the silence scream at them. All negotiators knew sometimes less was more and hostage takers could get uncomfortable in the silence. Some would rush to fill it.

"All right." One finally broke the silence. "But if anything happens—" "We understand," McFarland said. "We're sending them in now."

One stood staring at where Two had disappeared, then shook his head and moved farther away with a low comment to Three. The two men moved about twenty-five feet from the hostages, standing back-to-back, One facing Vanderbilt Hall, Three facing the hostages. It was a stance that kept the hostages covered, giving them greater security overall with only one gunman. Because who would shoot the man actively keeping a bomb from exploding?

One minute ticked by. Then two. Then three.

Gemma was starting to worry—why was this taking so long? Then movement caught her eye just at the edge of her peripheral vision and she looked to the southeast entrance to the concourse, at the end of the Lexington Passage, the entrance Gemma and Logan had used to enter the concourse so many hours ago.

An A-Team officer, all in black with full protective gear, carrying his M4A1 carbine at the ready—though not in place at his shoulder, to tone down the aggression of their entrance—was coming toward them under the archway with a woman. Between the distance, helmet, safety glasses, and the shading inside the archway, Gemma couldn't tell which officer it was, but knew the ESU would only send one of their best.

She focused on the woman who was still partly in shadow, instantly recognizing—as she suspected—they were not sending in the attorney general. This woman was smaller, slighter. She appeared to be wearing blue jeans and a red ski jacket and didn't carry the same confidence Gemma had always seen from Garfield.

Then they stepped into the concourse. There was a moment of silence; then One's shocked gasp echoed sharply.

Gemma's gaze jerked to One, who stood stiff, his lips parted, his eyes wide with surprise.

One must know this woman. Was she his wife? A girlfriend? His sister? She was too young to be his mother.

His knowledge of her identity was likely why they hadn't come through the 42nd Street entrance and Vanderbilt Hall, where they'd have been in view for a longer distance and One might have found a way to keep them out of the concourse. Now they were here, and there was nothing he could do.

Gemma looked back at the woman and tactical officer as a third person stepped out behind the officer to stand beside the woman. She took his hand, and they clung together.

It was a child. Well, likely a preteen, but still a child in Gemma's books.

Around her, several of the hostages gasped in shock and to her right came a horrified whisper, "He's just a boy!"

Garcia had pulled out all the stops on this one.

The A-Team officer marched the woman and boy closer as One stayed frozen in place, his gaze locked in horror on the newcomers, his arms spread wide as if in question, the wire connecting the dead man's switch to the bomb vest draping in midair. "What have you done?" His horrified whisper was barely audible.

As they came closer, Gemma realized she recognized the A-Team officer—Detective Sims, who she'd worked several incidents with recently. A solid cop, smart and capable, with lightning-fast reflexes when required. If they couldn't get Logan, Sims was an excellent alternative.

Three partially turned toward the newcomers, keeping his weapon on the hostages on the east side of the information booth, even as his gaze was drawn past it. As always, it was hard to read reactions behind the balaclava, but his squinted eyes and pinched mouth gave away his confusion, as if he knew something had gone sideways but wasn't sure what. For now, he took his cue from One and didn't confront Sims, but he pulled the P90 closer to his right shoulder, readying himself to use the weapon if required.

Sims stopped about thirty feet short of One with a quiet word to both woman and boy.

Silence stretched for long seconds before the woman finally broke it. "Owen, please don't do this." When One still didn't respond—Gemma couldn't tell if it was continued shock or fury—she continued. "I honestly didn't think you had this in you. They told me you were responsible, but I didn't believe them until they showed me the video feed and played me the audio picked up on a body cam when you were telling the NYPD not to shoot you. You need to stop this. Don't hurt these people."

Gemma noticed One had missed the salient detail about the video feed, but Three had not, and his eyes were already scanning the space, searching for any obvious sign of a camera. It would now be a lost advantage, but at this stage, it no longer mattered.

Things were going to resolve one way or another in roughly the next sixty seconds. In twice that, she'd either be getting ready to greet her family or they'd be planning her funeral.

Where's Logan?

If the bomb was going to go off, she hoped he'd gotten out. If so, she wouldn't blame him. Though, knowing Logan, if he was alive, he was still in the Terminal somewhere. Leaving to confer with his men wouldn't guarantee an easy way back in. If he survived the fight with Two, he was here in the shadows somewhere.

Gemma looked at Sims to find his gaze scanning the hostages. He met her eyes and she saw the question in his furrowed brow just before his gaze snapped back to One. *He's also wondering where Logan is.*

"How could you come here?" One's words lashed out, his shock dissipated, leaving nothing but fury in its place. "How could you bring *him*?"

The boy, still holding hands with his mother, visibly bristled, tugging his hand free and pulling himself up to his full height, which at most topped five feet by an eighth of an inch. "She didn't. I told her I wanted to come." Uncertainty filled the boy's voice. "When they told me what you...what you..." When he didn't seem to be able to bring himself to describe the horror of his father's plans, he waved a hand in the direction of the suicide vest. "You need to stop." He stood stiff, his eyes impossibly sad, his chin trembling as if he was fighting back tears. His clear blue gaze trailed over the hostages, pausing at the two teenage girls—so very close to his own age—and his jaw firmed. "Please stop, Daddy." His words were sure now. "They didn't do anything to you. Why would you hurt them?"

Three moved out from behind, stepping toward the hostages to stand beside One. "This is your wife? Your son?" he asked, his tone laced with venom.

"Yes." In contrast, One's single word was infused with defeat, as if his son's defiance—a truly courageous act in the face of certain death only feet in front of him—had stolen his fury, leaving him bereft.

Emotion swept through Gemma—victory, pride in her team, relief. They'd taken the minute details she'd been able to feed them through Alex's translation and Logan's Morse code and they'd put One's identity together. And somehow, they'd tracked down his family and managed to bring them in.

They'd known talking One down was going to be nearly impossible in the given time, but they'd also known they'd never be able to move in without him blowing the C-4, nor would they be able to get close enough to defuse the bomb without his consent. There was no motivation inside the Terminal to get him to stand down; he was ready to die for his cause. He was *committed.*

But was he so committed he'd take his own family with him? Take his son? Let them also be martyrs to his cause?

In all her years in law enforcement, through all the brave acts she'd seen from her fellow officers, Gemma didn't think she'd ever witnessed any one act as courageous as this boy, not yet on the cusp of manhood, defying the father he clearly loved to save him as well as those threatened.

"Tell them to leave." When One remained silent, Three swung his P90 toward the woman and child. "*Tell them to leave.*"

In response, Sims snapped his carbine into place at his shoulder, aimed directly at Three, center mass.

Standoff.

Beside the woman, the child shrank back, fear in his eyes at this unexpected threat. He had faith enough in his father to take this chance, but none in this stranger.

Without hesitation, his mother stepped in front of him, shielding him with her own body. "We won't leave," she said, unbending steel backing her tone. "Not until you give up or deactivate that bomb."

"And if I won't?" One's defeat in response to his son dissipated at his wife's resistance.

The woman craned her head over her shoulder toward her son, pausing there for a long count of three. When she turned back to her husband, her face was twisted with devastation and regret, but her eyes were determined. "Then we stay with you. We die with you if that's what you're determined to do."

The hand that had been shaking before twitched spasmodically and Gemma watched in horror as One's fingers went white with the exertion of keeping the trigger depressed. After hours of holding it together—keeping the bomb from detonating—his muscles were reaching the point of failure.

Gemma wasn't the only one who noticed. Abruptly, the woman broke away from Sims, who stayed motionless with the barrel of his rifle locked on Three. Leaving her son behind, she ran to her husband, dropped to her knees before him, and wrapped both hands around his right fist, taking the pressure of holding down the detonator away from him. He sagged heavily to his knees before her, raising his left hand in surrender as she let go of the detonator with her right hand to wrap it around his neck, drawing his forehead down to rest on her shoulder.

Their son bolted across the room to throw his arms around his parents, his head bending to theirs.

Even a man who acted like a monster to the outside world could still hold the love of his family. And love them enough in return to give up his dreams.

One moved his left hand to the back of his head, his message of surrender clear.

The teeth of the threat was neutralized—temporarily for now, and would be permanently neutralized shortly.

It was over.

But not for Three, who saw the danger he was in. One compatriot missing, the other surrendered, and a tactical officer thirty feet away held him in his sights.

Gemma could see the desperation in his eyes even before the P90 swung toward her, stopping in line with her head. At only ten feet away, there was no way he'd miss and death would be instantaneous. Three had no idea he'd threatened the one person left in the concourse the entire department would safeguard at all costs.

"Shoot me and she dies." Three's words dripped fury.

Apparently, Three knew he was running out of options.

Letting go of the P90 with his left hand, he dug in his pocket and tossed Gemma his knife. She caught it in both hands.

"Cut the zip tie," he ordered.

She met his eyes, calculating if she had any leeway, but the cold rage in their depths told her she had none. She depressed the button on the side of the handle, freeing the blade, quickly cut the zip tie around her ankles, then refolded the blade.

"Slide it back along the floor to me." When she did, he crouched down, keeping the P90 locked on her, not taking his eyes off her, searching with his left hand for the knife until his fingers found it; then he stuffed it in his pocket and rose to his feet. "Get up." He kept his eyes on Gemma but turned his face toward Sims. "My finger is on the trigger. Ever seen a P90 shoot? I can empty my magazine in seconds into this entire group. Shoot me, and that's what will happen. Even a kill shot between the eyes will cause me to jerk and pull the trigger. You want these people to live, you will *step back!*"

Gemma could see the conflict in Sims's eyes. Knowing Three wasn't looking at him, Sims flicked a glance at Gemma.

She shook her head very slightly. *Let me get him alone. We can't risk these people. He's going to take me somewhere. Alone, I might have a chance to bring him down.*

Sims lowered his rifle slightly, still at attention, still ready to move immediately, but giving them space.

Gemma scrambled to her feet. "He's lowered his rifle."

"Get over here."

Gemma exchanged a look with the man sitting beside her, who simply stared at her in horror. "You'll be safe," she murmured. She climbed to her feet and walked toward Three. The moment she got close, Three turned her back to him and banded his left arm around her neck, getting her into a headlock that nearly pulled her to her toes. She grabbed his forearm with both hands, levering herself up to get the unyielding bar of bone and muscle off her windpipe. "You don't have to strangle me. I assume I'm not worth anything to you dead," she wheezed.

Three's hold loosened slightly, but then it tightened again as he dragged her backward.

Where's he taking me?

For a brief moment, she hoped it would be out of the concourse and into the passageways beyond, where Logan possibly waited, but that hope died quickly as he continued to make a straight line toward the staircase in the middle of the West Balcony that led down to the lower Dining Concourse.

Where she'd be on her own.

Sims couldn't follow. He had to stay and make sure the bomb didn't detonate while the bomb squad, surely no more than a block away, came in at a run to defuse it. He'd make sure the A-Team was on her trail the moment they disappeared from view. Hopefully she wouldn't be on her own for long.

But if she was, she'd work with it. There was no one else who could get hurt. No other hostages to come to harm.

Now it was only herself and Three. One-on-one. Though he held an obvious advantage with the submachine gun.

She just needed to figure out how to get around that firepower to save herself.

Chapter 26

Three forced Gemma down the steps leading to the lower Dining Concourse, pushing her ahead of him down the left staircase. "Move," he grated in her ear. "Or I'll put a bullet in you."

Gemma doubted it, at least at that particular moment, but it wasn't a chance she was willing to take. Currently, she was a critical part of his escape plan, because that was clearly what he had in mind.

Three had to be beyond furious. All their planning, no doubt months of meticulous organization—site research and selection, date choice, bomb materials and production, weapon options, train schedules, participants— all falling down around him in the last crucial minutes of their takeover. It had been solid planning—rush hour on a Friday night in the run-up to Christmas when the good people of New York City would be heading home from work or heading out to Christmas shop or to their entertainment of choice. Until it all had unraveled. Now, because of One's unwillingness to kill his only child, their jailed Sinister 13 members would not only stay there but might still face the death penalty. Now these men would surely join them, potentially to the same end.

Or had Two already joined them?

Gemma had no way to know what had happened to Logan, only that he hadn't appeared while Sims was talking One into surrender. Not that he'd needed to talk. All that was needed was One to see the end of his line, the end of the people he loved, to decide unilaterally it was one step too far.

This was exactly what Three had been afraid of. He'd been willing to push, to lay down his life, but One was in control of the dead man's switch and he hadn't gone along to the end. Now with Two missing and One in the hands of the NYPD, Three was going to follow that aggression to his own personal end, be it freedom or death.

It was a fifty-fifty split on how this could end. For either of them.

Three pushed Gemma hard down the last step and into the Dining Concourse. The space was eerily quiet, ominously so, as if reinforcing how dire her circumstances were. Normally a constant bustle of diners at tables, or visitors of all ages standing in line for food—donuts, burgers, lobster, pizza, tacos, and much more—or running through to the doors leading to the lower train shed off to their left on the north side of the space, the Dining Concourse usually had an active, noisy, occasionally frantic atmosphere, a vignette of New Yorkers on the go, all to the varying scents of the nearby eateries.

Now, all was quiet, with the space behind counters still loaded with food prepared for the dinner rush, and the tables filling the eat-in areas of several larger restaurants in the middle of the concourse abandoned, with food scattered, drinks spilled, chairs askew, and personal belongings left behind in the rush to evacuate.

The combined lack of sounds and smells gave the space an otherworldly aspect. New York City should never be truly quiet. When it was, it was only because of death and disaster.

Three jerked her roughly to the left, compressing the blood vessels on the left side of her neck as he jammed the barrel of the P90 into her right kidney. Her left hand shot out, making contact with the century-old curving brass banister, its surface buffed smooth under the brush of millions of hands over the decades. Gemma gripped tight for a moment, regaining her balance but causing Three to ram against her from behind. "You don't have to jerk me around. Tell me what you want me to do and I'll do it."

"Like I'm supposed to believe you're going to do whatever I say." A sneer was heavy in Three's tone. "I never bought that act you were putting on."

"That was no act. I just want to survive. Like you, I'll do whatever I have to do to make that happen. And if that means keeping you alive, then that's how it goes."

They followed the curve of the banister to their left, Gemma's fingers trailing off as the metal ended; then Three dragged her through the next entryway. Because of Three's hold around her neck—tight and pushing her chin up so she had a better view of the beamed ceiling than the floor and her feet—only when they passed under the wide archway that read To Long Island Rail Road did she know Three was taking her out of the Terminal and down yet another level to Grand Central Madison.

Farther away from the NYPD. Farther away from Logan, if he'd been successful in winning his freedom. But also farther away from the hostages, the main group she'd been trying to protect all this time. Sims had watched her be taken, as had his A-Team colleagues high in the windows overlooking the Main Concourse. They'd seen her disappear down the steps. Granted, from here Three could exit the Terminal via the lower train shed and its associated exits and tracks, but Gemma suspected Three wasn't making it up on the fly.

She went back to gripping his forearm with both hands, pulling his hold slightly downward, allowing her to breathe with a bit more ease and to see what was coming in front of her. Two narrow escalators divided by a double-wide staircase led down to the next level. Three pulled her over to the downward treads on the right and Gemma let go with one hand to grasp the handrail knowing Three's hands were occupied between having her in a headlock and holding the P90 on her. If either of them lost their balance and no one was holding on, they could tumble face first down the escalator.

Or would that give her an edge? She made a lightning-fast calculation from the little she could see and the few times she'd been down this way. Like most New Yorkers who passed through Grand Central Terminal, Grand Central Madison had been a curiosity, and she and Frankie had made a point of making time to see the new concourse, the jaw-dropping 180-foot escalators, and the mezzanine level when they'd come to Midtown shortly after it opened.

They rode the escalator down, skimming under the sign that read ↓ Madison Concourse - Long Island rail Road ↓, taking them farther underground.

She needed to wait for the perfect time to get free. Step one had been to let him get her away from the hostages. Then if it all went to hell, it was only her own life on the line. Even so, she had no intention of being a martyr and was willing to wait for the right moment to attempt to take Three down. She was skilled in Brazilian jiu-jitsu, a martial art centered around using leverage, weight distribution, and the strategy of bringing the fight to the floor, making it a fair fight for a smaller individual. If it was just Three and herself, she knew she could even the odds despite his large size, meaty fists, and rage. But the P90 made things exponentially more difficult. How could she best someone in a fight, even a dirty fight—and she had no doubt he'd fight dirty—when he had a weapon that could end her in under a second? She was going to have to try, but she knew the deck was heavily stacked against her. Taking him down on the escalator could work to her advantage if he dropped his weapon and if they landed in a way that didn't result in her skull being crushed between the metal treads of the escalator steps and Three's heavy frame. However, the narrow space, with only enough room for a single person per step, made a planned fall essentially impossible without severe injury to herself even before she took the P90 into account. She needed to hang on a little longer, trusting that her fellow NYPD officers were incoming fast.

The best thing she might be able to do was to slow down Three's progress, to fight him every step of the way, if possible, without looking like she was, which would raise his ire even further. It would be a fine line to walk—the line between being a valuable hostage and too much trouble to keep alive—but she'd been successful so far this evening. Now she needed to see if that luck held.

She released the handrail and they stepped first onto the metal escalator platform, then onto tile flooring. In front of them lay two groups of three blue doors, each with a large window of wired security glass, all under a lit sign declaring the way to the MTA Long Island Rail Road. Heading toward the rightmost bank of doors, Gemma steered toward the leftmost door, the one that would require someone to pull on the handle to open it, a much more awkward passage for the two of them. But Three seemed to sense her direction, twisting her body instead toward the middle door.

Making sure she had a good grip on Three's forearm, Gemma pretended to inadvertently step too far sideways, her right foot landing on his left boot, causing her to trip, pulling down hard on his forearm to keep him from choking her, curling her chin down and into her fist, forcing a little space between her throat and his brutal grip.

Three swore viciously and yanked her back upright, nearly pushing her face-first into the glass in the door.

"Wait!" She let go of his arm, slamming her palms against the door, the tip of her nose just kissing the glass as she shoved backward. She closed her eyes, giving herself a single inhale and exhale to get the temper spiking at his treatment under control. *Don't let him see you. Don't let him see what you're capable of. Let him get careless.* "I'm sorry, I didn't mean to step on your foot."

"Be more careful."

Gemma stared through the glass at a second set of doors and beyond to a number of massive columns. "I'll do my best." She pushed against the door and it swung open. They moved into the narrow vestibule and through the next door to step into the transition into Grand Central Madison. Relatively newly opened, the train terminal still carried the cleanliness of its launch. Unlike the soaring ceiling of Grand Central Terminal, or even the height of its Dining Concourse, the entrance to Grand Central Madison, with its massive black stone support columns and low ceiling, gave the space a closed-in feel, something Gemma didn't appreciate at that moment with the hulking form of the gunman breathing down her neck.

Signs overhead pointed the way to customer services and the LIRR tracks, while the retail space on both sides of the corridor was still unoccupied—floor-to-ceiling posters covered the windows, with pictures of the goods that might be found inside one day. Ahead, a large map of the terminal pointed their way around a corner and into the concourse proper. Down the center of the corridor, an art exhibit of gold-toned, still life photos commanded the space, but Gemma hardly gave any of the images a glance and kept her attention fixed beyond, to the first archway, the true entrance to the Grand Central Madison concourse.

Three prodded her with the P90. Gemma sent up a silent prayer to one of her mother's favorite Catholic saints, St. Monica, the patron saint of patience and perseverance. Three could use the patience; she could use the perseverance. She swallowed a biting comment, realizing abruptly she'd lost her fear of the P90. Yes, it could kill her instantly, but she didn't think he was ready to slay her yet. If one of the A-Team officers suddenly appeared, Three needed her upright and acting as a physical barrier to keep him from being mowed down. One wasn't there any longer and there was no reason not to kill Three, as long as they could do it cleanly. Maybe Three was realizing the security he'd felt in the Main Concourse, where he was the center of attention with his two compatriots, had utterly disappeared. He'd had the security of knowing if anyone had killed him, they'd all die. That was no longer the case and he was a target.

He had no idea her presence was a protective force for him, because no NYPD officer would sacrifice one of their own to kill a suspect. But she was happy to let him worry.

Three forced her farther down the hallway and into the concourse proper, with its high curved ceiling, brightly illuminated by pot lights and the glow of recessed LED strip lighting at the apex of the side walls.

Gemma studied her surroundings. She needed to make a break from Three in a location where she could take cover from both him and his weapon of death. Best case scenario for her, she could get him to unload his weapon. It would only take seconds and his spare magazines were back in the Grand Central Terminal concourse. Then she'd have a fair fight on her hands. But it would be risky in the extreme—one wrong move and she'd be bleeding out on the glossy tile floor in a fraction of a second.

But would he let loose like that? He had to know law enforcement was coming after them. Nothing like a stream of bullets shattering marble, tile, and glass to shine a giant spotlight on your location. Would she simply lose him if he decided he was attracting too much attention and took off? And if he made it back to street level, would others die as a result?

This was John Boyle all over again. She thought of their frantic run through the Lower East Side, as news of their escape from the park in front of City Hall through the long-closed City Hall subway station carried over the airwaves.

Up ahead would be her best chance as they approached the 45th Street escalators. The bank of five long escalators leading farther down into the depths of the terminal were located at a spot in the concourse where there were extra supports in the form of more of those massive stone or steel columns, each easily three feet in diameter. More than enough width to hide behind entirely, and even the P90's bullets wouldn't be able to pierce through to the opposite side.

While there were no exits directly to street level at this location, there was a staircase tucked discreetly behind the upper rim of the bank of escalators, its polished steel railings leading down a full story, down to the 45th Street Cross-Passage. From there, more than a dozen staircases led up to the individual platforms in the lower train shed. If she could get free of him, she could loop back around to Grand Central Terminal, which was no doubt full of law enforcement officers.

But after all this, was that what she really wanted to do? Simply get free of Three, not see him brought to justice? When she'd run through the Lower East Side with Boyle, her intent hadn't solely been to save herself, but to take him down. She needed to do the same here. Step number one: Get the P90 away from him or make it useless.

She would try to find justice for those who died for the sin of doing nothing more than being in Grand Central Terminal's concourse at the wrong time. Only if she wasn't successful in that goal would she try to save herself, escaping through the cross-passage and finding her way back into Grand Central Terminal. She didn't think he'd follow her, as the risk of capture, running straight into the waves of incoming law enforcement, would be too great.

Ahead lay the deserted concourse. Completed in tones of white and gray with arches reminiscent of Grand Central Terminal and copious overhead lighting, the wide walkway stretched out of sight to the north over glossy tile floors. Directly in front of them, the concourse opened from a wide corridor to a shallow circular atrium with the number 45 on the floor in tones of gray marble. Above it, a circular cutout in the ceiling was rimmed in green light. Thick oval columns supported the structure on the outer edges of the space, two on each side of the main walking path. The bank of five escalators disappeared downward on the right, the entrance marked by two additional shiny steel oval columns. The massive steel-and-stone columns were only about three feet apart, just to the right of the waist-high, curving glass wall topped with a run of smooth blond wood separating the gap through which the escalators ran from the surrounding floor.

One of those columns would do nicely. As long as that's where we're going. And my money is on Three wanting out of this straight corridor, where he could be picked off by an A-Team sniper. Not even five hundred yards on a flat path with no cross breeze. Child's play for an average sniper. Logan could probably do twice that.

Logan. *Where are you?*

She had to proceed as if she were on her own, but she wished she knew where he was. Was he in trouble himself?

One step at a time. You can't afford to get distracted. If he's in trouble, his own guys will find him.

Three changed their angle, frog-marching her on an angle toward the escalators even before they entered the atrium. Gemma casually let one arm drop from his forearm, letting it swing free, noting the P90 wasn't digging into her side and there was perhaps a scant half inch between the barrel and her sweater. It would be enough.

Closer...closer... *Now!*

Just as they passed within a foot and a half of the steel column, Gemma grabbed the top of the P90's frame and snapped her arm outward as hard and fast as she could while hooking her left hand into the end of the shirt sleeve of the arm around her neck. They slammed into the steel pillar with a crash and a stream of bullets burst from the gun, shattering the tile at their feet as well as the last panel of the glass dividing wall. Glass and razor-sharp bits of stone sprayed outward, ricocheting off Gemma's tall boots.

Still holding on to his sleeve, Gemma yanked Three's left arm down and away from her neck to give her room to spin toward him.

Jiu-jitsu taught there were two ways to fight if you couldn't avoid a confrontation—out far enough your opponent couldn't touch you, or in close enough he couldn't put enough leverage behind any strike to do serious damage. Distance wasn't an option, so close fighting it was. If she could only get him down to the floor—there were numerous choke holds she could use on him—then he'd be unconscious in about six seconds. Even if she ended up underneath him, she could still be in control.

But they were still on their feet with a weapon in play.

On the spin, Gemma took advantage of Three's off-balance stance to switch hands, slamming her left hand against the side of the P90, smashing it into the pillar again, Three's right hand trapped between two layers of steel from the weapon and column.

"*Bitch!*" But Three's finger must have been off the trigger, as no more shots were fired.

Gemma turned farther into the spin, but before she went chest-to-chest with Three, she bent low, using the force of her right hand coming off the P90 to swing her right elbow into his groin.

Three's roar of pain ended in a breathless squeak.

Direct hit.

But Three's lack of balance played to his advantage as he staggered forward, pushing her with him, his inertia trapping her. Three steps and her back hit something solid, her head slamming backward into unyielding steel, his bulk knocking the air from her lungs. She desperately tried to keep her hold on the P90, but one downward pull and it was gone from her grasp over the top of the frame.

Then the barrel was digging into her left breast.

"Give me a reason to pull the trigger." Three's words were slightly higher pitched than before, punched between panted breaths. "Please."

She held very still, hardly daring to breathe, her heart pounding with such ferocity, she was sure he'd be able to hear it.

He pulled back a few inches and grabbed a handful of her sweater at her neck, twisting it tight even as he lifted, forcing her head up and restricting her airway. He yanked her toward him as he turned toward the escalator. She had no choice but to go up on tiptoe to release some of the pressure at her neck.

He walked her backward around the sign that had been her downfall—a large metal sign decrying 45TH STREET—then onto the closest escalator. Not being able to see where she was going, or even see her feet, she nearly fell when she stepped backward onto the moving tread, but she managed to lock both hands onto the rubber handrail on either side to keep herself upright.

"Try anything again and I'll end you." The fury in Three's voice was unmistakable. "You're not worth the trouble." A low laugh rumbled, full of satisfaction and malice. "Maybe I should give you a shove... You'd fall all the way down to the bottom. That would do the job for me."

Gemma gripped harder and braced herself, waiting for Three to put actions to words as the ceiling of the escalator shaft closed over her head. He was correct—a backward out-of-control fall on the longest and steepest escalator in the city could be deadly, especially as she wouldn't be able to see to catch herself. At the very least, the fall would stun her, leaving her an easy target at the bottom for an execution. He'd lost bullets, but she had no cause to believe his gun was empty. All he'd need would be a single bullet to shoot into her skull as he strolled by.

Up to now, she'd calculated she was worth more to him alive than dead, but in making the attempt to get free, she'd lost that advantage. She was now disposable. She'd known it wasn't a fair fight when he had that kind of firepower, but she'd had to try. She'd lost.

If she wanted to live, she had no choice but to try again, but the parameters around the fight had changed. Now she'd simply be fighting for her life and her freedom. Bringing Three to justice was a luxury she simply couldn't afford anymore. If she could get away, it would be up to other officers to finish the job.

As soon as they got to the bottom of the escalator, she'd make another attempt.

Her choice was clear now—escape or die.

Chapter 27

From inside the upper train shed, even under the gear and behind safety glasses, Logan recognized Sims through the P90 sight when Sims stepped far enough forward to be visible past the information booth. Logan didn't recognize the terrified middle-aged woman with him or the teenage boy. But from One's stance, he did.

He held both arms out wide, as if in surrender as he shook his head, his eyes wide with shock as they locked on the boy.

The woman answered him, her words low and indistinct at this distance. Logan could hear the beseeching tone, though not the message, but when he panned over to her face to study her and the boy, while she was clearly terrified to be standing so close to the bomb—to have brought her child into its circle—she was determined to do the right thing.

Realization hit home—somehow, he and Gemma had done it. Their intel had given the NYPD—possibly with aid from the FBI—a springboard to find a way to counter the threat these men offered. And the only child brought to Grand Central at this moment would be the child of one of these two men.

From One's reaction, from the way the woman and boy never took their eyes off him, they were his family. He had his confirmation when the woman ran to him, dropping to her knees to wrap her hands around the detonator, lending her strength to his to keep her child safe. One dropped to his knees, head bent, as his wife pulled him in.

Logan suspected the woman knew it would be her last chance to do so without him in restraints. She'd ended the bombing standoff and had saved his life, but in doing so, had committed him to jail for the rest of his life. He wondered if One would consider that a favor in the long run. From a strategy standpoint, he had to hand it to his NYPD colleagues. They'd figured out another way when there was no way to give these men what they wanted and no way to send in the A-Team to overpower the suspects without everyone dying. When given the choice between capitulation or devastation, they'd found a third option—surrender. They'd forced One's hand, ensuring everyone's safety by blocking his use of the bomb. Now the bomb squad could disarm it.

Standing by the hostages, a flurry of emotions ran across Three's face—shock, betrayal, rage. Then the sound of his voice—short, sharp, full of fury—and he threw something into the hostage group before stepping toward them and disappearing from view behind the information booth. Sims raised his rifle but didn't have a shot without risking the hostages, as Three was among them with his finger on the trigger. For a moment, there were only indistinct sounds, then a woman's cry of pain.

Anger whipped hot at the sound. Logan knew the sound of that voice. *Gem.*

Three walked backward into view and Logan's worst fears were confirmed. Three had Gemma in a headlock with his left arm around her throat as he dragged her backward. Logan knew very well she could get out of that position by turning into Three, kneeing him in the groin and using her right hand over his shoulder to yank his head back by the hair or side-strike his nose.

But the barrel of the P90 pressed into her side precluded any action. If she attempted any aggressive move, she'd be ripped apart by over a dozen bullets in the first second and there would be nothing anyone could do to save her.

Stay alive.

He knew she couldn't hear his message, but she didn't need to. He knew Gemma, knew she'd already be calculating how to get free, how to take control of the situation. Because he knew her, he recognized her calculation would be to let her be separated from the rest of the hostages. Then the only life on the line would be her own. With Logan missing from the group, Gemma didn't know what had happened to him and couldn't expect to depend on his help.

She had it nonetheless.

From the shelter of the upper train shed, Logan watched Three drag Gemma down the staircase in the center of the West Balcony and out of sight. Turning, he raced back past track 30 and into the northwest passage. A closed corridor between tracks 30 and 32, the northwest passage ran all the way to East 47th Street at the level of the upper train shed. But just past East 45th Street, it had stairs leading up to Park Avenue and another flight leading down to the lower train shed. That was Logan's goal.

He was the only officer on Gemma's trail at this point. His fellow A-Team officers would be on the move, but none of them could get down to the Main Concourse level quickly from their present locations. It could take minutes—too much time to lose. There were too many options for an escape attempt down below, and someone needed to know where they were going. Losing Gemma now might mean losing her for good. Three would only keep her alive for as long as she was useful. If they managed to disappear between now and then, she'd truly be on her own. Logan wouldn't abandon her to that fate.

Heading to the underground Dining Concourse meant one of two escape routes: He could take Gemma through the lower train shed and either down to the 45th Street Cross-Passage or straight up the elevator or stairs to Park Avenue, which would likely lead straight into the arms of the NYPD. They'd have officers blocking all entrances to the Terminal to keep bystanders out but would be happy to catch an escaping suspect. Alternatively, Three could take her farther down and into Grand Central Madison. There, the Main Concourse stretched for a quarter mile, running parallel to Madison Avenue, with exits leading to East 43rd, 44th, 47th, and 48th Streets. More exits gave him more flexibility and considerably more distance from the epicenter of the chaos.

But Logan judged he had another goal in mind—the tracks. Every train coming into Grand Central Terminal and Grand Central Madison had been stopped, leaving the tracks, while still dangerously electrified, deserted for several miles. Which meant they could be used as a means of escape. The trains had periodic ventilation support, including the ventilation tower erected on East 50th, as well as maintenance entrances, which meant there were multiple egress locations, all in spots blocks away that the NYPD might not be covering as it concentrated its operations around Grand Central.

If he was Three, it's exactly what he'd do. Escape the nexus of NYPD activity, remove the balaclava in the knowledge that his face was unknown, blend into the background of the bustling city...and disappear. Unless Three was an idiot, he would have to know he'd be on a list of possible Sinister 13 members, so maybe he'd planned on a change of identity after today. With the amount of planning that had gone into today's incursion, maybe he already had one set up to assume as soon as he was free.

He sprinted down the passageway, around the half wall cordoning off the paired escalator and staircase, and took the stairs two at a time down to the lower train shed.

Logan held the P90 close, ready to fire at any moment. He had lightning-fast reflexes and knew with his finger resting along the frame just above the trigger, rather than against it, even holding the weapon a little low to facilitate faster movement, he could snap it up to his shoulder and have his finger on the trigger in a fraction of a second. But he didn't dare risk an accidental shot giving away his location or that he was armed.

He exited cautiously onto the platform, listening for any sign of Three and Gemma coming into the lower train shed. Instead, he heard Gemma's voice telling Three he didn't need to be so rough; his weapon ensured her cooperation.

He pressed back against the stairwell, cursing the light streaming down from overhead when Three marched Gemma past the entrance that lined up with where he sheltered on the platform for track 112. They circled around to the left and disappeared.

Headed down another level and out to Grand Central Madison.

He retraced his footsteps back into the stairwell, following it down to the 45th Street Cross-Passage. Knowing he was safe for now with Three and Gemma in an entirely different corridor, he burst out into the passage.

He was halfway down the passage when a rapid blast of gunfire sounded in the distance and he jerked to a stop to confirm direction. The sound had been indistinct, but he was sure it was down the east end of the passage—either from the east end of the lower train shed or from Grand Central Madison.

His money was on Grand Central Madison. Had Gemma gotten free? Was she fighting him for the weapon?

He sprinted down the hallway, searching for the staircase to carry him up to Grand Central Madison's concourse.

If Logan was sure of one thing, it was taking Gemma was a mistake that could compromise Three's plans. Three could have selected anyone in the group but likely had several reasons to choose Gemma. She'd been the suspects' outward-facing representative for the negotiating team, and the connection to the NYPD and the voice they knew. He likely calculated she would be the safest hostage for him to take, the hostage the NYPD was most invested in.

The guy didn't understand the NYPD at all. Every life would be important. They weren't going to throw up their hands and go home because he'd taken the woman who spoke for them. They'd pursue, no matter who he'd taken.

But more than that, Gemma could represent their failure to free their men. If Three was going to blame someone for the disintegration of their position of power, while a good portion of it lay in One's hands, Three might find Gemma also partly responsible as the voice that didn't produce their required results. For this reason alone, Three might not only consider her disposable but might find pleasure in watching her die.

The thought left Logan chilled.

Of course, Three had no idea he'd taken the one person left in the group best prepared to fight for her life. Gemma was smart and strategic, and Logan knew from firsthand experience she had the hand-to-hand skills to put a man down. He'd been cocky himself the first time he went head-to-head with her on the mats during training. She'd taken him to the floor and grappled him into submission in an embarrassingly short amount of time for a man of his size and strength. She'd used his own prejudices against him and won. It had been a good lesson for him to learn in a situation when his life wasn't on the line, and he'd never forgotten it.

She'd used those skills against Boyle and had nearly gained the upper hand in their struggle in the pitch blackness of the crypts under St. Patrick's Old Cathedral until an elbow coming out of the dark had the bad luck to connect with her nose, slamming her back and giving Boyle the opportunity to escape to the cemetery, where he'd come under Logan's gaze.

She could use those same skills here. Jiu-jitsu taught how to manage close fighting, which is exactly the position they'd be in.

The problem was the P90, its compact design making it easier to control in close quarters. Gemma could be a jiu-jitsu black belt world champion, and she'd have no defense against the firepower of the P90. Her skills would only be useful if Three could be disarmed.

His money was on Gemma.

Up one more set of stairs to move from the cross-passage to Grand Central Madison's concourse level. Then he'd be right behind them.

Hang on, Gem. I'm coming...

Chapter 28

Logan shot through the double doors at the east end of the 45th Street Cross-Passage and ran up the right side of the double staircase, over the short landing, where he switched to the left side. Then he slowed as, above, the ceiling of the Grand Central Madison's concourse came into view.

Silence.

A cold shiver ran down his spine. Silence was bad. Silence could mean he was too late.

Only one way to find out.

He crept up the flight of stairs, then barely eased above the concourse floor. Shattered glass and tile told him this was where the P90 had been fired, but there was no one in sight. He crept up a few more inches.

Clear.

He stepped into the concourse, pausing again. For several seconds he froze in place, listening to the sounds of the Main Concourse beyond over the sound of his pounding heart in his ears. All was silent. Then he heard it, faint, as if coming from a distance—the sounds of a struggle and an echoing cry.

She's alive and still fighting for her freedom.

He jogged to the damaged section of the concourse floor, which, to his immense relief, carried no traces of blood, nor did any of the surrounding floors or columns.

Because of the risk of injury or death, Grand Central Madison would have been evacuated at the same time as Grand Central Terminal, using any of the street level exits. And as there were no trains coming in to disembark passengers, and all exits would be blocked by officers to keep both train stations empty, no one else would be coming in once all was quiet.

All exits would be blocked by officers... Yet another reason to believe the tracks would be Three's attempt at escape. Of course, that came with its own risks, as the electrified third rail would be an ever-present danger, with the capability of frying anyone who touched it with 750 volts of power pulsating through it. Logan knew from years of riding the MTA subways and trains that the electrified rail had a top cover to protect workers maintaining or repairing the tracks, but it was still partially open on one side to allow contact with the train itself. If Gemma struggled with Three while on the tracks and fell to the ground, landing on or against the third rail, simultaneously grounding the connection by touching one of the running rails or the track bed, death would be the likely result. It would also be much harder to track them in the dimly lit tunnels. Not to mention, if they disappeared at that point, Logan would only have a one in four chance of picking the correct tunnel to follow them.

Not good odds. The goal, therefore, was to catch them before they made it to the tunnels. That meant no waiting. No backup. He was on his own. Though he knew he had a solid partner in Gemma, who would be doing everything in her power to save herself.

He quickly took in the deserted concourse with its false storefronts showing where future businesses would reside, and an archway with signage pointing the way to TICKETING AND CUSTOMER SERVICES - LIRR TRACKS. A bank of five escalators lay under a sign decreeing MTA LONG ISLAND RAIL ROAD and a downward arrow pointing to tracks 201–204 and 301–304.

Three and Gemma were down there somewhere. The long empty space of the concourse made that clear, but deducing where Three was headed meant they weren't on this level. Which meant a trip down the longest escalators in the city.

Logan had been down them only once before but knew the details from the fuss around Grand Central Madison's construction and opening. The escalators dove down nearly eleven stories in height over nearly two hundred feet of length at a thirty-degree downward angle to the mezzanine level located between double tracks above and below in two locations. He remembered the ride down, the curved walls and ceiling that seemed to go on forever, the feeling of vertigo that had assailed him as he lost track of where the horizon was. He'd solved the battle between his brain and his eyes by staring at the stair treads with an occasional glance up to track his progress. For someone who had no fear of heights, it had been a disconcerting experience lasting more than a minute and a half.

The ride down was entirely exposed. A shooter standing at the bottom would be able to fire on him, and while he could fire back, the man below had places to shelter; he would not.

Indistinct sounds of a scuffle and a low angry voice floated from below.

No help for it. The best he could do was stay low. Running down the escalator would be fast but would call attention to himself and force him to remain upright in full view over the rails of the escalator. And if the vertigo hit while he was running down the treads with the P90 in both hands, he ran the risk of going down face first and taking himself out of the fight. Not worth it to gain at most an extra forty-five seconds.

He pulled the butt of the P90 in tight against his right shoulder and headed in a crouch for the middle escalator, its treads gliding downward, calculating that staying in the middle of the space would give him the most flexibility. He stayed low, only popping a little higher for a brief second to peer down at the mezzanine level far below—the semicircle of pale tile floor visible was deserted. Hopefully it would stay that way.

Logan stayed down, backing the edge of his left hip onto a stair tread as it rose up to full height, folding over the P90 pressed against his thighs as the escalator continued its descent. As Logan sank through the oval opening to the bank of escalators—past a white-on-green strip of the seal of the State of New York bordered in shining polished steel—the walls of the escalator shaft closed around him. The walls on either side were composed of long lines of glossy green tile while repeated pairs of pot lights overhead ramped downward.

Logan kept his eyes on the ever-widening arc of flooring below as he glided closer. A third of the way down... Halfway down... He perched lightly on the step, keeping his weight on the balls of his feet, ready to move the second he hit bottom.

Two-thirds of the way down, the mezzanine floor below opened out, revealing a wide space centered with a glowing green circular glass floor surrounded by a dark charcoal tile circle overlaid with a "45" in tones of pale and medium gray.

Almost there.

Suddenly two bodies staggered into view below and Logan shot to his feet, planting his boots and jamming the P90 back into place at his shoulder, peering down the sight.

Three still had Gemma in a headlock, but she was fighting back. Her left hand was locked onto the integrated sight and barrel, her elbow also locked, pushing it away from her body as she used her right hand to force his head up and back, starting to take him off-balance. Logan could see her intent—get him on the ground, stay in close so the P90 was useless but still occupied his right hand, and grapple him into submission or knock him unconscious, knowing help was only minutes out. Little did she know, help was seconds away.

But he couldn't get a clear shot. They were so entwined as they struggled, from this overhead angle he had no trajectory that didn't risk killing Gemma as well as Three.

A cry ripped from Gemma's chest as she struggled, putting an extra inch—then two—between them.

Come on, a little farther; then it's all over.

But in pushing Three's head back, Gemma must have given him a direct line of sight up the escalator shaft because his eyes flared wide. He released her, letting her own inertia wrapped in the force she was exerting in pushing him away take her down when his grasp abruptly evaporated. She started to fall, pulling the P90 with her, but Three got his left arm free and under the frame of the weapon, raising it higher. As Gemma fell, he went down on one knee, keeping her as cover as he opened fire over her head.

Logan knew he was a sitting duck. In the millisecond he had to decide between moving or pausing long enough to take the shot if Gemma could get down low enough, he knew he'd have to move, even though there was no guarantee of survival.

Releasing the forward grip of the P90, he braced his left hand on the moving railing and leaped, rolling over the slick steel dividing the two escalators as a stream of bullets blasted up the treads and over where he'd just been standing. He hit the treads of the next escalator—this one traveling upward—steadying his grip on the P90. A look down showed Gemma again struggling with Three for his weapon. They were still too close, and Logan didn't have enough time to truly catch his balance, but he got off two shots, aiming for Three's right shoulder, farthest away from

Gemma. The shots went wide as Three jerked sideways, catching Gemma around the torso, using her body as a barrier.

He dragged her a few feet sideways, swearing viciously as she tried to set him off-balance. Keeping the P90 out of her reach, he fired a one-handed burst at Logan, who was still unsteady with nowhere to go. But when bullets flew that fast, precise aim was optional.

Logan's torso exploded in agonizing pain as bullets slammed into him.

As he went down backward on the sharp treads of the escalator, he heard Gemma scream his name.

Chapter 29

Logan's body jerked with the impact of each bullet; then he dropped, thrown backward over the stair treads to lie unmoving as the escalator moved upward, carrying him away from them.

"*Sean!*" The frantic scream ripped from Gemma's throat, leaving it raw, but the pain barely registered as shock rocketed icy tendrils through her body.

A series of images shot through her mind: *Grappling with Logan on the mats at the academy, glee racing through her at the shock in his eyes when she pinned him. Watching him nail target after target at the range, his precision with a handgun and rifle obvious even early on. The shadows sculpting his face, only a whisper away in the dim light of his bedroom as his ragged breath feathered over her lips. Balancing on Logan's shoulders at Rikers while holding on to a rope fashioned from a bedsheet as Alvaro Vega slowly strangled to death. The supporting grip of his hand around hers as she told him it was the twenty-fifth anniversary of her mother's death. Exiting South Greenfield, his hand on Sam's shoulder, bringing the heart of the Capello family back home.*

The deafening crack of a gunshot only feet away, followed by the warm splash of her mother's blood. The way her mother's body crumpled bonelessly to the floor. Her open staring eyes. The way her hand cooled over the hours as ten-year-old Gemma held it while sitting beside her, alone, desperately wanting her to wake up. Knowing she never would.

Now Logan was gone as well and they'd never have the chance to see if there was ever anything between them. Beyond that, like her mother, he'd never have the chance to grow old, to see his children—hell, to *have* children—to make lieutenant as everyone expected and possibly to move even farther up the ranks. All that potential, brutally annihilated under a hail of bullets.

Rage rose in a thick red wave, clouding her vision as her mind snapped. For a minute, she went crazy, struggling in Three's one-handed hold while the P90 was still pointed in the direction of the escalators. She managed to twist toward his chest, and even as his fist forced her head upward, she landed a solid hit in his stomach with her left fist. Pain sang up her arm as she hit the armor plating of his vest she'd forgotten in her fury, but she pulled back and put as much force as she could muster with her nondominant hand into an uppercut under his chin, making contact with a satisfying crack. More pain, but Three's surprised grunt made it all worthwhile.

Gem, stop. This isn't the way. Logan's voice sounded in her head, but she didn't pay it heed over the roar of fury filling her mind. Reaching up, she dug her nails into his right cheek and raked down, feeling them gouge deep. Three's roar of pain sent a bolt of satisfaction through her.

Three managed to get a fistful of her sweater at her shoulder and jerked her around so her back was to him again and the cold metal of the barrel of the P90 dug into the soft flesh under her jaw.

She froze, the red haze of rage dropping away, her logical brain finally winning the fight for dominance.

Gem, to stay alive, you have to be in control. Stay alive.

This time Logan's words penetrated. She knew she wasn't actually hearing him—she'd seen him die—but was more hearing her training reinforced through his attitudes and beliefs. In this moment, when she was as alone as she'd been in that bank twenty-five years before beside her mother's corpse, she had something she hadn't had back then—fourteen years of experience as an NYPD officer.

She could manage this situation, but she had to stay calm. Stay calculating. The grief could wait. It had to or she'd be completely incapacitated.

She pushed all thoughts of Logan away.

"I could kill you." Three's furious words grated in her ear. "Blow your head clean off."

"You could." Gemma forced her voice to stay flat, emotionless. Hearing her own voice in control would reinforce that feeling for herself. "But that would be a mistake. Who's going to stand between you and the A-Team officers who are coming? My bloody corpse won't protect you." She purposely opted for the most brutal imagery. He stepped to his right, and she couldn't help the sharply indrawn breath as he dragged her backward, the barrel digging hard into her jaw.

"Move. Unless you want me to end you here and now."

They moved farther into the mezzanine; then he crowded her onto the upward escalator. Her head tipped backward and she nearly tripped, but she slapped both hands on his forearm again and kept herself on her feet.

The ceiling of the upper platform came into view with its lower overhead and double row of strip lighting illuminating the edge of the wide platform on both sides. In front of her was the elevator leading down to the mezzanine and the lower platform farther down.

But it was the deserted tracks on either side that concerned her. This had to be Three's goal—the darkened tunnels, where she would no longer be quite as useful to him. Every New Yorker who used the rail or subway systems knew about the hazards of the electrified third rail that powered the trains, the most distant of the three rails.

She'd failed to free herself in the concourse above. She'd failed on the mezzanine below. This would be her last chance, because once he got her into the tunnels, she'd be harder to find. If he shot her here and the incoming A-Team heard the shot, she'd be easy to find and there would be a chance of medical intervention. If he shot her in the dark of the tunnels, the odds were she'd bleed out before being found.

She'd run out of time and had to try to take him down here. She'd stalled and slowed him, but that was over now. If she let him toss her off the platform, only death awaited. If not from the third rail, from the weapon this man carried that would follow her into an unyielding dark.

The pressure under her jaw disappeared, only to return to her rib cage as they stepped off the escalator and he drove her toward the platform on the left. One glance to her right showed the end of the platform where the light receded and the track sank into the gloom of the tunnel.

That gloom would be his safety and could be her end.

They were only feet from the edge of the platform, and from the way Three was pushing her along, she had only seconds to make her stand.

She took a deep breath, thought of her father, her brothers. Of her mother's bravery. Of Logan.

And attacked.

Chapter 30

The crack of the sharp edge of steel against the back of his skull left Logan momentarily stunned, his vision dissolving into a black haze dotted with green pinpoints. Then the echo of Gemma's anguished scream and the sound of her continued struggle snapped him back into alertness, his vision clearing. For a moment, panic rose as he couldn't suck in air, but he bore down, calmed himself—*Get a grip. You're just winded*—and tried again, oxygen flowing into his lungs once his diaphragm stopped its spasm.

Not dead. But how?

Pain stabbed through his torso as if someone had whaled on him repeatedly with a sledgehammer, and he had to wonder if one or two of his ribs might be broken. He ran his hand over the soft cotton of his shirt, now punched through with ragged holes, the contorted shape of several flattened bullets beneath, below them the protective bulk of the armored Kevlar vest. *Has to be a level IV vest. Nothing else would stop these rounds.* The gunmen had come armed to withstand anything the NYPD could throw at them, which, in the end, also included the ammunition they carried themselves, possibly in case of coming under friendly fire in the chaos of the opening seconds of the attack. Or simply because of their determination to complete the mission at all costs.

He jerked upright with a groan. He still clutched the P90 with his right hand as the escalator carried him back up to the concourse, but below, he couldn't see either Three or Gemma. Were they still fighting on that level or was he dragging her toward the tracks, ensuring her compliance with the P90? Either way, he would be following them.

The back of his head throbbed incessantly. He probed the spot with the fingers of his left hand. His hair was wet, and when he pulled his hand away, his fingers were slick with blood. He didn't think he'd hit hard enough to be concussed, but the protruding teeth on the edge of the step had bitten deep, and, like any head wound, it was bleeding copiously. But not enough to be a serious issue in the next ten minutes when he was the only officer on Gemma's trail. He'd deal with it later.

He considered alternate ways to get down to the mezzanine—other banks of escalators or the elevators near the customer service desk—but all that would take too much time and he could lose Three and Gemma just at the moment she needed him most.

Screw quiet. If Three was dragging Gemma along and she was fighting him, he wouldn't hear Logan coming down the escalator. Besides, he likely thought Logan was dead. Or well on his way to it.

Gemma would think that as well. Fine, it would be a surprise for both of them, but not the same kind of surprise.

As Logan climbed to his feet, a series of metallic clinks around his boots reinforced that the vest had successfully stopped the bullets and was now shedding them as discarded shrapnel. Something for the NYPD to deal with as evidence later.

He ensured he had a good grip on the P90 and ran up the escalator steps. At the top, he skirted the railing and headed back down the flight he'd just abandoned. He compromised on safety, running his left hand over the rubber handrail as he ran down the steps. He tried to keep his footfalls light, but from the silence coming from below, Three had pulled Gemma away from the escalators or to one of the other levels. He couldn't risk the kind of long fall that could break his neck, and vertigo now would be deadly, so he kept his eyes on the edges of the steps, trying to keep the horizon firmly in place.

As soon as he was able to step off onto the steel decking at the bottom, he snapped his left hand back onto the grip, pulling the weapon in close. Now on tile flooring, he ghosted silently on his rubber soles toward the wall on his left. Spanning over the green glass floor, the center of the space was supported by a network of massive concrete struts. The surrounding passageways continued the arched style of the concourse above, with signs indicating the tracks beyond. Across to the right, a three-sided glass-and-steel railing surrounded a single escalator and a set of stairs leading down to tracks 301 and 302, but there was no sign of movement beyond. Inching down the wall, he edged slowly to the corner. Across from him was another deserted MTA desk, its officers evacuated to help deal with the crisis in Grand Central Terminal. He edged a little closer to see around the corner. No movement, but another escalator and set of stairs leading up to tracks 201 and 202. Directly across from him was a wide corridor leading to tracks 203, 204, 303, and 304, but Logan doubted he'd take Gemma the long way.

A muffled cry from above cemented that opinion. They'd gone up.

Leading with the P90, Logan took the corner quickly, scanning for any motion, but all was still. He ran for the flight of stairs; the escalator also led up, but he didn't want to be a slave to the escalator's inexorable upward travel. Better to be able to sneak up and stop just before being seen. As he approached the open staircase, he scanned for any movement above him, but no one was in sight. Instead, he could hear staggered footfalls and the heavy breathing and grunts of a struggle.

He had no doubt Gemma could normally hold her own, but if she'd been blindsided by his "death," she might not be fighting with the cool head a struggle like this would require. Emotional turmoil could be deadly because it could let your opponent outthink you.

Logan kept the P90 jammed against his right shoulder as he peered down the sight, both eyes open to take in the full field of view, and crept silently up the stairs. The staircase was nearly a full two stories high, having to pass through the vaulted ceiling of the mezzanine and come up to the upper level at the height of the raised platform. He slowed when he was about three-quarters of the way to the top, easing up the steps as the top of a masked head came into view. Another step and his heart skipped a beat.

Gemma and Three were twenty feet down the platform, struggling. Three's arm was still locked around her neck, and it looked like he was going to drag her down off the platform with him and she'd chosen that moment to make her final stand. It was a shrewd last-ditch strategy from his point of view. At this point, she believed she was truly alone, with his corpse lying at the top of the bank of escalators. Three still wanted to use her as a hostage; they were still too close to the center of the incident, and if law enforcement closed in, Gemma could be the only thing standing between Three and instantaneous death. There was no bomb now to convince the A-Team shooters not to take him out. Cops were dead and he was responsible. There would be no hesitation about lethal force if there was no compliance...unless he still had a hostage. That made Gemma paramount to his escape plan through the tunnels.

Gemma would know the farther removed she was from any assistance, the lesser her chance of survival. Better to bank on the fact he wouldn't step back and riddle her body with bullets—like Logan had just experienced—and try to take him down.

Gemma stood with her back to Three, his left arm wound around her throat as he dragged her toward the edge of the platform. There was no easy way down as passengers were not supposed to be on the tracks; the only way down was to jump or be pushed.

Being thrown onto the track could be incredibly dangerous unless you landed close to the platform, kept your balance, and avoided the electrified third rail at all costs.

They were about two feet from the platform when Gemma made her move. She planted one foot and simultaneously locked her left hand onto the frame of the P90 from beneath, jamming her fingers into the gap just in front of the trigger, yanking the barrel toward the floor as she stepped through and behind with her other foot to turn into his body. She slipped her right arm through the narrow gap between them, swiveling to come chest to chest with him.

Logan ghosted up three more steps, entirely unnoticed, and tried to get a bead on Three, but with Gemma pressed so close against him, there was simply no way to get a clean shot. The added complication was the knowledge that the vest Three wore would stop his shots. He not only needed a clear line of sight, it needed to be outside the armor plating of the vest—if he couldn't get a shot through the unprotected side section, it would have to be a head or leg shot.

Gemma kept up her downward pressure on the gun, using her smaller stature to bend him low. He resisted, pulling the gun toward himself, and a short burst of automatic fire exploded, shattering the concrete at the edge of the platform. Three swore viciously, then got his left hand up into her unbound hair from behind, yanking her head back brutally, loosening her hold on the P90.

Step back... Step back... Give me just a few inches.

Patience was everything. Patience could earn him the shot he needed.

Gemma's right hand clamped down on Three's wrist and tried to pull him off, but backward and behind her head, she simply didn't have the leverage she needed to free herself from his enraged grip.

"Not so strong now, are you, bitch?" Rage filled Three's voice. "Get on the tracks."

It was a fight Gemma could have won, but to do it, she needed both hands. Keeping one hand on the P90 left her vulnerable. Three pivoted, dragging Gemma with him, her scream of rage and pain ricocheting around the tiled walls and floors as he moved to throw her onto the tracks below.

If she was lucky, she'd avoid the third rail. If she was unlucky, she'd die in seconds. As it stood right now, she was off-balance and wasn't going to be able to control her landing when he threw her.

Just a little farther...

Three rotated, pulling Gemma away from his body, ripping the P90 from her grasp in order to raise the barrel toward her abdomen and deliver a fatal blow if she continued to resist.

Got you.

Logan squeezed the trigger.

Chapter 31

The sound of Logan's single shot boomed through the empty space, bouncing off every slick, glossy surface.

Still off-balance, Gemma jerked at the sound of the gunshot, her hands flying to her abdomen as if to hold in the blood she expected to spill. For a moment, she froze in place, just as Three did. Then he crumpled bonelessly, falling backward, yanking her forward and upright just before the hand in her hair went limp, releasing her. The P90 fell from his lax grip to clatter against the tile floor as he toppled backward off the platform.

Gemma's gaze stayed locked on Three down below as shock carved furrows across her forehead and slackened the set of her mouth. She didn't pick up the P90 for protection, but simply stared down at him—confirmation for Logan that Three was dead.

Logan climbed the last treads and stepped onto the platform. "Gem." He spoke quietly, not wanting to startle her when she stood so close to the edge of the platform.

She spun to face him, her eyes going wide, as if not believing what was right in front of her. "Sean?"

He simply grinned at her.

Then she was running, and he only had enough time to grip the curve of the frame of the P90 and spin the fire selector from semiautomatic to safe before she was on him.

He caught her, wrapping his arms around her, the P90 still gripped in his right hand to lie against her back as she threw her arms around his neck, pulling his head down to press her mouth to his. The kiss was like a dam breaking—thick with desperation, with the shattering of nerves held taut for hours, overlaid with her disbelief he was actually alive and their joint relief the crisis was finally over and they'd both survived. He banded her in tight, feeling like he couldn't get her quite close enough, while her hands couldn't remain still, running over his shoulders and neck before arrowing up the back of his head into his hair to grip the strands as she moved in closer, taking the kiss deeper.

A groan broke from the back of his throat, a sound threaded with pain, not pleasure. He stopped himself from clenching his teeth against the pain just in time to avoid catching her tongue.

Her hold loosened and she pulled back, searching his face, her eyes alert, concerned. "What's wrong?"

Reaching behind his head, he pulled her hand away, revealing fingertips smeared with blood. She'd been too invested in the kiss to notice the damp slickness under her touch.

"What happened?" Grasping his shoulders, she twisted him around, going up on tiptoe for a better look. "Oh, God. Look at you." Clasping his head in both hands, she carefully tipped it backward toward her.

He could only imagine what a mess it must be. "I left my cosmetics mirror at home. How bad is it?" He couldn't see her eye-roll, but he knew it was there, though after everything they'd been through that day, surely she couldn't blame him for trying to lighten the mood.

"There's a lot of blood." Her fingers gently parted the short strands of his hair. "It's not as bad as I thought it would be, though it's bleeding like crazy. Not a long gash, but a line of what looks like punctures."

"You know how head wounds bleed. Got it when I was blown backward onto the escalator stairs. I caught the edge of the step across the back of my head. Rang my bell a bit."

Gemma circled around him, wiping her bloody fingers off on her jeans. "I'm sure it did. What I don't understand is how you're alive." She met his gaze and he saw residual edges of grief there, also reflected in the slight huskiness of her voice. "I thought he'd killed you." Her gaze dropped to his chest, to his shirt, and she lifted one hand to lightly touch one of the bullet holes. "He tried." Her fingers ran sideways to the next ragged tear. "He *really* tried."

"He would have succeeded." He unbuttoned his shirt with his left hand, fully revealing the bulletproof vest beneath. "Except I 'borrowed' this from Two after I knocked him out cold. They paid for top-of-the-line gear. My own standard-issue vest wouldn't have protected me nearly as well, if at all. But nothing got through." In four locations—two over his pecs, one over his lower left ribs, and one over his abdomen—the cover of the vest was a cluster of ragged tatters, the gray armor plating revealed below. It, too, was damaged, the bullets having partially penetrated, leaving the heavy material shredded. But it had held, protecting the flesh beneath. "Pretty sure I must be bruised as hell though. Those bullets packed one hell of a punch. Knocked the wind clean out of me for a few seconds."

"Between this and your head, you need EMS to look you over. I've never been hit like that, but I've heard stories. You could have a couple of broken ribs under there." She laid both hands against the ruined vest and looked up at him. "Thank you."

"For what?"

Her laugh was thick with disbelief. "How hard did you hit your head? For coming after me. For tracking where we went. For putting your own life on the line. For nearly losing your life. All to find me." Sliding her hands to his shoulders, she went up on tiptoe and kissed him, long, slow, gentle, as if not willing to risk injuring him further.

When she finally pulled back, he felt like his brains had been slightly scrambled and he'd been transported back fifteen years. This was what it had been like between them before, this near instant incineration. They'd been young, stupid, and overly focused on their careers, not giving credence to the importance of a bond between them. In short, they'd both been insane to walk away from it and each other. And look where they were, years later—both single. From his perspective, while he'd had other relationships, nothing had clicked like it had with Gemma, likely why none of them had survived long-term. He had to wonder if it had been the same for her.

He tipped his head down to rest his forehead against hers. For a long stretch of seconds, they simply stood quietly, her hands still on his shoulders, his free hand on her hip. Then, blowing out a long breath, he stepped back, knowing as officers their day wasn't over yet.

He moved to the edge of the platform, looking down, needing to see with his own eyes for confirmation. Three sprawled over the tracks below, his body lying across the running rails with one extended hand touching the third rail. Every muscle in his body was spasmed tight, his face contorted into a gruesome death mask. If Three hadn't been killed by the bullet Logan had neatly placed under his arm—and Logan was sure it had been a fatal shot, skirting between the protective plates of armor on a direct path to his heart—he was definitely dead now, as high voltage power coursed through his body.

Nothing more to do here. Logan turned away from him. "We need to get word out. Our commanders, our teams, your family. They must be going crazy. And they still think we have an active op."

"In a second. First tell me how you found me. You managed to track us. And then took the risk to follow. I know how dangerous it was to come down those escalators."

"There was no time to find another way. If you'd disappeared into the tunnels..."

"I figured he would have killed me as soon as I wasn't useful anymore. Which likely would have been once we were well into the tunnels or when he found a way out. He'd be able to move faster if he was on his own and not constantly fighting a hostage."

"You made his getaway hell."

"That was the goal. I tried to slow him down to give someone a chance to follow." Her brow furrowed as her expression closed in. "I didn't know whether you'd survived your attempt to escape. I hadn't heard any gunshots, but Two also had a knife."

"So did I. I cut the ties with my knife as I went through the bathroom door." He lifted his injured left hand, which still oozed blood. "Got me in the process as well, but it worked to get free. Then I took Two down. He's still tied up on the bathroom floor."

Gemma caught his hand in hers, studying the raw patch running across the heel of his hand. "Looks like you sideswiped it with the blade and shaved off the top dozen layers of skin." She shook her head. "You're a mess."

"No denying that." Now that the crisis was over and the adrenaline rush was leaching away, pain was rushing to the surface as his head started to pound, his chest stabbed with radiating agony, and the knife wound on his left hand ached. "Wouldn't say no to an Advil or two. Or twelve."

"No Advil. At least not yet. We have to deal with this first; then I want you seen. Actually, I'm going to ask for someone to come in to treat you. But quickly, how did you know where to find me?"

Logan gave her the CliffsNotes version of his trip through multiple levels of the terminals until he caught up in Grand Central Madison. "You had me a bit terrified as I came up the stairs and found you struggling with him. I know you can fight; I know you can win. But that's in pure hand-to-hand. When there's a weapon in the mix, you never had a chance to get the upper hand."

"I tried multiple times, and you're right, I never had a chance. Not with a short, automatic weapon like that." Her gaze dropped to the shattered tile and cement marked by the spray of bullets. "I'm lucky that wasn't into me." She turned to look down at Three's lifeless body. "I'm lucky that wasn't me either. He was about to toss me in there, and who knows how I'd have landed? It could have been bad."

"It was for him."

"You think he was electrocuted?"

"No, he was dead before he fell off the platform. I had to wait for the shot, but once he rotated far enough away from you at the angle I needed to get around the body armor, I knew I had him."

"And there you are again, saving another Capello. What did you say at St. Pat's? You carry a piece of every life you take with you? Even if your hand was forced?" Her dark eyes were full of regret. "I'm sorry you had to take that on for me. For us, because my family will also consider themselves in your debt."

"No one's in my debt. I was doing my jo—"

"Really?" The curve of her eyebrow told him she didn't believe his knee-jerk response for a second. "Was that all it was?"

He pulled in a breath that lanced bruised muscles with arrows of pain. "Okay, I wasn't just doing my job. My job gave me the skills to manage the situation. And yes, I would have made that shot to protect any hostage. But it was different, more personal...because it was you."

"As I said, I'm sorry for any burden that brings you, though I'm grateful you saved my life." She took in his stance, stiff with discomfort with the conversation and physical pain, and gave him a half smile. "This is making you uncomfortable, so enough said." She turned back to the man on the tracks. "We need to get the power turned off, then retrieve his body. We don't have any way to contact anyone from down here, but teams are incoming." She studied him for a moment. "I'll meet whoever is on their way. You need to sit down."

"I'm fine."

"You don't look fine. You also don't have to prove anything to me. I watched you get shot and go down hard on those steps. There's no seating except up in the concourse waiting area, so maybe sit here on the stairs and take a load off for now while you hold the scene. And before you dig in your heels, do it for me?"

Pain was stealing his breath. He definitely needed to rest, even only a minute or two to pull it together. "Okay."

"Agreeing that easily tells me how much you're hurting. Now sit."

She waited as he sat down on the top step, the P90 across his thighs; then she descended to the mezzanine and headed in the direction of the main bank of escalators.

Only once she was out of sight did he let himself sag against the brushed metal post supporting the end of the stairway railing, curling in on himself to ease some of the pain radiating from his chest and ribs. But beyond the pain, beyond the exhaustion, came relief and satisfaction. They'd done it. It was over.

Together, they'd beaten the odds and survived.

Chapter 32

Gemma rode the escalator back to Grand Central Madison's concourse, calling out her designation as per A-Team protocol when exiting a location. She'd come this far and didn't want to get shot by an overenthusiastic A-Team officer when she suddenly appeared. "Detective Gemma Capello, coming out! Hostage taker is neutralized."

As she approached the top of the escalator, she noted four mangled bullets dancing at the end of the upper escalator decking where the steps cycled into the concourse floor. Fortunately, they were too large to slide between the interwoven fins of the treads. She stepped over them as the sound of footfalls came from her left, but took the time to slam the side of her fist against the STOP button to the left of where the handrail dipped down at the top of the escalator. The crime scene techs could deal with them later.

An A-Team unit appeared to her left, coming in fast from Grand Central Terminal, Lieutenant Cartwright leading the group. His eyes panned up and down her body, searching for injury, pausing briefly at her forehead. "Capello. Good to see you."

"Good to be seen."

"You're okay?" When she nodded, he continued, "You took down the hostage taker?"

"Negative. Detective Logan did. The hostage taker is deceased on track 201."

"Logan? He got free?"

"Yes. Then he tracked me through the Terminal and down below." She held Cartwright's gaze, knowing that while there would be an investigation into Three's death, Cartwright would be solidly behind his officer. Still, there was no harm in reinforcing that opinion. "He saved my life."

Cartwright nodded sharply, the expression on his face saying he expected nothing less from those under his command. "Take me to him."

"Affirmative. But first, can you radio for EMS? Detective Logan has taken a beating. Took four rounds at relatively close range to the chest through a vest, but the vest held. And there are other injuries. He's mobile, and his injuries aren't life-threatening, but I want him seen."

Cartwright didn't question, simply keyed the radio high on his vest. "Unit 3 to command. 10-13Z, immediate EMS requested. Grand Central Madison, track 201, via the 45th Street escalators."

10-13Z—Civilian clothes officer needs assistance.

"10-4, Unit 3. Immediate EMS to be dispatched. Do you require additional assistance?"

Cartwright looked at Gemma.

"We need someone from the station to come and turn off the power to the third rail so we can retrieve the body on the tracks. But maybe you should come down first."

"Unit 3 to command, 10-6 on assistance until we've had a chance to view the scene. Please pass on to Chief Capello that Detective Capello is safe. Suspect was neutralized by Detective Logan. Detective Capello is taking us to him."

"10-4, Unit 3."

Cartwright released his radio. "Let's go."

"Come see this first." Gemma led them to the second-from-the-left escalator. "I stopped the escalator when I got off to maintain the evidence. Those are the four rounds Detective Logan took. We'll want the crime scene techs to collect them."

"We'll make sure they're not overlooked."

Gemma led the team of men down the escalators to the mezzanine, then over to the stairs leading to the platform between tracks 201 and 202.

Above them, Logan sat on the top step, his head bowed, his right hand cupping the base of his skull.

Thinks he's alone and doesn't have to hide how much pain he's in.

At the sound of the approaching team, Logan's head snapped up and he pushed to his feet with a wince to stand straight, the P90 gripped in his right hand, pointed down at the step. "Sir."

"Stand down, Logan." Cartwright eyed him critically. "You're okay? Capello called for EMS."

"I'm sore and a little battered, but nothing that won't heal given a week or so."

Cartwright studied the tears in his shirt and the armor plating visible beneath with an experienced eye. "Those were 5.7x28 rounds?"

"Yes, sir."

"Good vest. Where'd it come from? It's not one of ours."

"I took down one of the gunmen in the Station Master's Office and left him there, unconscious and bound with his own zip ties. I helped myself to his vest and weapon. Good thing I had his vest. Wouldn't have survived otherwise."

"I've taken a round in the chest while wearing a vest. Hurt like a mother. Did it break any ribs?"

"Broke a rib once. As much as I hurt now, I don't think it's that bad, but I could be wrong. Bruised the hell out of them at the very least."

"EMS can confirm. Either way, you've earned yourself a little time off to heal." Cartwright caught Logan's expression of displeasure and cut off any oncoming argument. "That's an order, Detective."

"Yes, sir."

"Suspect is neutralized?"

"Yes. I got behind him while he was grappling with Detective Capello. She was holding her own, but hand-to-hand with someone with a submachine gun is challenging. She nearly got control, but he managed to raise the weapon for a torso shot. She had no vest; I had no choice but to take the shot."

"Agreed. You did what you had to do to safeguard a fellow officer."

"The suspect then toppled off the platform onto the tracks below."

"Did one of you check him?" Cartwright asked.

"We didn't because of the risk," Gemma said. "When he fell, he landed on the third rail. That would have killed him, but he was dead before he made contact. Logan's aim was sharp as usual."

"No surprise there. Wilson, please relieve Logan of his weapon. We'll need it for evidence. Now, show me the hostage taker."

"Up here." Logan handed off the P90, then turned and stepped onto the platform.

"What happened to your head?" Cartwright marched up the stairs, his men following, stopping behind Logan to study the bloody head wound. "That looks nasty."

"It's worse than it looks, I think. I was standing on the escalator when I caught those four rounds. Blew me backward and my head clipped the edge of a step with all those little teeth."

"Concussion?"

"Don't think so. I certainly didn't lose consciousness, though I was winded initially."

"Not a surprise, considering." Cartwright stepped to the edge of the platform, studying the corpse while his officers lined the edge of the platform and Gemma closed ranks on Logan's other side. "Yeah, not worth the risk until the power gets shut down. Chisholm."

"Yes, sir." A man stepped backward out of the line of officers.

"There won't be any radio access down here. Head up. Get officers to the Station Master's Office and take that suspect into custody. Get someone down here to cut the power to the third rail. We need crime scene to collect those bullets and then come down here to document before we can recover the body and the weapon on the platform. After that, stay up top to direct the teams down here. Including EMS."

"Have EMS go to the waiting room in the customer service area just past 46th," Gemma suggested. "Keeps this area clear for the techs." *And gives Sean a chance to sit down.*

"Good call. Got it, Detective?"

"Yes, sir." Chisholm jogged off.

Cartwright turned away from the body. "What happened here, Detective?"

"I was in the upper train shed when Detective Capello was taken hostage," said Logan. "I was able to get to the lower train shed in time to track her being taken into Grand Central Madison. I backtracked down into the 45th Street Cross-Passage and entered Grand Central Madison from the staircase behind the 45th Street escalators. I pursued down the escalators, but the suspect fired on me when I had no cover. Luckily, he didn't realize I wore a vest, so he aimed for mid-body instead of a headshot. Took me down briefly, but then I was able to follow."

"He found me while I was struggling with the hostage taker," Gemma continued. "I'd already attempted a takedown two previous times, but I couldn't get the upper hand because of the weapon. I suspected I had value to him and bet on the fact he didn't want to kill me outright because he knew he was still overwhelmingly surrounded in Grand Central. If he came face-to-face with officers, he'd want to use me as a shield. He got me in a choke hold from the start, and never let go, likely because he was afraid if there'd been even a few feet between us and one of your guys popped out of a corridor, he'd be an open target. So he kept us close. I stayed on the lookout for a good opportunity to jump him, was hoping for a flight of stairs that might put us on different levels, but it was escalators all the way.

"I tried upstairs in the concourse. He had me positioned backward all the way down that massive escalator, threatening to push me off the whole way, so I had to hold on with two hands until we got to the bottom. Then when he headlocked me again, I fought him. That's when Detective Logan arrived and was shot. The hostage taker then dragged me to this level and I knew it would be my last chance to act. Especially when he tried to throw me onto the tracks, partly because of the third rail and partly because I didn't want to get forced into the dark tunnels with him, as there would be less need of me as a shield. I made my final stand with him here on the platform. I'd tried the whole time to slow him down."

Her gaze shot to Logan. "At the time, I believed Detective Logan had been killed, and while I knew you and your officers were in the Terminal, you needed time to get down from above, determine where we'd headed, and follow. By the time I was fighting with him, I had to hope you'd figured out where we were and were closing in. I knew I couldn't hold him. He was big and extremely strong. And while I'm good at hand-to-hand, as Detective Logan can attest, it's much harder to do when you're also managing a deadly weapon. I'd gotten some strikes in by the time Detective Logan arrived and, honestly, I think he was going to shoot me because he was in a rush and I'd pissed him off fighting him all the way. At that point, I was no longer an asset. Had Detective Logan hesitated for even a second more... Well, I think the corpse you'd be recovering would be mine." She caught Logan's sharp sideways glance and continued, "Luckily, that's not how it went down."

"Agreed," Cartwright said. He turned to his team. "Wilson, Burnham, and Huskinson, I want you to hold the scene while we go up."

"Yes, sir."

"Logan, time for you to get checked out." Then he turned to Gemma. "You, too."

"I'm fine. He didn't hurt me."

"You haven't looked in a mirror lately." Cartwright's gaze darted up to her forehead. "Your head wound?"

Gemma reflexively touched her fingers to the gash on her forehead, the sharp snap of pain reminding her of the open wound. "I'd forgotten about it with everything else. A little cut wasn't important."

"It's not as little as you think. Let's go meet EMS."

Ten minutes later, she and Logan were seated in separate rows of the waiting area just off the concourse, a position that had given Gemma a chance to extract her flip case from her boot and slip it into her pocket.

She sucked in a breath as a female FDNY paramedic in a navy uniform cleaned her wound with disinfectant.

"Sorry," she said. "I know it stings."

"I'll say." Gemma watched the woman's concentration. "I know you're being careful... Sorry, I don't know your name."

"Delia."

"I know you're being careful, Delia. Thanks for that. How does it look? Is it going to need stitches?"

"We can go one of two ways here. We can get you to the ER where a plastic surgeon can work on you, or we can deal with it here. In my opinion, some tissue glue and a couple of butterfly bandages as backup support will do the job. The slice is a little over an inch long, but it's not too deep. You're lucky the glass didn't do more damage. You're luckier still you didn't catch it in the eye, because you might have lost it. Your call on the repair. When it's the face, some people only want the best."

"Let's do the tissue glue and butterfly bandages, if you think that will be sufficient."

The woman leaned in, testing the area with gentle fingertips. "I do. If it was me, I don't think I'd want to kill six or more hours waiting at the ER."

"You won't need to with Delia."

Gemma turned in her seat to study the man standing in front of Logan. Tall and rake-thin with short-cut red hair and an identical uniform to Delia, he grinned over Gemma's head at his coworker.

"She's good?" Gemma asked.

"The best. If she says she can do it, she can."

"Then she will." As the man swiveled to face Logan again, Gemma got her first look at him. He sat facing her, shirtless, his shirt and Kevlar vest in two large evidence bags held by an officer nearby. She couldn't hold back the gasp at the sight of his chest and abdomen. Four wide areas of brutal bruising spread across his skin, each with a bloodred center that then spread outward in bands, almost like a bullseye, surrounded by ragged oval smudges of yellow, then peachy-pink, then purple. "*Dio mio*," she breathed.

Logan looked up at his paramedic. "Uh-oh. Must be bad. She's breaking out the Italian."

As the paramedic laughed, Gemma glared at Logan. "I'll give you Italian, you *dolore ostinato nel culo*." She turned back around in her seat.

"What did you call him?" Delia murmured.

Gemma matched her volume. "A stubborn pain in my ass."

Delia's crack of laughter had silence coming from the men behind them until Logan asked, "You going to translate that for me?"

"No." Gemma grinned at Delia.

"I just saved your life."

"Busy over here, Logan." Gemma pointed at her forehead. "Do your thing, please."

Delia grinned back. "You got it."

Five or six minutes later, Delia set the last butterfly bandage in place, then stepped back to look at it. "That will do nicely. Keep the area dry for forty-eight hours, then you can get it wet when you shower. The bandages should fall off naturally around the ten-day mark. Let that happen, don't pull them off; if parts come loose, trim those sections off. Any concerns, get it checked by your family doc. Most of the blood is off, but you may want to do some spot cleaning when you get home."

"Thanks. I appreciate the care you took."

"I heard what you did in there. We appreciate what both of you did, working from the inside to save as many as you could."

"Word is traveling already?"

"That guy from ABC7 is broadcasting live from outside the Terminal."

Coulter. Of course he'd be doing his breaking news thing. "Now why doesn't that surprise me?" Gemma stood. "Thank you. Need to check on my pain in the ass over there."

Delia chuckled, then seem to notice the concern in Gemma's eyes. "He'll be fine. I'd put my life in Connor's hands in a heartbeat."

"Good to know. Thanks."

Gemma circled the end of the double row of chairs and then sank down in the seat next to Logan. Connor was on one knee, gently palpating the darkening bruise oozing over the lower ribs on Logan's left side. Logan sucked in a breath through gritted teeth as Gemma wrapped her hand over his where it gripped the armrest. His left hand lay palm up in his lap, the knife wound there already cleaned and bandaged.

"The best way to tell if it's broken or bruised would be an X-ray," Connor said.

"And if I go to the ER and kill the rest of the night there and find out it's broken? What difference will that make?"

"Well...none. The treatment is the same whether they're broken or bruised—rest, ice, and, especially in the first forty-eight hours, pain meds. Prescription pain meds if it's really bad."

Logan threw Gemma a sidelong glance. "So...Advil."

"In the long run, yes. It will also help with the pain and inflammation. But I'm going to give you a morphine injection now so you can finish your day. I highly recommend a follow-up with one of the NYPD surgeons tomorrow. He could prescribe something better than Advil."

"Noted. I'll evaluate tomorrow based on how I'm feeling." Logan glanced down at the vibrant bruising. "I have a feeling this is nothing compared to what it will look like tomorrow."

"Pretty much." Connor prepared and then injected the morphine. "You'll feel that kicking in about ten to twenty minutes from now." He safely disposed of the syringe. "Going to go around behind you and clean that head wound."

As Connor circled around behind Logan, Gemma studied Logan's injuries. Amazingly, for all the bruising, the skin hadn't been broken, so there was no external blood. "Hopefully you're going to come out of this without any scarring." Her gaze slid to his left shoulder, where the thin pink line—all that remained of the knife strike he'd taken in the final Rikers tactical breach—lay at the edge of where his vest would normally lie. The injury had healed well, the color fading, but Gemma suspected he'd always bear the mark of that incident.

"Well, if I do, they can join the rest." Logan's tone was light. "Hard to live an active life like this and not come out of it a little banged up." Detective Perez, one of Logan's A-Team guys, entered the waiting room and jerked to a halt as his gaze landed on his teammate. "Jesus, Logan. They said you'd been shot, so I wanted to check up on you. But...hell."

"Look that good, do I?" Logan joked back, but pain laced his words.

"You look like you must be in agony."

"Just imagine how I'd look without the vest."

"Without the vest, we wouldn't be having this conversation." Perez's gaze shot behind them to where Logan's tattered shirt was bagged. He flipped the safety on his M4A1 carbine, pulled it and the sling off over his head, laying it across the arms of an unoccupied chair, then carefully unstrapped and lifted off his Kevlar vest, the pockets loaded with spare magazines.

When Perez pulled the tails of his long-sleeved uniform shirt out of his pants and unbuttoned it, Gemma realized what he was doing—literally giving Logan the shirt off his back. Because in the NYPD, your teammate was family, and family took care of its own.

Perez shrugged out of his shirt, leaving him in a black T-shirt. "We're about the same size." He winked at Gemma as he tossed the shirt to Logan, who draped it over his thigh. "Wouldn't want you scaring the ladies looking like that."

"You mean my fantastic physique?" Logan quipped back.

"I mean the color of your fantastic physique, because... Jesus, man."

"I hear you. Thanks, Perez."

Perez strapped himself back into his vest. "Anytime. I guess you're going to be off for a bit."

"I'm guessing. Not too long though."

"Can't keep a good man down." Perez picked up his carbine, slipped the sling over his head and arm to lay cross-body. "Don't overdo it, and take whatever meds they offer you. And let us know how it's going. Everyone will want to know."

"Will do." As Perez strode out toward the concourse, Logan looked sideways at Gemma, studying her bandaged forehead. "That's not too bad."

"This is a paper cut compared to you. As Perez said, you must be in agony."

"I admit...it hurts." Logan winced and stiffened.

"Sorry," Connor said from behind them. "Just want to make sure it's all clean and doesn't need stitching."

"Does it?"

"I think you're fine without it. At most it would be a stitch or two in each spot, but I think it will heal nicely. I can bandage it, but I'd have to anchor the bandage around your head. Can't stick it to your hair."

"And if we don't bandage it?"

"You'll need to keep it clean to make sure it doesn't get infected. You don't have great visuals on it, so have someone else keep an eye on it for the next few days."

"Can do. I'm off duty for at least a few days, so I won't have to wear a helmet. That will help."

"Sure will. Okay, all done. You're good to go."

"Thanks for patching me up."

"Happy to." Coming back around, Connor flashed them a grin, then set to working on organizing his equipment.

"Let's get you into that shirt." Gemma grabbed the shirt and stood, shaking it out. Logan stood with his back to her, and she held it out for him as he slipped it on.

He turned back around, and she brushed his hands away from the top button. He stared down at her busy fingers. "I'm not that badly wounded. I can button a shirt, you know."

"I know."

She secured two more buttons before he spoke again. "This wasn't what I had potentially in mind for us tonight. Or at least not you buttoning me *into* my shirt."

"Me either, but there's time later for that." Her hands stilled, and she tipped her head back to look up at him. "Was that where we blew it all those years ago? We rushed to scratch an itch, which then made it easier to walk away?"

"I actually didn't find it easy to walk away, but yeah, you may have something there. It was easier than it might have been otherwise."

"Then I'm all for not rushing."

"If I'm not going to convince you to possibly take pity on this poor abused body and come home with me tonight, will you at least tell me what you called me a few minutes ago?"

"That's a pretty poor consolation prize."

He laughed, then winced in pain. "You're telling me. And don't make me laugh. It hurts just to breathe, forget about laughing."

She raised a single eyebrow. "This is why I'm not coming home with you tonight. I might kill you by accident." Gemma worked hard to stifle the laugh that rose at the twisted expression on Logan's face so he wouldn't laugh as well. "I can put you out of this misery at least. I called you a stubborn pain in my ass."

"I try to be." He grinned at her, then it slipped away, leaving his eyes shadowed. "I was terrified I wouldn't be able to get to you in time. That there were too many places to lose you, and if you disappeared into the dark, I wouldn't ever get you back. I knew he'd only keep you alive as long as he needed you. After that, you were just an inconvenience, one easily ended."

His honesty made it easy for her to meet it with her own. "I thought I'd lost you entirely. That I'd watched you die right in front of me, just like I had my mother twenty-five years ago. Something snapped in me at that moment. The fury and anguish almost made me careless, but in the midst of it, I could hear your voice in my head telling me to get it together. I thought you were gone, but it felt like a part of you was still with me. It got me through."

"Think the universe is telling us something?"

"About wasted chances? If it is, I think we're both getting the message loud and clear." She paused, unsure if she was projecting her own emotions onto him, but willing to take the chance after everything that had happened that day. After what she thought she'd lost. "At least I am."

"Me too." He cupped his right hand around her neck, his thumb stroking her cheek as he pulled her in, ignoring every officer around them as well as the paramedic team packing their equipment away behind them as he dropped his mouth over hers.

"Hey, Capello! I have a message from—" Perez cut off abruptly as he entered the room, then simply stood staring as Gemma and Logan only pulled far enough apart to look at him. Perez cleared his throat. "I...uh... I have a message for you from Chief Capello. He says he'll meet you at Lexington and 42nd." He flapped a hand at them with a wide grin. "Now... as you were." He gave them an eyebrow waggle, turned on his heel, and strode away for a second time.

Gemma's exhausted laugh carried an edge of resignation. "Every single one of your teammates is going to know about that kiss inside of about ten minutes."

"If not sooner. And it's going to be the only thing I hear about for the next month. Maybe two. As a group, we live to torment each other."

Gemma knew this kind of camaraderie was how teams that had to often deal with the hardest aspects of law enforcement survived the stresses of their jobs. "It's a good thing you actually like each other then."

"You bet. So...shall we go meet your dad?"

"It's more likely to be everyone. But yes, I'd like to."

There was nothing like a life-or-death crisis to make one really appreciate the good things in their life.

Her family was her rock.

She couldn't wait to see them.

Chapter 33

They climbed the steps into the concourse of Grand Central Terminal, now alive with sound and moving bodies. Not totally back to normal—that wouldn't come until the next day—but the buzz of NYPD activity was more calming than the otherworldly silence of the hostage standoff.

The bomb squad had already done their thing and removed the explosives. One—Gemma needed to think of him as Owen McCadden—was nowhere in sight, so he'd also been removed, likely followed by the family that had been the downfall of his scheme but who had also saved his life. Gemma had to wonder if McCadden thought death preferable to the looming prison sentence awaiting him. He might not have pulled the trigger to kill any of the victims, but he'd masterminded the plot and there would be a host of state and federal crimes piled on. She doubted he or Two would see the outside of prison walls ever again.

The crime scene techs were spread out, documenting the scene from every angle in detail. They'd started with the fallen, as techs from the Office of the Chief Medical Examiner attended the dead, doing their on-site examinations and then preparing to package and move the deceased. The hostages had been removed from the concourse to have their statements taken before being released, but all their belongings remained until the scene could be fully documented.

Gemma's gaze found her jacket and bag and Logan's jacket. "Going to be a chilly ride home tonight."

"At least it's not mid-January or we'd be really cold. Fortunately, we have an in to get our stuff back tomorrow once the scene is documented."

"In the meantime, it's going to feel like I lost an arm not having my phone." She glanced back at the information booth where they'd huddled for so many hours. "We're never going to be able to look at this place the same again."

"Definitely not."

"Oh, here's a question for you—who's Isaac Lyford? I used my middle name and my mother's maiden name. Is that a family name?"

"Mr. Lyford was my high school varsity basketball coach. Tiny man with the spirit of a giant. Mr. Lyford was always someone to look up to."

"Even as you looked down on him?"

"Exactly like that."

They walked a wide circle around the outer edge of the concourse, staying well clear of the techs bending over the dead, bodily fluids, and hostage belongings, passing in front of the ticket counters, then turning toward Vanderbilt Hall.

There they found the hostages. The NYPD had settled them into the tables tucked into the wine bar on the west side. Some talked to a detective on their own, some in their natural pairings. While they looked exhausted, they mostly looked relieved, except for Deborah Cowell, who wept into her hands while a female detective spoke to her quietly and rubbed her shoulder, the only comfort she could offer.

Only a few A-Team officers remained, their role here now mostly ended, but each of them came up to Logan and either shook his hand or slapped him on the back—gently, so news of his injuries had apparently accompanied that of his actions—before turning more serious to compliment Gemma on a game well played. Then pointedly gave them both a hard time about the kiss.

"You're a celebrity," Gemma said as they pushed through the doors into the Onassis Foyer.

"You can see how long that lasted. Long enough for kudos, then they were needling us about that kiss." He shrugged. "It's what we do."

"Sharing their movie knowledge, too," Gemma said dryly. "'I've heard relationships based on intense experiences never work,'" she quoted *Speed* in a deeper intonation, imitating Logan's male colleagues. "It's like they think we just met."

"They know we haven't. You should look at it this way—being poked at like that is inclusion in their group."

"I'll take it as a compliment, then." Pausing before the outer set of doors, Gemma held out her right hand to him, watching his gaze shoot down, hold.

"We're going out to your family." Logan's gaze rose to hers. "You sure you want to do that?"

"Are we starting something here, Detective Logan? Something better late than never?"

"That's my take on it, Detective Capello."

"Then my family is going to find out sooner or later, so let's get it over with now. You're never going to be more in their good books than you are now after saving my life. My family is a huge part of my life. We don't hide things from each other, and I'm not embarrassed to show them our connection. You shouldn't be either."

"I'm definitely not embarrassed. I just respect your four brothers. I could take down Alex or Mark. Joe is an even match. The FDNY brother could be my downfall."

"Teo? He's a kitten." Her grin held a wolfish slyness. "A kitten who can bench press three hundred."

"That's what I'm talking about."

"You leave them to me. They know better than to mess with my man. Granted, it's been a while since there's been a 'man,' so they're likely out of practice. That also plays in your favor. Not to mention that after what Perez just saw, they're going to find out by tomorrow at the latest. Why not now?" When she raised her hand another inch, he clasped it, the bandage wrapped around his palm brushing her skin. Realizing any pressure on that hand might cause him more pain, she let go, but he held on.

"It's okay. I'll let you know if it's not."

She closed her hand around his, keeping the pressure light, trusting him to tell her if she hurt him.

They walked through the doors onto 42nd Street under the Pershing Square Viaduct to the organized chaos of a full police response. Police vehicles of every size and shape filled 42nd Street, and red-and-white lights strobed rhythmically.

A chill gust of wind caught them, a shiver running down Gemma's spine as they turned down the sidewalk hugging East 42nd Street, then passed a cruiser and one of the A-Team armored vans.

"Hey, you know, the pub is open until 4:00 AM. Still want dinner?" Logan asked.

She tossed him an incredulous look until she saw the grin on his face. "Good, you're kidding. I'm exhausted. You must be exhausted, and battered on top of it. Let's save this for another night."

"How about tomorrow? I already have my walking orders. Pretty sure the powers that be will also want you to stand down after this for a day or two at least. I mean, we'll have debriefings and paperwork tomorrow, but that will be during the day."

"I'm free tomorrow night."

"I'm sure my buddy will find us a table, even if they're booked solid. They often are on a Saturday night."

The morgue van was pulled up next to the curb for easy loading. Beyond it, filling the middle of the street, was a cluster of NYPD SUVs and unmarked detective vehicles. To their left, the Hyatt Grand Central was weirdly quiet, the rotating main entrance doors still, with no lineup of cars and cabs disgorging people and luggage.

Up ahead lay Lexington, where a crowd of people was visible. Another block distant, the lights of moving cars and the sound of horns drifted toward them; the NYPD had opened some of the roads to let traffic resume, but this close to the incident, thoroughfares were still locked down.

As they stepped out from under the second-floor balcony that sheltered the entrance to the hotel, the night sky opened over them, the edge of the Chrysler Building glowing like a beacon above.

When they were about fifty feet from the corner, a dark shape separated from a group on the far side and sprinted across the street, ignoring the red light. Gemma released Logan's hand and ran to meet Alex partway. They threw their arms around each other, clutching tight.

"I knew you'd figure it out," Gemma whispered into his ear, her arms locked around him.

"I wasn't so sure it would be enough. Then we weren't sure our plan would work." A shudder ran through Alex's frame. "I was terrified I was going to witness your death like you'd witnessed Mom's."

"You and the team got us part of the way there. Sean did the rest."

Alex pulled back, keeping his left arm around Gemma, extending his hand as Logan caught up to them, having slowed his approach to give them a moment. "Logan, I don't know how to thank you."

Logan shook Alex's hand. "No thanks required."

"You have it anyway. From all of us."

They turned toward the new voice to find Chief Tony Capello directly behind them. Gemma slipped from Alex's hold to find herself wrapped in her father's arms. She held on for a moment, her eyes closed, as he rocked her back and forth like he had when she was a child. Then he set her back, scanning her face, his gaze locking on her bandaged forehead. "Are you all right?"

"Yes. This is nothing. I got hit with a little flying glass—didn't even need stitches." She thought it best not to mention that stitches had been an option. "It's Sean who's hurt." She purposely used his first name, breaking the typical cop convention of calling everyone by their last name. Stepping back to Logan, she took his injured left hand in hers, held it, making an overt statement.

Tony's gaze took in his officer, bandaged, slightly hunched, and wearing a borrowed ESU uniform shirt. "Detective."

"Chief." Logan's tone was formal, not just a detective to his chief, but a man to a father.

Tony stuck out his hand. "Thank you. You kept safe someone very precious to us."

Logan clasped his hand but then looked sideways to Gemma. "To me, too."

Alex slapped Logan on the back. Logan winced in pain, not able to hold back a low groan.

"Oh, crap. Sorry." Alex looked genuinely contrite. "I forgot. We heard you took a few rounds through the vest. Anything broken?"

"Jury's still out on that for now. It's certainly possible a rib or two is busted." Alex grimaced, so Logan let him down gently. "It's fine, really. I'm sore, but it'll heal. They gave me some morphine. It's kicking in."

"I was shot like that once," Tony said. "It's extremely painful. Wait until you see what you look like tomorrow."

"It's already not great now. Should be pretty colorful by then."

"Especially with multiple hits." Tony turned around and waved across the street.

Gemma peered over her father's shoulder to find Joe, Mark, and Teo jogging toward them. There were hugs for Gemma, while after a warning, Logan received careful handshakes and sincere thank-yous.

"Capello!"

Six heads turned at the sound of the family name.

McFarland, jogging across Lexington with Garcia, Shelby, Taylor, and Williams behind him, shrugged, his palms spread wide, a huge grin on his face and an expression that read *Whatcha gonna do?*

Gemma stepped away from her family to greet her team, gleefully ignoring McFarland's discomfort to give him a tight hug, and then repeating the gesture with every member of the team. Her team was family; they had been before the incident, but that bond was only stronger now.

Garcia told Gemma in no uncertain terms she was to take the weekend and then all of next week to rest and recover from the stress of the situation.

"Are you sure?" Gemma asked. "I don't know I need that much time. I admit I'm exhausted now, but—"

"No buts." Garcia used the tone his people knew was set in stone. There would be no budging him. "You just survived a crisis. You watched people die; you thought there was a good chance you'd die yourself. If you're going to get on the phone with a hostage taker, I need to know you're not carrying any baggage from this negotiation. In fact, watch for the department to require both you and Logan to have a sit-down with the department psychologist before being cleared for active duty. Take the time. If needed, I can rotate you off active negotiations for a little while. Let's see how it goes. You'll be honest with me about how you're feeling?"

"Yes."

"Then I won't require more time than that. As long as you're honest that you're ready when you come back."

"I will be. Lieutenant..." She paused. She was talking to her senior officer, but this was too personal and went beyond their on-the-job relationship. "Tomás...thank you."

"There's no need to thank me." Garcia's voice carried a touch of roughness.

"But I want to anyway. You put together the team that made the difference to every life in there. You found the people who knew me best, knowing they'd collectively have the best chance of reading between the lines. Just as importantly, you let Alex assist to help stack the deck in our favor. Many other cops wouldn't have let someone from IAB into the room." She turned to the greater group around her. "I need to thank every one of you. You worked together and you worked with my brother to pull this off. Every one of you played a part in saving our lives, and I know this time it wasn't just a job. It was a team effort and you helped save the city from a disaster, the likes of which we haven't seen in decades and hoped we'd never see again. I'll always be grateful to each and every one of you."

Shelby caught her in a hug. "We're just glad to have you back. *I'm* glad to have you back. Who else would I bitch about the guys with?"

Gemma's laugh was full of relief and gratitude. "You got that right."

A repeated shout from across the road finally registered. Gemma turned to look across the intersection to the far corner of Lexington and East 42nd Street. The flash of electric blue identified who was calling her name.

"Is that Coulter?" McFarland asked.

"Pretty sure it is." She stared across the road for several long seconds, then blew out a breath and set her shoulders. "He's not broadcasting currently. I'll be back in a minute."

"You're going over there?"

"Yeah."

"But you hate Coulter."

"I think it's mutual. But if he hadn't spotted me and told you guys I was in there, this whole thing could have ended very differently. I owe him a thank-you for that."

"You're sure?" Garcia's expression said Coulter could rot in hell in his books.

Gemma met his gaze. If there was anyone who disliked Coulter as much as she did, it was Garcia. "Sadly, yes. I'm not planning on becoming his BFF. If I'm not back in three minutes, come get me yourself."

"Gladly."

She crossed the intersection on the diagonal, passing the cop on the corner who was locking Coulter and his cameraman in place, not letting them get closer to the action. Normally no camera crew would be this close in, but Gemma had to assume it was the compromise the NYPD had agreed on in exchange for his assistance. "Mr. Coulter."

"Detective Capello." He watched her cautiously, as if he wasn't sure she wasn't a snake preparing to strike. Caution morphed into shock when she walked to him and extended her hand. "What's this?"

"This is thank you for assisting in saving my life in there. For helping in saving all the hostages' lives. The fact that you recognized me and carried that info back to the NYPD let every other move in this game of 3D chess we were playing fall into place." She extended her hand farther. "Thank you."

Coulter still looked unsure, but he clasped her hand and shook it. "Are you thankful enough to tell me what happened in there?"

"On the record or off?"

"I'd like on, but I'll take off if that's all you can do."

"Tonight's not the night to ask me for anything on the record after what happened. Maybe in a few days... I don't know. But what I can tell you off the record is when you told the NYPD I was in there, they assembled a negotiation team I could talk to on two levels. They assembled a team that allowed my brother, a detective in the Internal Affairs Bureau, into the group because he knows me best and could understand some of the hints I laid down. Alex also knew I was with one of the A-Team detectives, so the NYPD knew they had two plants in the hostage group. Saving everyone in there was a group effort from the two of us inside, to you, to my team, to the A-Team, to the rest of the NYPD, to the FBI. Take out one of those pieces and the whole thing would have fallen apart. But it didn't. And we got all but one out alive, and the one who didn't make it died because he tried to exert control and was killed for his interference." Coulter drew a breath to interrupt, but Gemma cut him off. "I can't tell you the names of the deceased. They'll be released, but next of kin has to be informed first. Anyway, I wanted to say thank you for what you did tonight. And that I recognize even though you wanted the story, it took guts to walk into the Terminal knowing what was there. Well done."

"Thanks. Can I use any of that? Just call you an NYPD source?"

Gemma had to squash the urge to roll her eyes. Some things weren't going to change. "No. You can't use it." He deflated slightly. "Contact the department in a few days—" She held up a hand when he started to splutter. "In a few days, Coulter. Then maybe we can work something out. Okay?"

"Okay."

Gemma gave him a nod and stepped off the curb. She was two steps away when he called her name and she turned around.

"I'm glad you made it out."

"Thanks. Me too."

She crossed back to the other side, feeling Garcia's eyes on her the entire time.

"How did it go?" he asked. "Did he hound you?"

"Fine, and yes, but only slightly. If I'm in the mood, I may talk to him in a few days." At Garcia's raised eyebrows, she shrugged. "Yeah, me too. It's like I've lost my mind. Yet I can't get over the feeling I owe him something for his part in this, because without him, our chances of survival approached zero. Maybe he'll turn out to be not as big an asshole as we think he is." Garcia's boom of laughter coaxed a chuckle from her as well. "Yeah, you're probably right. Once an asshole, always an asshole. But we'll see how I feel in a few days."

She turned when she felt a hand on her shoulder to find Alex standing behind her. "Everyone is going back to Dad's. We're all wired for sound and no one is ready for bed. Frankie's going to join us. She's desperate to see you."

"I wouldn't miss it." She turned back to her team. "Thanks again, guys. Really. I'm going to hang with my family now, but I'll be in touch over the next couple of days."

She returned to her family, circling the group to stand at Logan's side. "We're heading to Dad's now?" At the affirmative response, she grasped Logan's arm and pulled him back a pace. "You didn't come the last time I invited you to Dad's. I'm asking you again." She paused at the caution in his eyes. "I know it's going to feel weird having a beer with your chief, but you'll get used to it."

"You have no idea how much I'd like a beer after the day we've had. Sadly, after that morphine shot, I'll have to take a rain check on it. Are you sure you want me to come?"

"Yes."

"Then I'm there."

"Good." She threaded her arm through his where his hands were jammed in the front pockets of his cargo pants to stay warm. "Who's driving us?" she called to her brothers, smiling when Joe, Mark, and Teo all offered.

It was a relief to leave the area, to walk back to where cars had been left just inside the police barricade, back toward the noise and lights and normal chaos of the city she loved. To walk toward that chaos with the man who had given his all, nearly given his life, to save hers. To give them the chance to see what lay before them.

Only time would tell if this was the beginning of something more certain, more realized. For her. For her family, who had welcomed new partners in the past, many of whom became permanent family members. Each had changed the dynamic slightly—most had improved it; those who hadn't had left the fold. But overall, the bonds of those couples who lasted had only made the family stronger. Brought new life into the family.

Could it be the same for her and Logan? It was very early days, and only time would tell.

But it was a damned good start.

Acknowledgments

It's such a joy to write the book you always wanted, but for which you didn't think you'd have the opportunity. So my very first thanks goes to editor extraordinaire, James Abbate, who resurrected the NYPD Negotiators when he advocated not only to bring *Lockdown* back into the Kensington fold, but the following book I already had planned. James, in the most basic sense, this book would not exist without you, and I'm so grateful for the opportunity to bring Gemma and Logan full circle. As always, your camaraderie, flexibility, crazy work hours, and counsel are beyond appreciated!

Shane Vandevalk is another invaluable partner. Shane spent many hours with me planning the physical setup of a hostage situation in such a compromised space, including poring over Grand Central Terminal maps and photos from my two visits to the site. Shane also continued in his role as weapons specialist, ensuring my details were correct. No lie, it would be impossible for me to convincingly write a police procedural without Shane and his strategic thinking. Many thanks!

My husband, Rick, was once again a willing accomplice as I dragged him around New York City on yet another research trip. We went through every nook and cranny of Grand Central Terminal we could access (get caught trying?), as well as Grand Central Madison so I could bring this incredible architectural beauty to life. The use of the P90 was also his idea, so thanks to him and to many reruns of *Stargate SG-1* for that suggestion!

My critique team, Kathi Alexander, Rick Newton, and Sharon Taylor, enthusiastically jumped in on an extremely short reading window due to my overstuffed schedule and still managed to beat that short deadline. Thank you for such an in-depth read. Your comments always go the distance in strengthening my manuscripts!

Thanks to my agent, Nicole Resciniti, for always working her magic in the background and for her constant support and advice. I couldn't do any of this without you!

And, finally, the Kensington Team—Alexandra Nicolajsen, Madeleine Brown, Renee Rocco, Susanna Gruninger, Vida Engstrand, Kait Johnson,

Kristin McLaughlin, and Andi Paris. It's always such a pleasure to work with you through the various stages of every publication. Many thanks for all the effort you put into all my books!

About the Author

Sara Driscoll is the pen name of Jen J. Danna, coauthor of the Abbott and Lowell Forensic Mysteries and author of the FBI K-9 Mysteries and NYPD Negotiators series. After over thirty years in infectious diseases research, Jen hung up her lab coat to concentrate on her real love—writing "exceptional" thrillers (*Publishers Weekly*). She is a member of the Crime Writers of Canada and lives with her husband and four rescued cats outside of Toronto, Ontario. You can follow the latest news on her books at saradriscollauthor.com.